THE HARD HAT GIRL,—POWER ENGINEER

THE HARD HAT GIRL,—POWER ENGINEER

A Novel
BY McCULLOCH BYERS

—1976—
Fairfield House, Publisher
3 Fairfield Drive, Baltimore, Md. 21228

COPYRIGHT © 1976 BY R. McCULLOCH BYERS
ALL RIGHTS RESERVED

Except for brief quotations in reviews, no part of this publication may be reproduced, stored in any retrieval system, or transmitted in any form or by any means without written permission of the publisher.

All characters, incidents, places, and organizations in this novel are fictitious (except for those obviously named for general recognition), and any resemblance to actual ones is purely coincidental.

Book and cover design by author

Manufactured in the United States of America
by
Publication Press, Inc., Baltimore, Md.

Fairfield House, Publisher, 3 Fairfield Drive, Baltimore, Md. 21228

First printing—1976

Library of Congress Catalog Card Number: 76-29554

To the memory of my father, who guided me into his family's traditional profession of engineering, now represented in our fifth successive generation,

and

To the memory of my mother, who encouraged me to write about it

Author's Preface

IF AN AUTHOR NEEDS any reasons for writing a book, mine here are fourfold:

First, though not a few literary critics have suggested that I must have placed this goal *last,*—I wanted to produce that rarity, a readable engineer's novel by, about, and for engineers—and for anyone interested in the profession of engineering or its practitioners, especially the rapidly growing ranks of thousands of women engineers.

Second, after a life of preparation and work in the engrossing field of electrical engineering of power plants and substations,—I wished to pass on to young people and their counselors today an insider's glimpse of this fascinating and challenging career so vital to America's future as the third century begins for the nation.

Third, although numerous published references try to inform us about the energy crisis, including the many problems confronting our electric utilities in securing fair rates, attracting construction capital, fighting inflation, and finding rational answers to plant siting and ecology questions,—my aim here was to sugar-coat a factual presentation in a fiction format to help the reader through an otherwise technically formidable and forbidding subject.

Fourth, after over forty years of utility engineering,—I hope I may be pardoned for my desire to present some of my observations,—a euphemism for constructively critical "gripes,"—of certain improvements I consider desirable in all sectors of the power industry, including utilities, consultants, educators, contractors, suppliers, and government regulators.

In evaluating this novel, I am aware that the conventional elements of interpersonal conflict, characterization, and suspense have been tailored somewhat to fit the latter three objectives: the messages on career guidance, utility energy-crisis problems, and my industry criticisms. However, my purpose was to provide something for everyone,—enough technical meat to satisfy the engineer's appetite while not inflicting indigestion upon the general reader.

After all, this *is* a realistic suspense story of an appealing heroine's daily struggles to "hack it" on her new job of leading her skeptically antagonistic all-male group of power-plant electrical engineers. Therefore, in a typically engineering empirical approach, I sampled a score of random subjects—from homemakers, typists, and teachers to engineers, lawyers, and students. Although most non-engineers admitted to some difficulty in skimming over the *technical* passages, one teacher complained of too much *tennis*! On the other hand, an attorney-businesswoman, whom I've never met, wrote, "This is a belated note to tell you how much I enjoyed it. The *tennis* scenes and the garage incident remain especially vivid in my recollection. The topic is certainly as current as one can get. It should have a big reading audience with women."

And a young mechanical engineer stated, "It's uncanny how my work parallels THE HARD HAT GIRL,—POWER ENGINEER. I could empathize with Marion so much. I understood pressures she felt to perform superhuman technical feats, how she was responsible for results and not just doing the best she could,—how she could take pride and satisfaction in doing something that really couldn't carry a personal mark. I suppose these things apply to other professions but not in the way they seem to apply to engineers."

Undoubtedly my greatest encouragement to publish this "engineer's novel" was the firm support given by Mr. Bruno M. Zambotti, Chairman of the Public Relations Committee for the Power Engineering Society of the Institute of Electrical and Electronics Engineers.

And now I can only hope that each reader will find entertainment in some facets of this engineer's yarn while gaining new insight into the electric power industry so essential to our nation's future.

McCulloch Byers

July 4, 1976

Contents

AUTHOR'S PREFACE — vii

CHAPTERS

1. THE RISKY SNEAK PREVIEW — 1
2. IT WAS THE MORNING OF THE FIRST DAY — 15
3. SOLID STATE SNAFU — 29
4. CLIFFSIDE ENCORE — 46
5. MASSACRE AT GREEN KNOLLS — 58
6. THE THIRD DAY'S THE CHARM — 72
7. ORPHEUS AND EURYDICE — 85
8. LOSE EVERY BATTLE,—BUT WIN THE WAR — 93
9. HER FIRST T.G.I.F. — 110
10. TOUGH DAY FOR ANY PRINCIPAL ENGINEER — 123
11. FRANK FRIGHTENS A SUPERVISING ENGINEER — 136
12. UNCLE BOB — 148

THE
HARD HAT
GIRL,—POWER
ENGINEER

CHAPTER ONE

The Risky Sneak Preview

IT WAS HOT as hell. Blinking and squinting her eyes, Marion Francis peered through the shimmering heat waves and blue traffic fumes to read 105 degrees on the revolving digital thermometer which hung above the bank across the busy downtown street. Patting her perspiring face with a soggy handkerchief, Marion felt rivers of sweat running down between her breasts. Having just arrived from up north, she wasn't prepared for this kind of summer inferno below the Mason and Dixon Line.

Jostled on all sides by the irresistible tides of heedless shoppers flowing around the busy corner, Marion turned away from the curb and just then became aware of the dazzling white skyscraper towering above her. Why, it was right up there on the fifteenth floor that she had landed her job with the electric power company last week. She still couldn't believe how easy it had been at the interview. All over the country millions of people were out of work; and, like thousands of other electrical engineers, she had been given her notice at her utility up north. After a year as a graduate engineer in professional training and two more as an associate engineer, Marion had just been promoted to the grade of engineer only a week before the ax had fallen; and it had been that senseless tantalizing timing that had made the blow all the more crushing. Her boss obviously had been very embarrassed at having to perform his unpleasant task; his halting speech had been full of praise for her work and promises to call her back at the first sign of any let-up in this worldwide, "stagflationary," energy-crisis recession. It had been all she could do to endure the ordeal stoically and afterwards flee to the ladies' room for a good cry.

And now, while still technically employed up north before her notice period would run out next week, Marion would start work here next Monday—exactly one week from today—with an incredible promotion to senior engineer. Her salary would be $20,000—an inflationary, lordly, 33% boost over her last year's annual stipend of $15,000. She had won this promotion here on the strength of her present position as engineer, backed by three years of experience in electrical engineering for a utility as well as her previous university record, which included her bachelor's and master's degrees with honors in electrical engineering, concurrent with two years as an instructor on an industry research fellowship. True enough, after much soul-searching, she *had* requested this promotion to senior engineer as compensation for making the job switch with its loss of seniority and pension rights and its attendant relocation costs; but, under her present circumstances, she actually had not expected any such good fortune at all. Even if she had not been fired, she would have faced at least five more years of hard work and unsettling uncertainties before she could have hoped for this promotion from engineer to senior engineer.

Violently bumped again by the scurrying crowds, Marion found herself at the building's revolving door; and, on an impulse, she synchronized her step with the whirling glass paddles and was quickly ejected into the pleasantly cool, dimly lit lobby in company with numerous fellow travelers. Beyond the long patient lines of customers, keeping their cool while paying their electric bills at the counters on her right, she saw two black receptionists, one male, one female, sternly blocking her path to the elevators—like Cerberus, as it were.

Marion shivered involuntarily, but that was a natural reaction to coming in, all sweaty, out of the blazing heat into this delightful chill. She just had to learn more about her new job—by meeting her immediate boss and her co-workers—and, by so doing, try to appraise her capability of successfully performing what duties were expected of her, as well as to ascertain why the company had so eagerly accepted her application, promotion and all, with so little questioning.

Walking hesitantly up to her fellow woman, Marion waited until the receptionist looked up inquiringly from a lurid paperback novel before asking, "Would you please check if Mr. Joe Knight, the Chief Electrical Engineer, could see me for a few minutes?" She spelled out her name carefully.

"Please remind him that I am the new engineer who will report next Monday."

Quickly thumbing through a directory, the woman spoke inaudibly into a telephone and replied solicitously, "Mr. Knight is out of town all week. Can anyone else help you?"

Rummaging desperately through her large tote bag slung from her shoulder, she luckily found her little black notebook. "How about Mr. Ben Board, the Supervising Engineer for Generation and Transmission Substations?"

After a somewhat longer period, the guard triumphantly announced,

"He is out of town also this week, but the Engineering Department receptionist says she will try to get Mr. Sellers to come down. Why don't you be seated—over there, ma'am? I'll direct Mr. Sellers to you."

Suddenly her knees did feel sort of rubbery. She smiled gratefully. "Thank you."

Following the kindly receptionist's pointing finger, she walked across the lobby to a row of a dozen, bucket-seat, plastic-and-metal chairs arranged beside a pool of running water, bordered by a rubber-tree-like jungle. She seated herself in the only vacant chair among a group of brief-case-clutching men, all sales "reps", she thought. Reluctantly braving the searing downtown heat today on a shopping mission for her aunt, Marion had selected one of her briefest—and coolest—miniskirts. However, now she tried to smooth out and stretch the inadequate material to a more modest covering of her thighs; but, failing, she placed her feet and knees firmly together and sat primly erect to watch the continual flow of visitors to the twin reception desks across the lobby. Now she noticed that there were several chairs beside the male receptionist, but they were all occupied by men. She was the sole woman visitor. With nothing else to do for the moment, she began to question why she had ever thought she could fill this job. Then, as at many other times of late, she firmly reminded herself that Father had done this work all his life and had often reassured her, insisting that she could do it also—and just as well as—if not better than—any male engineer.

Now a tall thin man was at "her" desk looking over in her direction and scratching his head in apparent bewilderment. She tried to tell herself that he must be eyeing one of her male neighbors, but her feminine intuition at once assured her otherwise. Slowly, as if burdened with great reluctance and disbelief, the man walked towards her. Probably in his early sixties with graying brown hair and lines about his mouth, he must be some years the senior of the Chief Electrical Engineer and nearly a score of years older than the Supervising Engineer, Marion thought. With a mighty effort of willpower, she arose, gracefully she hoped, and smilingly walked to meet him. Really he was not bad looking; and, when he grinned now, his lean serious face lit up all over, making him look years younger. His brown eyes glanced down at her left hand clutching her bag's shoulder strap. Then, as they shook hands, he looked down at her from his six-foot-plus height and asked in a pleasant voice, "Miss Marion Francis? I am Robert Sellers. It *is* 'Miss', isn't it? Not 'Ms'? I have a niece—about your age, I think,—who prefers 'Ms'!"

She smiled. "'Miss' will do nicely for *me*, Mr. Sellers! Or better still—just 'Marion'".

He was still grinning, but the head-scratching now resumed as he released her hand. "The Engineering Department receptionist said that the new engineer in my group wanted to see me. I understood the name *M A R I O N* to be masculine—as I once knew a boy by that name in high school. So—I was surprised—to put it mildly—to behold a beautiful blue-eyed blonde! But—Marion *is* more of a feminine name; I also knew a woman by that name. I like the name; it has a nice sound!"

Marion took a deep breath, still smiling. "My parents were golfers—and named me after Marion Miley, an attractive golf champion back in the thirties—even before I was born! They reasoned 'Marion' would do for either sex! They could have picked 'Jan' or 'Gayle' or 'Beverly'—or 'Allison'—or 'Lloyd'—or 'Merle'—or—'Terry'—"

He nodded. "I recall Marion Miley. She was murdered in her home by a burglar. She was very talented—and pretty. Very sad . . ."

Then, as frowns replaced smiles on both their faces, she blurted out, "But, Mr. Sellers,—then you didn't know I had been hired—to learn the ropes,—so I'll be ready to take your place when you retire this fall?"

He gazed over towards the elevators. "No, Miss Francis, I must admit I did not know of your hiring. But I did know they were trying to find a qualified engineer—of suitable education, experience, inclination and—characteristics—for the job." He paused and obviously forced a grin. "And I should have known any one taken on now would have to be a woman—if at all possible."

Feeling herself blush, she forced herself to say, "You sound bitter, Mr. Sellers! I was told you were a bachelor—but not a woman-hater."

Now it was his turn to show embarrassment. "Oh, no! Not at all, Miss Francis! And—pardon me—if I sounded that way. It's—just a case of cumulative frustration bubbling over, I guess; and I . . ."

Quickly she interrupted, "I'm sorry I spoke hastily. As a woman engineer, I suppose I'm always on the defensive. But why couldn't an experienced *man* be promoted from within your group?"

He shook his head. "They're too few—and with too little experience. Ten years ago I had a good group of six old-timers. All gone now—from attrition. They said our Company's pay scale then—couldn't compete with the electronics and aerospace industries. So—no replacements. Just overtime without pay. Quantity versus quality. Hectic times—with consultants. On top of all that, I was demoted from the ranks of supervisors—and put in 'technical direction of' instead of 'supervision of' my decimated group for generation electrical engineering, which was then put under the Supervising engineer for Transmission Substations. It would seem *obvious* that the power-plant electricals should be located with the *other* power-plant engineers,—civils, mechanicals, 'nukes', environmentals, I&C,—*not* with substation electricals!"

"Why was that merger made, Mr. Sellers?"

"They said we should be with the substation engineers to simplify interfaces between the design of the plants and their substations; but—now *we* handle our own switchyards and substations, too! Also, to lighten the Chief Electrical Engineer's load—by eliminating one supervisor reporting to him. And to facilitate workload transfers between the groups, so they said."

"Mr. Sellers, is that why you decided to retire early now?"

"It was the final straw! My reward for forty years of service. But, too, what with the Company's liberal early retirement pension after age 60 and 40 years of service and Uncle's graduated income tax, why work when my net, take-home, disposable pay was very little different than if I loafed at home?"

As they laughed, he said, "But I'm boring you with office politics and such. I mustn't impose on your polite ear!"

"Oh, no! That's why I dropped by today—when I'm not due to report for work until next Monday. I—wanted to meet you—and my group—and learn all I could about my job before I start. Then—with no experienced help—are you actually doing all the power-plant electrical engineering by yourself—besides training newcomers?"

He laughed mirthlessly. "Sometimes I think so—even though I do dump *everything* on my three new staff men,—each with less than a year's experience! One is a Corps of Engineers Reserve lieutenant from Fort Belvoir's nuclear power-package program,—an E.E. 'grad', a good man—but no utility experience. He's rated as engineer. The second is a bright, young, black, E.E. 'grad' of last June. The Company only looked around for a black after being prodded by government, racial, antidiscrimination regulations—like the new sex rules that led the company to hire you!"

"I resent that," Marion protested. "I am well qualified."

"I'm sure," he dismissed it. "But getting back to that black. Personnel really beat the academic bushes to find him,—a real prize,—rated associate engineer now. The last man is weekly rated as technician. He's going to night school now for his B.S. in E.E., due in three years. They are all ambitious and eager to make good; but it takes time to get the necessary experience,—not taught much in college in my day—and less so today! Meanwhile, they all need technical direction—from someone—when I retire."

"It all sounds like a real challenge for me, Mr. Sellers!" Marion fervently hoped the authoritative sound of her brave words had that reassuring professional ring of today's managerial jargon.

He smiled faintly, looking her over from head to foot. Embarrassed again now, she asked softly, "Mr. Sellers, I sure hope you're not in any real *hurry* to retire right away—because *I*'ll need a lot of your 'technical direction'. But—but—just what *is* keeping you—on the job—now?"

Solemnly he stared over her head. "I—I really don't know. 'The Puritan work ethic'? You know,—the more you earn, the higher the tithe. 'The sweat of your brow'! A need for self satisfaction—of leaving my job in qualified hands—for my small part of the Company—after 40 years."

He smiled now. "Then, too, I'm a stockholder from all the employee purchase plans! You know, I've seen the Company's generating capacity expand twenty times the size it was when I started work—with the number of engineers increasing almost as fast. And all that will be nothing compared to the task facing you!"

She nodded understandingly.

Now he looked down into her eyes. "So, Miss Francis, you see why I'm glad they've found an experienced and qualified woman for the job—since, as I've said, Personnel must have felt obligated by the anti-sexual-discrimination codes to find someone like you,—a practically impossible task, I'd think. Personnel must feel 'tops' at discovering and signing on such a prize as you! The Company's very first woman E.E. in power plant and substation design and construction. A true 'rara avis' in the industry, I'm sure."

Try as she might *not* to ascribe any male chauvinism to his words, she thought she could detect that subtle sarcasm she had been encountering from men ever since she had decided to enter an arena almost exclusively reserved for men. She said questioningly, "But, Mr. Sellers, in this big company of 8,000 employees, am I really the only woman graduate engineer in any discipline now?"

"Yes, Miss Francis, you hold that distinction—among all the hundreds of male engineers. We once had a girl engineer in overhead-lines design—before she married a fellow worker and had to resign by our antinepotism rules. Actually she was a B.A. 'grad', majoring in math,—and not an engineering 'grad'. She only did office calculations and design,—not field engineering. We now have a young woman in our new environmental engineering section, but Ann Teach is actually a BA major in environmental sciences—like biology. Actually there has not been a big rush of women for such hard hat engineering graduate jobs in any field or discipline or industry. Perhaps a few now in petrochemical—and even mining engineering. Some—maybe—in this country. In Russia,—more, I'm told. You are truly in the vanguard, Miss Francis."

Somehow he seemed so down-hearted, so dubious about her as his qualified replacement that she fumbled in her bag and handed him two typed sheets.

"Mr. Sellers, since you were not at my previous meeting in Personnel with your supervisors, would you care to examine an extra copy of my resumé? It has endorsements signed by Personnel's Mr. Keener with my starting date, salary, rating of senior engineer, and so on."

"Thank you, Miss Francis." Rapidly scanning the pages, he murmured, "You're the same age as my niece,—28! An excellent record in a fine engineering school. An E.E. master, too! Honors! R & D utility fellowship. And three years in the engineering department of a good utility system. Three years! That's a real fast time to make engineer up there. A lot of hard work there—even with your prior qualifications in college. I feel greatly relieved. Frankly, I am impressed with your credentials—and with you in person, Miss Francis!"

Marion blushed as she stuffed the papers back in her bag. "Thank you very much for your confidence in me already, Mr. Sellers. And now that I'm in your group under your 'technical' direction, could you call me 'Marion'?"

"Thank you,—Marion. And—how about calling me 'Bob' as all the others in the office do?"

She smiled. "Maybe—later? But—not just now—if you don't mind. You remind me of my father. Can you understand?"

He nodded gravely. "Alright, Marion. Now—do you still want to see your desk—and meet your three-man group? Or can you stand the suspense of waiting another week? It's now after 2 o'clock."

"*I* have enough time, I think. Can we go up now—and satisfy my feminine curiosity? That is, if *you* can spare the time?"

"By all means. Let's go."

Signing in at the desk of the black male guard this time, she followed Mr. Sellers into a waiting elevator; and soon they were walking along an eleventh floor corridor. They stopped at a door with a nameplate reading "Electrical Engineering Dept.—Generation and Transmission Substations Unit." Holding the door open for her to enter, he followed and scratched his "lobby" entry off a logsheet at a typist-receptionist desk, unoccupied at the moment. It was a bright sunlit room, perhaps nearly a hundred feet in length and thirty feet wide with twenty sickly-greenish desks, each with a reference table and non-matching file cabinets, all piled high with rolls of drawings and stacks of papers.

There was a glassed-in office by the receptionist's desk—for the Supervising Engineer. Here and there, fake palm trees sprouted weirdly from the beige wall-to-wall carpet, which was subdivided into aimless patterns by shoulder-high, garish, orange-and-black, plastic separators. Truly a far-out color scheme, Marion thought, probably designed in-house by male engineers who deserve it!

"How do you like our fancy new décor?" Mr. Sellers tossed over his shoulder with a disapproving air which invited no response—fortunately. Feeling that all the occupants were giving her the usual "once-over" now, she demurely fixed her eyes upon Mr. Sellers' back as he led the way down the chair-cluttered aisle towards the far end of the room, which had fixed full-height windows on three sides and a row of file cabinets and costumers against a partition on the interior side, common to another similar adjacent room. All but two of the watching faces were young, Marion noted from quickly stolen glances; she supposed these two veterans to be the principal engineers—for the two substation groups—just as Mr. Sellers was for the power plant group. She wondered how long it would take to earn her promotion to principal engineer, the grade held by Mr. Sellers after forty years! Then Marion smiled as she heard the reassuringly normal, low, wolf whistles behind her as she hurried to keep up with her tall, long-legged guide. As he halted near the windows, his three group members arose and stood beside each desk. As everyone smiled expectantly, Mr. Sellers announced in a slightly amused tone, "Gentlemen, I see this time I don't need to ask for your attention. This is Miss Marion Francis. Of course, Joe and Ben no doubt will introduce her officially when she reports for work next Monday; she's just dropping by for a few minutes this afternoon for orientation. From her Personnel papers I note that she has been hired to replace me—so that at long last—now I can be let out to pasture in 'the promised land'—after wandering 'forty years in the wilderness'. Marion comes as a senior engineer with both a B.S. and M.S. in E.E. as well as two years of industry-sponsored R&D and three years in the electrical engineering department of a northern utility. Now, Marion, this is Tom Fields, our expert in batteries, controls, and such."

Smiling, she shook hands firmly with the cautiously friendly black, repeating his name clearly to impress it in her memory. She approved of him. His hairdo was conventional—not Afro. He was stocky, an inch or two shorter than she—even in her low heels. She felt an instant empathy for the black; they shared something in common here: trailblazing in a new field, he for his race, she for her sex.

"And this is our 'nuke', Art Core, Marion." The Army Reserve officer was an inch or two taller than she—and very slender and erect, she observed. They shook hands politely and repeated each other's names. By his reserved appraising manner, she sensed that he already was assessing her arrival in terms of a threat to his chances for promotion. This, Marion knew, would be a delicate situation which she must face with sensitive understanding.

"And here is our nocturnal scholar, Ed Eager, Marion." At least five, perhaps six inches taller than she, Ed was rather mod-dressed and very handsome with his red waved locks cut collar-length in back but with clean-shaven face. Somehow, she feared that he would be hard for her to handle,—especially in "extracurricular" situations. She had encountered some such problems in college when she was a graduate instructor. With no little difficulty, she succeeded in extricating her hand after the same salutations just as he turned to Mr. Sellers and laughingly volunteered, "Boss, I have that vacant desk next to mine, you know,—if you'd rather *keep* your prints here on this one!"

Everyone laughed as Mr. Sellers replied, "Never mind, Ed. I'll get all that stuff over to you this week. She sits here by me until she moves into my desk—very soon now."

At once the irresistible technician responded laughingly, "O.K., Bob, you're still the boss! But, anyway, the view from my dark desk—way over here by the files in lower Slobbovia—will sure be improved next week!"

As the laughter subsided, Marion said softly, "Well, gentlemen, I'm certainly glad I dropped by to meet you all this afternoon, and I look forward to next Monday when I can begin working with you."

Just then the Army Reserve officer asked seriously, "Marion, we're working with Planning on the specs for our new, fossil-plant, 800-MW. generators now,—and we're making up cases for our stability studies. And—uh—we're trying to reach a consensus to limit the number of costly computer runs—but still—uh—include all the parameters for a practical range of ratings. What was your policy up north on SCR's and response ratios, Marion?"

Oh, no! Not already! Even before she could get into her job—or even sit at her desk, this ambitious military officer—with the management text book on his desk—was starting right off by firing the first gun to challenge her capability of providing the technical direction and leadership needed by her inexperienced young group. And unerringly his aggressively probing thrust had penetrated a fatal weakness in her vulnerable defenses; before her entire group he was about to expose critical deficiencies in her otherwise impressive credentials. All at once her vital credibility was suddenly at stake. Everything could be lost in this desperate moment. He could "bag" her right now.

She breathed deeply and tried to speak casually, "Art, that sounds like an interesting study you're into there. I'm sure it demands more time than I've got right now. Could you—fill me in on it—next Monday? We should have more time to go over it all then. O.K., Art?"

What must Art think of her now, she wondered, for obviously sidestepping a simple question? And Mr. Sellers? She glanced appealingly up into Mr. Sellers' impassive face. Anyway, she really needed his help now.

At once he spoke up matter-of-factly, "That's right, Art. Marion has another appointment this afternoon,—and right now she and I have some other important things to discuss. You've been struggling with that problem for months; I'm sure it can await Marion's contributions next week. Now I'll have to deprive you all of her charming company. Ready, Marion? We'll use the boss's vacant office so as not to disturb these fellows, who all are just itching to get back to work!".

Smiling at all three of her group, she said brightly, "It's been good meeting you all! See you next Monday! 'Bye now!"

Walking into the glassed-in office, he closed the door behind her; and they silently sat down opposite each other, he in the swivel chair and she in a straight side chair with soft plastic upholstering. Between them was a large, empty, reference table.

At last he said quietly, "Marion, everyone can see us; but they can't hear us—if we don't talk too loudly. We don't have any lip-readers out there!"

He was obviously waiting for her to begin discussing now those "other important things" which he had mentioned to Art.

Dully she said, "Thanks for extricating me from the Army's clutches—at least for the moment, Mr. Sellers. I am aware that by saying 'SCR', Art wanted to test my knowledge of a generator's short circuit ratio,—not of silicon-controlled rectifiers,—the SCR's, by the way, with which I am more familiar—from my R & D work in that area. Somewhere from college, I vaguely recall that the SCR of a generator is a ratio of field currents—and that the response ratio somehow relates to excitation characteristics; but—the years have left it all pretty hazy in my mind right now. I—I'll have to dig for it—by next Monday—to answer Art. You see, I've—never worked—in—in that field. I—I—"

Mercifully, he interrupted in a mildly reassuring tone, "Marion, your college,—like most others today,—didn't have a power option, did it?

You got good electrical engineering fundamentals—with a strong tilt towards electronics. Right?"

Nodding in miserable assent, she fixed her eyes on the table as he relentlessly continued, "And your power-company work has been all in planning,—load forecasting, statistical analyses, substation area mapping, ten-year growth projections,—all that sort of thing,—crystal ball stuff. Up there,—as here—until our Planning Department was split off from Engineering a few years ago,—up there all planning and construction engineering are still together in the Engineering Department. Am I correct, Marion?"

Again she nodded affirmatively, not daring either to speak up or look him in the eye. Again he resumed in an objective tone, now sounding for all the world like her sympathetic defense counsel, eliciting favorable testimony from her on the stand in some courtroom series on TV.

"Your impressive resumé is correct and all in order beyond any reproach. Education? A brilliant E.E. record in a fine school. Phi Beta Kappa. Eta Kappa Nu. Honors. Experience? A truly remarkable performance in the electrical engineering department of a progressive utility. And—you are a woman,—just what the doctor ordered,—I mean Uncle Sam,—as a first token move towards compliance with the law of the land—as to elimination of sex bias—in our engineering department. We have thousands of women employees, but now at last we have a female construction engineer—and in my power plant electrical engineering group! Therefore, in conclusion, I find no deception in your resumé whatsoever!"

As he paused expectantly, at last she spoke softly, looking up at his grave face, "But—but you do think my resumé deceived your management—by what it *didn't* say—rather than by what it *did* say, Mr. Sellers?"

Ignoring her question, he posed his own, "But, Marion, how did you think you could just step immediately into this replacement position? It would even take *me* months to fit into such a job up in your former company!"

At once she protested, "My resumé did state that I wanted engineering work in power-plant design and construction, but I didn't know this group-leader job was the only such opening—until the interview here last week. Then—everyone seemed so pleased at discovering me—that I—I just couldn't disappoint them all!"

She added appealingly, "I—I guess—I thought that there'd still be time enough—for—for you to—to educate me—before you retired. I'd try very hard to learn."

"This job is very important to you, isn't it, Marion? Why?"

For the hundredth time—down in the lobby—she had rehearsed it all in her mind. "Mr. Sellers, I need this well-paid position here in town—where I can be with my aunt, who was recently widowed—and now has health and financial problems. She needs me here. And there's nothing to hold me up north now. My parents both died these past two years—after long costly illnesses. I had to let the old mortgaged home go. And—with hundreds of other recent employees, I've just been discharged from my job—effective next week. As you know, jobs—of any kind—are hard to find now."

"Marion, I'm truly sorry to hear of your misfortunes," he said sympathetically. "And our Company is facing that 'firing' problem, too. There's a job freeze on now; your hiring is only because the Company bowed to the law of the land as to sex bias and pressure from the feminist groups."

"I see," Marion said, "where I'll have to face a lot of opposition. Art's question was clearly meant to embarrass me."

"Yes, I'm afraid so," Mr. Sellers conceded.

Now he looked puzzled. "This is of academic interest only, I suppose, since all jobs are frozen in our Planning Department; but why didn't you apply for area-planning work, in which you have experience?"

She searched for the right words. "I did find the work interesting at first. But—maybe I should have been an architect—or a civil engineer! I like to visualize—and plan—and design something needed by mankind—and then engineer it into reality,—to see it materialize,—to blossom before my eyes! And Father wanted a son to follow in his footsteps. You see, he had your job up north—before his illness. He said building more low cost, efficient, reliable power plants was the best way to fight the energy crisis—with electric heat pumps, electric trains and cars, electric power—to save oil. And to feed the world's starving billions in the future—by electricity on the farm, in the fertilizer and machinery factories. And even to improve the environment by sending clean electricity to the cities from the country—and for sewage disposal plants and so on. But you know all this! Father took me on tours of his plants and told me about girls on factory test courses—and Edith Clarke's calculations—and set me on the way—to where I am now, I'd say! Now it's all up to me—to make good—somehow—as he wished for me. Only—I've got his sister depending on me here now, also. What do you think of it all now, Mr. Sellers?"

In the ensuing silence, she looked up at him again. For awhile his thoughts seemed to be far away; but suddenly he leaned forward, and his brown eyes met hers.

"Marion, I'm sure you'll make it. You've got what it takes. Now about Art's questions. Do you want to use this phone to call someone up north there in Generation Planning? And ask if they're paying any premium now to maintain an 0.64 SCR or accepting 0.58—or less today? And whether a standard response ratio of 0.5 fits into their stability studies or whether they're paying for 1.0—or higher?"

"I think not, Mr. Sellers. I've taken up far too much of your time now,—and it'd probably take a while for me to find the right one to answer these questions. I'll write an urgent letter to a friend there tonight—and ask for a reply in a day's time!"

He nodded approvingly. "Now—don't feel badly about it all, Marion. Your Army man didn't know any of the *questions*—not less the *answers*—a few months ago!"

As they both laughed easily now, her tensions all seemed to blow away in the cool air. At last she relaxed limply in the chair as he continued, "Since most colleges now neglect power engineering, I've gotten together my own version of a correspondence course or reference text or guide manual—for the engineering required in my group—with sections indexed on generators, motors, switchgear, transformers, wiring systems, controls, and—cookbook procedures for various calculations on IC-faults, regulation, reactances, system-voltage rating selections, economic maximizing parameter studies—and so on—even down to cable-shielding grounding computations and such details. You could start with the generator section—with the concepts of stability aids and studies—to—uh—refresh your memory on the background theory and application of SCR's and response ratios—and their values on our system—among other items. Of course, that's just if time should hang heavy on your hands this week—before we start loading you with work on Monday!"

"It sounds great! How could I get a copy?"

"I have several bound copies at home. Where do you live? Being a bachelor, I'm free nights. I could drive over to your home."

"That would be marvelous, perfectly marvelous." She gave him her address and arose.

"Now, I really *do* have an appointment—to drive my aunt to her doctor before getting supper." Her eyes met his. "And—thanks—for everything! Truly—I am very grateful, Mr. Sellers."

He smiled. "I'm the one who's thankful—that you're here! And—the sooner you make good in taking over my job, the sooner they'll liberate me! Can you find your way out now? Just be sure to sign out at the elevator desk—or they'll accuse me of loosing some rate protester in the building to plant a bomb in our billing computers!"

Smiling, she said, "I'll make it, Mr. Sellers! And—thanks again! Goodbye—until I see you this evening."

Walking on clouds of relief now, she floated down on the elevator, signed out under the watchful eye of the male Cerberus, and strode triumphantly out into the blazing sunshine, totally oblivious of the searing heat and jostling crowds.

CHAPTER TWO

It was the Morning of the First Day

This was the historic morning of her very first day at work, and already half of the morning was "shot" with the wall clock well after ten. Still Marion remained in the clutches of the Personnel Manager and his assistant, a Miss Wright, apparently in charge of females. Each was clucking over her like a hen with a single chick. All this executive attention was very flattering but also was vaguely disquieting as Marion wondered what lay in store for her after last Monday's harrowing preview.

"Won't you have some more coffee, Miss Francis?"

"No, thanks, Miss Wright." Soon she would have to escape to a ladies' room; the doctor's test sample taken over an hour ago had not afforded anywhere near enough relief to provide for all her subsequent drinking. Mr. Keener was still shuffling her papers. "Ah, yes. The medical report looks to be O.K. You have no problems, I see."

"No, sir." Her height was still a respectably tall five foot eight, but her 123-pound weight was 5 more than usual. She'd have to work on that with sports and diet.

"Mary, have you got her photo I.D. pass now?"

"Yes, sir. Here it is. The colors don't flatter her much, but it's a lot prettier than mine!"

"Miss Francis, here you are. Now you won't need anyone to sign you in anymore. Just please don't lose it. I think the likeness is rather good. Do you like it, Miss Francis?"

"It's alright, Mr. Keener."

"Now, let's see. You're all ready to go to work as our first woman ever to be a bona fide, hard hat, graduate engineer."

Now Miss Wright beamed proudly. "Yes, Miss Francis, for all us women, I'm counting on you to make good in a big way. Everyone in the Company will be watching you."

"I'm certainly going to do my best, Miss Wright. You can be sure of that, alright." For my *own* good,—and for Aunt Dinah,—and for Mr. Sellers,—as well as for the Company and its thousands of other women employees!

Miss Wright added brightly, "You know—we've recently hired our first two women as power-plant roundsmen,—I mean—roving operators. And four women meter readers. Of course, we've 'always' had women designers on your engineering drafting tables. And meter 'lab' testers—and chemists—and computer programmers—and—"

"Uh, Mary, didn't Ken ask to see Miss Francis at ten-thirty, I believe?"

"Yes, sir. Miss Francis, you've never met your Vice President of Engineering and Construction,—Mr. Blood,—have you?"

"No, I haven't, Miss Wright."

The doctor had worried about her fast pulse of nearly 100 before exertion; she had to sit quietly for fifteen minutes before her nerves had allowed her heart beat to subside into the low 80's. Now her pulse was suddenly racing away again.

"Mary, I'll introduce Miss Francis to Ken now. I know you've got that monthly status report to get out today."

"Yes, sir." Miss Wright obviously looked disappointed at being deprived of the honor of showing off Personnel's prize find,—the Company's first woman engineer.

Miss Wright turned to her. "Miss Francis, please call me if there is anything I can do for you or any questions I can answer. And good luck now. Have a nice day!"

"Thank you, Miss Wright." She could use all the luck available anywhere. Now she was following Mr. Keener out to the elevator and up to the rarefied atmosphere of the executive level on the 20th floor. The fancy colors of Mr. Blood's ornate outer office were no less bizarre than her own.

"Midge, this is Miss Marion Francis. She is to replace Mr. Sellers when he retires in September, you know."

Oh, no! Not in less than two months!

Turning to her, he said, "Miss Francis, this is Miss Mitter, Mr. Blood's secretary."

Pleasant, plump, fiftyish, with black hair streaked with silver, and nearly her own height, Miss Mitter arose and shook hands, saying warmly, "Oh, my, Miss Francis, you'll cause quite a stir around here! It's good to meet you."

"Thank you, Miss Mitter. Please call me 'Marion'." It would be good to have Midge on your side, she decided.

"Oh, Mr. Keener, you and—Marion—go right in. Mr. Blood is expecting her."

But not Mr. Keener? She wondered why—uneasily. Mr. Blood was standing beside his large mahogany desk. About fifty, thin, with black hair and sharp features, and nearly as tall as Mr. Sellers, he wore the same bewildered smile of all those she had met lately.

Proudly Mr. Keener announced in ring-master style, "Ken, this is Miss Marion Francis, the experienced woman engineer you requested to take Mr. Sellers' place in September."

"Now, Bill, are you sure she isn't the Hollywood actress you need for our public relations movies on TV spot commercials this winter?"

"Well, now, that's an idea, Ken! As you've suggested, she does look as though she could double in brass to save on the cash-flow problems we're having in the Company!"

As the two men laughed, she seemed to be ignored altogether. At last Mr. Blood extended his hand. "Please excuse our levity, Miss Francis. It stems from our relief at finding a qualified engineer—and a woman, too!—for your important work. After 40 years, Bob Sellers surely will be missed in the Company; he's had an important influence on the way we do things—in the power plants and substations. Yes, indeed, his shoes will be hard to fill; I'm sorry to see him go."

He paused while she wondered if he really didn't know why Mr. Sellers was retiring early.

"But now we're counting on you, Miss Francis; oh, may I call you 'Marion'?"

"Please do, Mr. Blood. Yes, I met Mr. Sellers briefly last Monday; and—I'll certainly try to absorb as much knowledge from him as I can during the next two months."

Smiling thinly, Mr. Blood now turned to Mr. Keener. "Well, thanks, Bill, for pulling a rabbit out of your magic hat. No pun intended on the famed bunny girls, Marion! Now, Bill, I know you're busy this time of month on your status reports; so—I'll escort her downstairs so that she can get to work now. That's what you want, isn't it, Marion?"

"Yes, sir, Mr. Blood,—by all means. But I can find my way down to the 11th floor; I know you're very busy, too."

He frowned.

"Well, I want to see Joe Knight, anyway."

Abruptly leaving Mr. Keener standing beside Midge, her V.P. strode towards the elevators; and she almost had to run to keep up with his brisk pace. In the 11th floor corridor, he at last broke his stony silence, "Howard Richards, your department manager, is out of town today. Anyway, you've already met him,—Marion?"

"Yes, sir. Briefly—at my interview with Mr. Knight and Mr. Board—in Mr. Keener's office—two weeks ago."

"Howard is on the 10th. Your department is now scattered over five floors—with other non-engineering people sandwiched in between on each floor. An inefficient set-up, but I'm always after the Chief to consolidate us—whenever money gets more plentiful again. Well, Marion, you're young and active enough not to mind the shuttle bit. However, I must say,—from your perfect figure,—that you don't really need the exercise of running up one and down two,—our rule!"

"Thank you, Mr. Blood. And, I might say, you don't either!"

As he laughed briefly, she wasn't going to admit to wanting to shed those five extra pounds as long as he hadn't noticed them. She added perversely, "I have to confess I haven't seen anyone running up *or* downstairs as yet!" He frowned.

"We *try* to get everyone to walk up one and down two floors—unless health problems require the use of the elevators. Well, here we are at your Chief Electrical Engineer's office. Midge phoned for him—and your Supervising Engineer—to await us here,—Marion."

Here comes the next hurdle for me to jump now, Marion thought.

Sure enough, the two men stood by the table as Mr. Blood escorted her into the small office, saying, "Morning, Joe, Ed."

Smiling, they both chorused, "Good morning, sir," their eyes on her.

"Well, gentlemen, Personnel's red-tape clerks and 'medicos' have now pronounced Miss Francis, or, Marion, here,—to be officially fit to plunge right into her work up to her trim elbows. And she agrees she's willing and able to tackle her job. I see she doesn't even have to roll up her sleeves before digging into that heavy work load you have ready for her."

They all smiled. The paper had predicted another scorcher; so she had selected a light, blue, sleeveless dress for the sweltering bus ride home this afternoon. And, if the office air conditioning got too frigid, she had a thin, matching, cashmere sweater in her bag. Now the Chief Electrical Engineer hesitantly suggested that they all sit down; Mr. Blood grimaced.

"Alright,—but I only have a couple of points to make." As they all sat down promptly, the V.P. began, "First, Ben, by noon—will you get out a memo for all bulletin boards, stating that—immediately—Miss Marion Francis,—and include her phone and room numbers,—will assume the technical direction of the Generation E.E. Group—period. Mr. Robert Sellers will retire September 1. Got it, Ben?"

Mr. Board had hurriedly scribbled the announcement on a small scratch pad with a ball point he apparently had ready for the occasion. "Yes, sir, but—"

"But what, Ben?"

"Well, sir, it's been customary—in the past, you know,—to refer to 'effecting an orderly transfer' for that period—so that Marion wouldn't actually take over by herself from Bob until September 1. I understand that Marion is—uh—qualified and experienced enough to take over at once, but what will Bob do for the next six weeks, sir?"

Mr. Blood smiled triumphantly as she held her breath. "That's my other point. Today Bob will move up to my office—and take that desk behind Midge. He will screen technical mail for me and handle special assignments until he retires. That way Marion will be able to take over her job completely today—without having to sit around on the bench the rest of the summer waiting for Bob to leave the team. Any more questions?"

Mr. Knight grinned. "Well, sir, you intend—just putting Marion right up on the firing line—as we used to say in the Army."

She wondered miserably why the environment here was so favorable for clichés. Even she could scarcely refrain from repeating that hoary collection: How am I going to do any work if I'm on the firing line, keeping my nose to the grindstone, my eye on the ball, my shoulder to the wheel, my ear to the ground, my hand on the plow, and—

Nodding vigorously now, Mr. Blood spoke emphatically, "You're right, Joe!"

Marion felt a sinking tug. She suspected that these top execs probably wanted Personnel to fail—in finding her as a suitable woman for the job; and they resented Personnel claiming credit with the Chief for her discovery—and then forcing her down their throats—when all along they had some *man* in mind for the position.

Marion doubted that Mr. Sellers had breathed a word about their interview, or that Art had posed a ticklish question; it was more that they must be skeptical of her capability to handle the job. They must mean to expose her promptly—and then find someone else before Mr. Sellers left.

It wasn't fair. She had done nothing to deserve such shabby treatment. Maybe her resumé could have been more complete, but it was accurate—with nothing but the truth—as Mr. Sellers had said. They could have asked more questions at her interview. And now they were out to humiliate her, ruin her reputation—just when she had thought she had it made. Well, she wasn't about to back down and make a clean breast of it all now; she'd go down fighting at least—even if she couldn't hack it. Why, they've even got me thinking in their cliché jargon now! Did they guess that Mr. Sellers was probably in her corner now? Maybe he could still help her even from the 20th floor, but she'd better make a stab at trying to keep him safely beside her as long as she could. She drew a deep breath to help her racing heart.

"Mr. Blood, I *am* anxious to get down to work, and I *do* think I can handle the job. Frankly, I also appreciate your position, too. You think that, while my credentials for this job seem to be all in order, the proof of the pudding is in the eating. And you'd like to be sure—before Mr. Sellers retires—so that, if I should fail, there'd still be time to—to make other arrangements. You'd want to use the experience of Mr. Sellers— in his last several weeks—to break in someone else. Nevertheless, in all fairness, even if Mr. Sellers would move to my old company, he would be the first to concede that even he would need several months to learn the ropes, the organization, the set-up. Also, to get the background,—the policies, and the methods before he could put together an effective contribution or 'take over the job' completely on his own."

Pausing to catch her breath, she saw that she was still holding their attention and so rushed on, "May I suggest a slight change then in your second point, Mr. Blood? That I take over at once, as you said, but that Mr. Sellers remain at his present desk—to brief and advise me—for the next three weeks at least. Then, if I fail to swing it, you'd still have Mr. Sellers for an equal period of three weeks to break in another replacement. If you agree, Mr. Blood, there'd still be no need to revise the *wording* of your announcement memo."

She still could detect no change in Mr. Blood's expression; it was as though his face were chiseled from marble. At last Mr. Board found his voice.

"I think Marion has a point there, Mr. Blood. That way we'll have a better chance at keeping that heavy work load flowing smoothly. Even with *both* Marion and Bob, we're at least one position short in the group, you know, with all that attrition—and Harry's retirement just last winter."

He looked at Mr. Knight in an obvious bid for assistance.

The Chief Electrical Engineer scratched his head nervously. "Yes, Ben, I agree we're in a tough spot in that chronically understaffed group;—and I do think Marion's—suggestion will maximize our maneuverability there in any contingency. We all know that Bob's three men are very inexperienced; each has less than a year's experience on the job—or any such work, for that matter. Mr. Blood, don't you think we can go along with Marion's idea?"

As three pairs of eyes studied the V.P.'s impassive features for clues, Mr. Blood abruptly arose.

"You win, Marion. You are irresistibly persuasive!"

Turning to her two supervisors, he said, "Now, gentlemen, it's up to you to get the harness fitted to her shapely shoulders. Let her begin pulling her weight around here, starting right away! And, Ben, get that memo out *now,* so that everyone will know to work with *her* and not Bob from now on."

Now already she was "the old gray mare" harnessed up to the—The V.P. was extending his hand, so she stood up quickly; he really had a firm grip.

"Marion, we're all counting on you! Now Joe and I have some other things to discuss—if you and Ben will excuse us."

"I'll surely do my best, Mr. Blood!" she said stoutly.

Out in the hall again, she could understand now why Mr. Blood had to escort her down here—without Mr. Keener. Entering the now familiar doorway, she saw that her name was already on the sign-out pad as Mr. Board scratched out his entry.

"Pat, will you phone downstairs for any messages? And can you read my scribbling here? I need this memo out for all bulletins by noon. Oh, Marion, have you met Pat,—Mrs. Holder? Pat, Miss Francis is replacing Mr. Sellers—as you'll see on the memo."

Smiling, she murmured, "Pat, it's good to meet you!" The receptionist-stenographer was an attractive black girl, perhaps twenty-five, with about her own build but a couple of inches shorter. Pat had a soft polite handshake.

"Pleased to meet you, Marion. I never heard of a girl being a real 'genu-wine' engineer; but, anyway, it'll be good having another woman in this roomful of demanding men—always wanting something right away like."

Pat turned to the grinning Mr. Board.

"I'll get this right out, Mr. Board. You *know* I can decipher your *worst* scrawl by now—after the year's practice I've had! And I have another such memo to use as a guide. This goes to Construction, Operating, Purchasing, upstairs, downstairs, crosstown,—the works! Right?"

"Right! Good girl, Pat,"

Turning towards her now, Mr. Board said, "Marion, please sit down in my office here while I go get Mr. Sellers to join us."

The dark, handsome Mr. Board seemed to be sympathetic but rather insecure. He was about her height and around forty. On the other hand, the blond Mr. Knight appeared to be more aggressively calculating and unapproachable; he was perhaps only several years younger than Mr. Sellers and also several inches shorter.

This time she did not arise but simply smiled up at Mr. Sellers, who was entering the door first.

"Well, good morning, Marion! I see you've made it this far, looking—as always—pretty as a picture!"

"Thank you, Mr. Sellers, but somehow I'm afraid I *feel* like they've all taken the zip out of me already this morning!"

"Oh, no! Not that! Who'd do a nasty thing like that? We wouldn't want to do *that,* would we, Ben?"

The supervising engineer grinned wryly, "I hope Marion's not talking about *us.* Say, Bob,—you didn't tell me you'd already met Marion!"

"You didn't ask me, Ben! Like *you* never told *me* that *you* had hired Marion two weeks ago!"

Mr. Board stroked his brow nervously.

"Well, Bob, I was asked to keep it all quiet—until Management approved all the terms. I guess we didn't want to arouse your hopes prematurely!"

As the two men sat down, the Supervising Engineer cleared his throat, stared down at the desk, and began to speak in formal tones, "Bob, there'll be a memo on the bulletin boards at noon, announcing your September 1 retirement and Marion's immediate assumption of your position. Ken Blood wanted you to come up to his office in a 'consulting' capacity today, but we all persuaded him to delay that order for at least three weeks. Then a final decision will be made as to your last three weeks. Meanwhile, he wants you only to brief and advise Marion, but you're no longer to do, or re-do, any of the group's work. And you're to let Marion handle the other three men. That procedure should give Marion the best opportunity to get a handle on the job, to learn by doing. Right away, now."

As he paused, Mr. Sellers spoke up lightly, "Now, Ben, you know *I* haven't turned out a lick of work myself for years! I've dumped everything on my fellows—to train them. Anyway, the only trouble is, they've all 'graduated' from my group as fast as I've trained 'em! Even the mechanicals downstairs complain that I've gotten *them* to write my electrical letters to their mechanical vendors! With such superlative, executive, delegating abilities, I don't know why I couldn't even maintain my supervising functional rating for my own group! As for my 'graduates', one went on to be Manager of the Test Dept., another to be an Operating Department supervisor. One,—no, two, quit for high-earning law partnerships—after getting law degrees at Company expense at night school. And—"

Frowning now, Mr. Board interrupted, "Now, Bob, you know you're actually *doing* most of the work now—even though it all comes out over the names of your fellows. I can detect your wording, ideas, practices, policies in all their papers, letters, estimates, job orders, studies, reports, recommendations for purchases,—you name it! Yes, you used to dictate dozens of letters a week. I admit that's all stopped now, but—"

"Well, a lot of that dropped out when consultants began taking over our bigger projects. When that happened, I had *them* turn out the paper work to suit my requirements. If they're getting the pay and credit for the job, let them do the man-hour work. When errors slip past us, *we* get blamed! And don't fool yourself! It costs us more to pay consultants profit on our work! They—"

"Yes, yes, I know how you think on all that, Bob. But you *do* understand now what Ken Blood wants? Marion is to take over the group at once. You're only to brief and advise her about the job when she asks questions. O.K.?"

"Alright, Ben. I'll go quietly—without the handcuffs."

Mr. Board looked relieved as Mr. Sellers left the room ahead of her. "Marion, Bob will take good care of you; but, if you need anything, just let me know."

"Thank you, Mr. Board," she called back as she hastened to catch up with Mr. Sellers.

To the waiting trio, he proudly announced with an obvious tone of relief in his voice, "Well, you guys, it's official now. Marion takes over my job as of this moment. I'll just brief and advise her about the job for awhile—when she wants me to."

After a chorus of "Congratulations, Marion!" she smilingly replied, "Thank you, fellows! I'm counting on you all!"

As the men returned to their desks, Art quietly murmured to her, "Marion, I really didn't mean to put you on the spot last Monday; I was just trying to pick your Yankee brains!"

She *wished* she could believe him, but her knowledge of psychology and her equally extensive knowledge of men warned her to be cautious. He and—later—Ed Eager and Tom Fields all were likely candidates to replace her should she fail. She knew how invidiously jealousy streaked the human mind. For some time to come she would have to be wary. Extremely wary. But as long as Art was outwardly conciliatory, she would be also. She exclaimed, "Your question deserved deep study. I scribbled down some notes here on our practices; I hope you can decipher my scrawl. Then we can go over any additional questions later."

"Say, this is great! And you write a beautiful hand—just like you look! Thanks a lot, Marion! I'll digest it all now."

Quickly he stepped over to his desk while examining her notes as though they were as valuable a find as the Rosetta Stone.

Cautiously she glanced over to Mr. Sellers, and they both smiled. She whispered, "Your guide is a great source of information. I've scanned your whole encyclopedic set of references. It's all so lucid even *I* can grasp it all. It's all even more fascinating than I had ever imagined! You should be a college 'prof' now!"

"Don't wish that on me!"

"I mean it! Oh! And did you intend to include that stack of papers with your collected arcane formulae and technical data?"

He nodded; and she asked, "May I have another set of texts,—one for home and the other for the office?"

"Like any author, I'm flattered."

"Mr. Sellers, whenever did you find time to write it all?"

"Oh, mostly in hotel rooms—or trains—or planes—on business trips. Seldom at home. Dictated in a machine here—mostly before and after hours—or on lunch time."

When his phone rang, she hurriedly walked back down the aisle, wondering if she'd have to write "Little girls' room" on the signout sheet. Pat was not at the desk, so she quickly slipped out into the hall and into the ladies' room.

That certainly was a relief, she sighed, as she emerged from the stall, still trying to smooth out her tight dress and half-slip—and now checking herself in the wall mirror.

"Honey, you sure do have a lovely figure! But the devil of it is,—how to keep it, isn't it, darlin'?"

Glancing over to the couch, she saw a reclining Pat, relaxing with a cigarette.

"Oh, hello, Pat! I wondered where you were."

"Why, Marion, this is a nice refuge for us 'libbers' to escape to. And, I'll tell you,—all those overbearing men don't have it anywhere near as good in their dinky 'ole' room!"

They both laughed. "Well, Pat, don't go to sleep! And, remember, *I*'ll know where to find you! See you!"

Back at her desk, Marion noticed that the wall clock showed 11:45. Art and Ed were missing, together with most of the office force.

"Mr. Sellers, are they all at lunch already? What are our hours?"

Stretching his long arms and legs luxuriously, he replied, "Oh, nearly everyone's out to beat the noon crowd in the restaurants. The hours in this office are eight—to a quarter of five—with three-quarter hour for lunch—at any time. Ed punches a time clock morning and night."

Seeing Tom still at his desk, she whispered, "Why doesn't someone go out with Tom?"

He smiled. "Oh, they tried to at first. Then they all found out that he was avoiding them—because he was lunching with his fiancée! He now prefers to get a can of soup from the second floor lunch room and eat at his desk. Sandwiches are made by his wife."

"Well, when—and where—do *you* eat, Mr. Sellers?"

"I usually go out at one or a little later. That way there's also no crowd. And the office is empty and quiet now, so I can get a lot of work done without interruptions by phone calls or visitors. Also, I find I can reach our Construction guys in their shacks then—as they empty their lunch boxes. At other times they're unavailable—out on the job. Of course, that's a two-way street; they know they can get me then, too. Also, my late lunch makes for a shorter afternoon. I eat a good breakfast."

"Well! Sounds well engineered! And the location?"

"If it's 'falling weather', I have to put up with the vending machines down on the second floor. Not bad, really. Soup, ice cream, sandwiches, milk, and so forth. But I like to walk several blocks to a cafeteria on the tenth floor. I get a quick dollar lunch of soup, milk, crackers and cornbread."

"Also sounds good, Mr. Sellers. May I accompany you today? Dutch treat, of course?"

He smiled. "I'd welcome your company, Marion. It gets a little lonesome eating by myself. I used to eat with several, other, old guys, but they've retired. And my young fellows here have eaten with me, but usually they can't wait that long. Just give me five minutes to see Rob Wonder, who just phoned."

No sooner had Mr. Sellers left the room than his phone rang insistently. Now for the first time *hers* was jangling her taut nerves; and she managed to say calmly, "Good afternoon. This is Miss Francis."

"Wayne Landfall here. We haven't met yet. I'm Vice President of Operations. I called Bob Sellers, but he isn't in right now. Anyway, I just got the memo about you! Congratulations! Now I hope you can help me."

It was a pleasant but urgent voice. He *would* call right when Mr. Sellers had just left, and you don't keep V.P.'s waiting. "Yes, sir. I'll try!"

"Fine! The Chief's secretary has just transferred a call to me from the Governor's Energy Council chairman. He wants to know why our Company doesn't run at 5% lower voltage *all the time*—to save fuel oil—rather than just over these hot afternoon, air-conditioning, peak periods like we're doing now. I've asked him if he can hold on a few minutes—since I've got another call:—*you*! He said he's glad to 'hang in there'—rather than go back to the governor's meeting without an answer!"

Desperately she tried to shift her brain into high gear. She had come prepared, aware that she would be asked some tough questions, many designed to embarrass her. She cradled the phone on her shoulder and sought out a booklet containing the information. She read as she spoke:

"Well, Mr. Landfall, I'll admit I've never given the subject much thought, but let's see if we can 'blue-sky' the right answer now. We reduce voltage 5%—and at once all resistive loads—like incandescent lighting and resistance process heating—draw about 10% less power by the I-square ratio. Even the heavy induction-motor load falls off *slightly* with the 10% increased slips—as we can see by the curves in the handy G.E. pocket book I've found here. So—the peak load is maybe 3% less over the hot afternoon,—and we have enough generating capacity to get by until the temperature drops near sunset, thermostats unload air conditioners, offices close for the day, and so on. But, if we kept the voltage at 95% *all the time,*—then automatic or even manual controls would run the equipment,—pumps, heaters, even air conditioners,—for longer periods to get their jobs done:—tanks filled, water evaporated, and so on. Motors run satisfactorily at 90% voltage but 2% less efficiently at lower than rated voltage—as these G.E. curves show. Therefore, more kilowatt-hours will be needed and *more* fuel oil burned in our furnaces to do the same work less efficiently. Customers may even have to install more lighting or pumps or heating to satisfy their needs.

"So—our voltage reductions are to get us through temporary peak-load periods of several hours each day by reducing power demand temporarily by 3%. But in the long run the voltage reduction uses more—not less—fuel to do the job less efficiently than designed. Also, at my previous utility company we always had some overloaded feeders where corrective relief work was being scheduled to improve low voltage conditions. There—continuous 5% lower voltage would cause motors to run at less than 90% voltage, resulting in motor failures and customer complaints. So voltage reductions are to reduce the short-time peak loads so that our available 97% generation capacity can supply the customer requirements—but not in an efficient manner—until we can install more generation to avoid this undesirable, *fuel-wasting* expedient. As a continuous long-range practice, more energy and more fuel are used up by the less-than-design-voltage operation. It's only a *short-time capacity-reducing* not a *long-term energy*—or *fuel-saving* method. How does all that sound, Mr. Landfall? I'm sorry I took so much time, but I've just never thought it through before! For a politician, he's got a good question!"

"Right! I see where the IEEE Power Engineering Society Winter Convention in New York had a panel of experts expound on that very question. I'll bet they came up with your answer. Thanks, Miss Francis! And I'm looking forward to meeting you soon. But right now let me get back to our patient man—with your explanation. 'Bye now!"

"Goodbye, Mr. Landfall." Limply she hung up the phone and collapsed against the back of her swivel chair, tossing the little G.E. book on her desk.

"I couldn't have done as well or as clearly. Congratulations, Marion!"

She hurriedly rotated to stare up at Mr. Sellers, standing behind her table and smiling down at her.

"Mr. Sellers! You were there all the time—and let me struggle through it all! I thought you had gone downstairs!"

"I met Rob outside our door here! He had to come up to see someone else. You were doing fine,—so why should I butt in? You should repeat the incident to Joe and Ben after lunch. They'd appreciate how you saved them from embarrassment—since they couldn't have come up with it like you did. Incidentally, Wayne is a good man. He used to be a mechanical engineer here in this department. Before that he was one of our power-plant chief engineers. Now, doesn't that pep you up?"

"Yes, it does! Thanks! I know I couldn't have swung it if I hadn't boned up on your power course all last week!"

He handed her two memos. "Here are two copies of your appointment notice that I got from Pat. Now you won't have to push through the mob to read it on the bulletin boards! And you can let your aunt see one—and send the other to your friend up north."

"Thanks again, Mr. Sellers." It did give her apprehensive morale another boost to see her name thus in print. Seeing is believing.

One could say this memo was the Company's declaration in black-and-white for all to see, affirming its official confidence in her ability to hold down the important job of engineering the design, purchase, and installation of millions of dollars of power-plant electrical equipment and systems with the optimum efficiency, economy, safety, and reliability to serve the energy needs of millions of people.

"Well, Marion, shall we go to lunch now—before all the others return from theirs with full stomachs, ready to kill the afternoon with you and me?"

Smiling, she arose, slipping the strap of her bag over her right shoulder. Striding behind Mr. Sellers past the table with the "T. L. FIELDS" sign, she commented cheerfully, "That soup smells good, Tom. What is it?" On his desk she saw one of those flashy books exposing just who controls America's wealth.

He grinned. "Just beef-vegetable, but it's better than that cheap stuff you'll get where Bob's taking you! Don't say I didn't warn you, Marion!"

Maybe, but the onions are too powerful in Tom's soup, she thought, as she wrote an "L" opposite her name on the sign-out sheet. Mr. Sellers was holding the door for her as she walked out into the corridor. He was obviously a relic of the old school, but she had to admit that she still enjoyed the deference of these little courtesies. An old-fashioned country girl at heart, she herself must be an anachronism in some ways—but certainly not in every way!

Behind her, Mr. Sellers let the heavy door close with a decisive slam, thus ending the first morning of her first day with no inkling of what new challenges awaited her.

CHAPTER THREE

Solid State Snafu

SEVERAL STEPS AHEAD of her, a rather tall, balding, middle-aged, executive-type gentleman was walking resolutely towards the last table à deux at a window. Increasing her pace, Marion overhauled him halfway down the long carpeted aisle; and, as she passed him in the home stretch, she casually looked away towards the windows as though she hadn't noticed him. In full view of all these diners, it would definitely be unladylike for her to engage this V.I.P. in an unseemly waiters' race—even though they were toting their trays by hand instead of on the crowns of their heads. Winning by a good ten feet, Marion triumphantly landed her tray on the table top and unslung her shoulder-strap bag to her chair back.

Behind her now she heard Mr. Sellers say, "Good afternoon, Mr. King. We've got another hot one. I see all our old reliables are on the line out there."

"Yes, thank goodness! They need it up north again as usual."

Now Mr. Sellers touched her elbow.

"Oh, Mr. King, this is Miss Marion Francis, my replacement. Marion, this is Mr. King, Chief Executive Officer of our Company."

"How do you do, Miss Francis? You set a fast pace!" Mr. King was smiling amiably. "But you'll need to—to replace Bob Sellers."

Flustered, she smiled. "How do you do, Mr. King?"

"We'll hate to lose Bob, and we're counting on you now! I'd invite you two to sit with us, but I see my fellows have left just enough space for my chair at that big table over there. I'll be seeing you both!"

As he turned away still smiling, she realized he couldn't shake hands because there was no place to set down his tray. Marion shook her head as she unloaded her full tray.

"Well, Mr. Sellers, that was the wrong race to win; but I lucked out, I guess! Not too much damage done since this wasn't the table he wanted after all. He'll just think I'm another of those pushy 'libbers', trying to elbow their way past the men into places where only Uncle Sam thinks they should be!"

Mr. Sellers laughed. "Don't worry! He's an engineer, though not electrical. He won't think any such thing. But he will remember you after this! Here! Let me get rid of your tray for you."

"Thank you," she murmured as she watched—for next time—where he stacked the trays on a special rack by the water table.

Returning, he handed her a glass of water.

"Thank you—again; you're spoiling me!" She smiled as he moved her chain under her and up nearer the table. It was a heavy, armed, "captain's" chair with a dark polished mahogany finish and luxurious black leather upholstering.

"Why, Mr. Sellers, it's really very nice here! Quiet, a posh-looking place, at reasonable prices! Wonderful view of downtown and the river docks." She sighed audibly.

"The only bad thing, Mr. Sellers, is the trouble with any cafeteria: I eat too much! I should have *followed* you—and your example! Instead, while I selected your split-pea soup, milk, and cornbread muffin,—and then went on to this harmless fruit salad,—this delicious-looking chocolate pudding tempted me,—and I couldn't resist! I'll gain more pounds here than I can lose working in my aunt's yard!"

Mr. Sellers smiled. "Marion, I'm sure you don't need to worry about your weight! Do you like to work in the yard?"

"I think it's good for me to get outdoors. Last week I replaced a rotten step board and riser, painted a porch, trimmed some shrubbery, weeded flower beds, and mowed the lawn—with a hand mower, too! Aunt Dinah doesn't like gasoline mowers with their obnoxious noise and smelly fumes. And the big kids in the neighborhood will not push an 'Armstrong' mower these days—despite all the publicity on physical fitness, gasoline-energy crisis, the environmental-ecological air-pollution bit, not to mention the inflationary cost-of-living and the recession with 9% unemployment!"

"Yes, I know! Well, your aunt must be glad you're here! Your yard work sounds like my 'bachelor's hall'! I suppose you're ready to rest after you get supper, especially after all that work in the yard these days."

"Yes, we just sit on the patio and talk until the mosquitoes drive us in to the screen porch after dusk. Nothing exciting in my night life now!"

He was faintly smiling as he stared out the window. She wondered if someday she could bring herself to ask why he had never married, but there would be the risk of his questioning stones penetrating her own vulnerable glass house. As they ate rather silently, considering the soup, he at last spoke, "In spite of the inference in your resumé, you aren't really a Yankee, are you?"

She grinned, "You're very perceptive! I can't hide a thing from you! No, I'm from Dixie! I'm returning home again below the Mason and Dixon Line—where I was born and raised. Father moved north to greener pastures after I went away to college nine years ago."

"I thought so, Marion. Your voice doesn't have that hard nasal twang, and your aunt is a true Southern belle. I'm delighted that I met her."

"Mr. Sellers, do you mind if we talk shop at lunch?"

"Not with someone as charming as you, Marion. What's on your mind?"

"My job—on which I'm determined to make good. And I will! I know that I'm going to face opposition. Loads of it. That doesn't faze me. What does worry me are those who will pose as friends—with a drawn knife poised to strike."

"Heavens," she quickly added, "I don't mean *you*, Mr. Sellers; you're about to retire, and so you hardly want *my* job."

"But others do, I concede," Mr. Sellers said, and shook his head sorrowfully. "Rivalry is the way of the world, I suppose; but I'm glad you're aware, Marion. At all times, be very cautious." He deliberated a bit and spoke again, "As you must know from your extensive experience, Marion, there are interdepartmental rivalries in all large corporations. Frankly, I must say that I am still fuming over Personnel hiring *you*." He paused before adding the obvious, "*I* should have been the one to pick my successor—or at least have a 'say' in the selection."

"Your brief is well-taken and *justified*," Marion conceded, "but surely you would not want me to fail over *that*?"

"No, not over any personal 'gripe', Marion; *that* I can swallow and live with. But you should know that, retirement or not, and, bypassing an accumulation of personal slights and insults, my first loyalty is to the Company. In the last—or first—analysis, I must always think of what is best for the firm which employed me for the past forty years— and which, I might add, will be paying me a very liberal pension—plus dividends, I hope!"

"And you think that a *man* would have been more suitable?" Marion prompted.

"Frankly, I do. And this hasn't anything to do with your *competence*, Marion. You're competent enough, but—"

"But I'm a woman."

"Yes, and it's a handicap that has nothing to do with efficiency proper. Let me illustrate my point. You are very attractive, Marion. Built the way we are, it is inevitable that some men you work with will regard you as a *woman*, not a qualified technical expert."

"I've faced that problem before, Mr. Sellers. Many, many times. I take pride in knowing how to handle myself."

"Good," Mr. Sellers applauded—and went on. "There is also the matter of *drinking*. Time after time secretaries have been called to rush to a certain restaurant to steer some executive home."

"I've lived through the matter of guys having a few Martinis too many on my old job, too."

Mr. Sellers had more to say, "Personnel says hundreds in the Company have a serious drinking problem, and a manager was retired on disability pension for alcoholism. Maybe you'd better call on our special, Company, confidential counselor on alcoholism; he might tell you which co-workers you are to guard against."

"I may do just that, Mr. Sellers. Execs or not, I know how ugly men—and some women—can get once they're 'stoned.' But I'll do this a bit later; let me get my bearings first."

"You're wise, Marion. I'm betting on you to overcome *all* obstacles. And I'll help in what ways I can, using one overall yardstick: the best welfare of the Company."

"Thank you, Mr. Sellers. I can't think of anything fairer. If I fail to be an asset to the Company, I *should* be thrown out on my ear."

For answer, he patted her hand, which just then rested on the table.

Soon, despite more conversation, they had finished eating their leisurely lunch. "Are we ready to go back to the salt mines, Marion?"

She arose, saying smilingly, "In many ways you sound just like my father: judicious and determined. I am his daughter, all the way, without any generation gap."

When they returned, Mr. Sellers said, "See! It's only one-thirty. We used only a half hour for our lunch."

However, no sooner had they sat down, than all the others began straggling back. Now Art was standing beside her desk.

"Boss lady, I'm on my way to a two-thirty meeting at Cliffside to discuss two excitation failures these past several days among our dozen, 1,250-horsepower, 'circ.' motors, our first power-plant synchronous motors, I understand. It's a hot subject since a decision must be made soon on our new River Shore Plant—of synchronous versus induction; and, also, of course, we mustn't let motor failures jeopardize Cliffside startup operations now. We're on the spot because the Operating Department never has wanted any synchronous motors. For all previous plants, Bob has gone along with them in evaluation studies—of prices, installation costs, maintenance, losses, reactive value, control, and so on—where the net saving was only a thousand dollars or so. But at Cliffside—with the number, size, and very low speed of the pumps—

SOLID STATE SNAFU 33

there was nearly a third of a million dollars in net savings for the synchronous type. So now, where do we go from here, Marion?"

She certainly hadn't anticipated such a plant inspection,—involving trouble-shooting, blame-placing, problem-solving sessions,—on the afternoon of her very first day on the job. Why hadn't Art alerted her this morning?

She thought she knew the answer; it was a deliberate attempt to push her into a corner. And she strongly resented his use of "boss lady", but she knew that it would be a mistake to make an issue of it now. She spoke evenly, "Well, Art, do you really need me at your meeting? I hadn't planned on it, you know,—with all these papers on my desk—on my first day."

Art looked obviously disappointed as he mumbled, "Suit yourself, Marion. I just thought this would be a good chance to show you our hottest new project—where we don't want any electrical problems getting us any bad publicity in the management echelons. But if you—Oh, yes! I've even picked up your hard hat downstairs—and put your nameplate on it! I found your form filled out on your desk!"

"Thanks, Art! O.K., you win. You twisted my arm. Lead on, MacDuff!"

They both grinned as she grabbed the yellow plastic helmet and began adjusting the straps to fit her head. She then phoned home and luckily was able to get Aunt Dinah alerted about a late supper.

Arising, she picked up her bag and turned to Mr. Sellers.

"Art is taking me to Cliffside now. I'd say we'll be 'kinda' late getting back..."

Mr. Sellers spoke solicitously, "I'm sure you will—with such a late meeting. Will that be alright at home tonight? If not, you could let Art go alone. If necessary, he could phone you about any urgent decision required of you this afternoon. After all, this *is* your first day here!"

"I'll be O.K. I think Art wants me along. So—all cleared for takeoff! See you in the morning, Mr. Sellers."

She felt his eyes upon her as she followed Art down the aisle to sign out for Cliffside. Ten minutes later, inching through the downtown traffic, she looked over at her chauffeur.

"Thanks, Art, for showing me the ropes, so I'll know how to get a car out of our basement garage here after I pass my 'steering-committee' test. And for telling me about the main garage and all the others. It's all a lot of red tape: car tickets from Tim on the tenth floor, time-punch 'em, fill out the odometer readings and account, put one in the rack,—and more of the same when we return. Right?"

"Yes, and there's more rigmarole if you need gas or repairs on the road. You're expected to change a flat tire yourself! And to hand-pump your gas at a power plant. And fill up before turning the car in at night. And call Tim a day in advance to reserve cars; otherwise, take pot luck. There's more stuff, too!"

"I'm glad you're my driver today—to show me around, Art!"

"That's the old World War I West Harbor Plant on the left. And Gold St. farther east—over there. We have a full tank, so we won't stop now! We're late as it is, anyway."

The venerable plant looked different now from alongside than from the tenth-floor cafeteria. Father would have commented that the stack plumes had a good Ringelmann appearance; the haze was very faint since the precipitators were removing most of the fly ash, the firing rate must be steady now, and the weather was good—and hot.

"Did you have any ancient plants like this up your way, Marion?"

"Oh, yes, Art. And spruced up with newer high-pressure units and some of those gas turbines, too, like West Harbor."

"Boss lady, did you work through consultants up there—or did you do all your own engineering? I'd prefer doing all my own work; I'd learn more that way, I think. And many of the consultants' personnel on our jobs had never even been inside a power plant! How about that?"

Watch out, Marion, she thought, he's probing into your past again—without Mr. Sellers alongside to help me.

"Oh, my company does it both ways—like here—now. Consultants now are used to handle big jobs,—the overloads,—so the in-house staff wouldn't have to be hired and fired during the work-load peaks and valleys. Like you, I'd like to do our own work; we'd do it better and at less cost—and live with the feedback! But—it's a challenge to—to get a reasonably priced job turned out the way you want it—by consultants, who must get experience—just as we do! Will the consultant, contractor's engineers, and the vendor service engineers all be at this meeting?"

"Yes. Our operating and construction people like big meetings. Especially when there's some trouble or delay they can pin on us in the Engineering Department. When it's their fault, the meetings—if any are needed—are small and confidential. Now this thing this afternoon. You and I didn't select these synchronous motors over squirrel-cage ones; but *we*'re gonna get blamed just the same! Do you like these delicate, temperamental, synchronous motors for power-plant work? Have you used any? Or just rugged induction motors?"

Ignoring his questions, which she couldn't answer right off the bat, Marion decided to counter with her own. After all, she was the boss insofar as his being under her "technical direction"—but not "supervision"!

"Well, Art, 'money talks'; and it's hard to come up with arguments louder than a third-of-a-million dollar saving! Have you got your circulating-water-pump motor file here for me to peruse? I'll be cold at the meeting, you know."

"The folder—with all the studies, vendor drawings, test reports, and correspondence—is on the back seat with our hats—and your bag. Can you reach it?"

Twisting against the safety belt, she just made it.

"Right. Thanks, Art." She thought a while and added, "Art, this is hardly a pleasure trip for us; and, since we are in a Company car, using Company gas, let's talk about us as we relate to the Company."

His look of curiosity was an invitation for her to go on.

"Human nature, being what it is, I won't fault any engineer for resenting my coming in from the outside to take over Mr. Sellers' spot as group leader. I would have felt hurt also had I been in your shoes, or those of Tom and Ed,—and many others. But *I* got the job instead of someone being promoted from the ranks. Now my chief problem is to get cooperation,—especially from you, Art."

"I'm flattered, but why especially *me*?"

"Because," she said, "I think we both suspect you're the runner-up."

Art did not answer, and in that silence she began to study the contents of the folder.

Burying herself in the papers, she was only vaguely aware of riding through farm country now.

"Marion, on the left are the two 500-kv lines 'to' Cliffside. We hope they'll be 'from' soon! They don't look too bad, do they?"

Where exposed near side roads, the poles were of ornamental, light gray, tapered, construction; and, where partially hidden by trees or hills, the lines were on less expensive, conventional, latticed-steel towers. Of course, "beauty is in the eye of the beholder"; but the long, graceful, bundled-conductor catenaries had esthetic appeal to her because in their sweeping cable sags she could appreciate the mathematical purity of their natural hyperbolic trigonometric functions.

"Art, I wouldn't mind having them out my picture-view window—as long as the clearance is such that my TV signal is greater than the corona noise and 'ghosts' in bad weather!"

"Amen, Marion." He chuckled as she silently resumed her scanning of the voluminous file papers, extending back over six years. Then, when she had put the folder away, he said, "You're not wearing a marriage band, but that doesn't mean anything these 'mod-morals' days. I'd guess that you have a husband who is *only* an engineer, and you want to 'up' him at his own game."

"I'm not married," she returned. "If I were, I'd want my husband to be a *partner,* not a *rival* in any way. Is your wife a "pusher"—if I might ask?"

"Quite the reverse," Art said. "Jane's very timid,—afraid of her shadow."

Marion detected a hidden resentment in everything Art said. She felt that it was a tough spot for both of them. Right now she couldn't see just how she was going to win him over—to work with her—rather than against her,—to help her—instead of always trying to expose her. Soon he spoke, "Here we are—at our three-quarter-billion dollar plant—that's still not on the line eight years after the turbine generator order. And let's not allow anybody today to pin the blame for any delay on us electricals!"

"Now I'll say 'Amen' to that, Art."

Soon they were inside the Company grounds; Art said, "I think we won't need to show our passes to the contract guard at *this* gate—as long as we're in this marked Company car."

She smiled at the guard, and he waved them through. It was quite a sight as they rounded a curve along the forested entrance road, and all at once below them she saw the big, domed, concrete, containment cylinders, sitting between the clean-lined auxiliary buildings and turbine buildings with the sparkling blue waters beyond, a bright blue sky overhead, and a pretty, two-toned blue switchyard to receive the swooping 500,000-volt lines.

"Art, I wish I could come up with an aesthetic substation color scheme like that—for equipment and structures—and that orange accent, too, on lights and bushings! Did the consultant think of it all?"

"I understand that we asked for some color treatment, and the consultant's long-haired architect got their steno-girls to select the final colors from a $500-set of standards books we bought 'em!"

"Great!" She laughed. "Girl power!"

As they slowed down, she said, "Art, it's a handsome plant."

"'Handsome is as handsome does'! We've got to get it on the line for that. There's the visitors' overlook pavilion,—over there on the cliffs."

She knew the site area included a thousand acres; but, as they got out of the car after showing their passes to the Company's plant guard, the massive structures looming above them dwarfed their puny figures.

"Well, Art, I'll be lost here this first time for sure; so—please keep me securely in tow at all times this afternoon."

He smiled his big, masculine, protective smile for the weaker sex. "Don't you worry your pretty head over that, boss lady! Will do, except if you vanish into the 'little girls' room'! There's a nice one here for the plant clerical staff. I saw it as the lighting system was being installed—

prior to its christening, of course! Here,—I'll carry the file folder for you now."

Adjusting her hard hat onto her head and slinging her bag strap over her shoulder, she paused to encourage him to open the heavy turbine-room door for her. Maybe such clinging-vine feminine tactics might help win him over to her side yet, she dreamed hopefully. Inside, the two gigantic turbine-generators stretched out city blocks long under their huge over-and-under cranes high above them. But there was no time to gawk as she carefully stepped over boxes and lagging on the deck—because soon Art opened another door for her; and now they walked into the Service Building, down a narrow corridor, and all at once stood inside a large air-conditioned conference room, filled with the buzzing of dozens of talkative men, seated comfortably around a very long row of tables. It was no wonder the project was behind schedule; every man-jack of them must be in here out of the heat keeping their cool.

The babble subsided at once, and all eyes turned upon them. At presumably the head of the table, a slightly built, black-haired, little man in his forties looked up at the wall clock's hand pointing at 2:40 and smilingly announced, "Well, now that the Engineering Department's brains have condescended to favor us with a belated appearance, the meeting can come to order. Art, where's your boss?"

Art grinned mischievously. "Standing right here beside me! Bob Sellers is retiring early; and Miss Marion Francis, here, is his replacement, effective at noon. The notices are out. Marion, our genial host here is Mr. Doug Roberts, Chief Engineer of Cliffside."

She put on her best smile and apologized sweetly, "How do you do, Mr. Roberts? Sorry I made Art late! But this is my first day on the job; and everything's been coming at me thick and fast. Don't get up, gentlemen. We'll find chairs."

A big middle-aged man, seated beside Mr. Roberts, said, "Well, Art, all I can say is your boss has certainly gotten to look a lot prettier! Doug, I saw the memo just before I left West Harbor at noon; Bob *is* really bailing out on us alright. A damned smart move—if you ask me! I only wish I were a few years older now!"

As everyone chuckled, Mr. Roberts spoke up very politely, "We're pleased to have you aboard, Miss Francis. And you guys all watch your 'cruddy' language now!"

She laughed. "Don't bother on my account, fellows! I can stand anything you all can; I've just come from a Yankee power company. And, please, just call me 'Marion'."

By now Art had grabbed two metal camp chairs in the corner of the room, unfolded them, and set both in a second row half way down the tables. When he began dusting hers with his handkerchief, she hurriedly sat down, whispering, "Thanks, Art; but, please,—no Sir Walter act for me!"

He grinned and hissed, "I didn't want you to ruin your nice mini-skirted dress on this dirty chair, all mucked up by these filthy apes down here."

Mr. Roberts was obviously chairing the meeting as he spoke up again, "We'll all miss Bob. He's a top engineer—even though he wouldn't always give us everything we wanted, like rugged squirrel-cage motors instead of these flimsy, gingerbread, synchronous ones. I hope Miss—I mean, Marion—can help us get these damned things running, and keep 'em running, and specify good 'ole' cage motors for the next job at River Shore. Now we'll pass around copies of this meeting's attendance sheet. You'll each have to add Art's and Marion's names. Also, you'll each get a copy of our two trouble reports."

Letting her hat clatter to the floor by her bag, Marion took her copies and hurriedly scanned them. Some guys kept their name-plated hats on their heads; and so,—with the help of the passed-around, sign-in sheets, she could now identify the horde pretty well.

Now Art asked, "Friday morning, when I heard of the first trouble, I got the vendor's service engineer down here to work over the weekend. How is he doing—robbing parts from No. 2 motors for No. 1? I realize that our own Environmental Section needs Unit No. 1 pumps running for ten days now for their discharge water-effects tests for the government people."

Construction's George Foray replied, "Our crafts forces finished motor 11 on Saturday. Test and Operating checked it out and got it running that night. Then, when 13 failed that same night, we all started on it. I hope we'll get it back on tonight."

From the order of the list, the big gruff bear seated beside the chief must be Joe Johnson from the Operating Department's engineering staff headquarters at West Harbor. Now he asked in a loud protesting voice, "Yeah, but when is the next unpredictable critter going to 'crap out' on us? And how are we going to *keep* the plant running that way—if it ever does get on the line? Remember—it'll cost us $150,000 a day in purchased power to lose a unit!"

No one spoke up; so she said calmly, "But, Mr. Johnson, an outage of one of six pumps—even now in mid-summer—would reduce unit output by only about 8%—per the pump studies here. Not that $12,000 a day isn't a neat bundle! Now, these trouble reports indicate that the six Unit 1 motors have run about twenty to twenty-six hours,—about a full

SOLID STATE SNAFU 39

day. Of course they all ran on test at the factory, also; and the excitation 'black boxes' no doubt got some separate preliminary testing in advance. I've done some R&D lab work,—QC-QA-sigma probability stuff,—on various solid-state semi-conductors,—M.O. types,—diodes,—zeners. And they all have a short period of 'weeding out' the 'weak sisters'—'woops!'—You men have got that silly cliché foisted off on us women!—"

Everyone laughed—but mostly *with* her, she hoped, smiling.

"But then,—after that initial trial span to eliminate the originally faulty components, most of the remaining units have a long life of many years."

At once she heard someone at the other end comment, "In other words,—as usual—we're doing the testing in the field instead of at the factory! Can't you beat on the vendor about that?"

Art whispered, "He's the Chief Shift Electrician, Ted Mohr."

"Mr. Mohr, we can try—next time—before an order is placed! Of course, all service is testing—in a sense, isn't it? And where do you stop? We don't want to pay for too much costly factory-floor testing, which—in the ultimate—would be a life-time test run! But maybe the 'black boxes' should be tested separately for longer periods—before installation in the motors—without taking up expensive motor time on the factory test floor. Can I see one of the 'black boxes'—and ask the service engineer if he has—or will get—some QC answers from the factory now?"

George Foray promptly replied, "The two failed boxes have gone back to the vendor's shop already. The service engineer and the crew have got the second replacement back inside the rotor by now—and are busy installing it. So as not to interrupt the rush work now, we could get him to phone you in the morning, Miss Francis. O.K.?"

Relieved, she was about to agree when Joe Johnson chimed in, "But I've been thinking,—you know, how our operator had to trip both smoking motors. What was all that fancy cubicle relaying doing then? Sleeping on the job? What if our operators hadn't been at the motors for this special test run? They won't be there all the time normally! Would the whole motor burn up eventually,—and not just the 'black box' stuff? Each motor costs way over a hundred thousand dollars, doesn't it? And then the repairs might run for months,—not days!"

She hesitated before asking, "Is a relay engineer here?"

When there was no reply, she continued, "Well, from glancing at the elementary diagram on the way down here, I'd say my first shot at it is—that a faulty diode failed, resulting in an incorrect solid-state 'switching-in' of the shut-down field-discharge resistor. But,—since the motor was still running—and not de-energized for coast-down,—the small wire to the 'black box' soon went 'poof'—and so cleared the trouble—before the loss-of-field relaying could—or even had to—to trip the motor—for its protection. The smoke from the burned-open small wiring at last belatedly escaped from the 'black box' and motor to warn the operator to trip the breaker.

"Now, *that's* when the motor was exposed to possible damage—by the transient-induced overvoltages—when being de-energized without the field protection normally afforded by its discharge resistor; but—a new motor should be able to stand such an inadvertent test. That's my theory! The service engineer could fill us in on what the 'black boxes' looked like—and tested, I'd think,—and get us some factory word on their QC testing—and what relaying tests we can make to check now. But, as George said, I could phone him tomorrow morning—so as not to interrupt his rush work right now."

Art whispered again, "I guess the relay guys are all out at the motor now."

It was almost three o'clock now. She was already patting herself on the back for her success in wriggling out of this mess—for this afternoon, at least, when Joe Johnson stood up.

"Aw, let's get up off our—'duffs'—and go right out there—to check her story! I bet those guys out there need a smoke-and-coffee break by now, anyway! That way, the little lady here—can climb up on that motor platform—and poke her pretty face down inside that motor to see for herself!"

As everyone began to chuckle and whisper to each other, Joe Johnson looked at her, grinning broadly. "You'd want to see for yourself—after coming all the way down here, wouldn't you?"

She could hear someone next to Art whisper loudly, "When she goes up that ladder,—and stands on that grating,—and bends over double to look down inside that motor—with her figure—in that mini-skirt! Wow! There'll be more guys crowding around below and behind,—all ogling her,—than ever paid to sit under the 'bump-and-grind' boardwalk at the 'ole' Burley-queu! Better than the trick blower grill at the Roller Coaster Park!"

In spite of her sternest efforts at suppression, she felt a maddening flush suffusing her throat and cheeks.

Now Art was whispering, "Come on, boss lady! Let's leave these kid-stuff jokers and hit the road. We've done all that's needed now. You don't have to go along with his fun-house gag for the amusement of all those clowns out there!"

She whispered back, "Thanks, Art! But I'll go anywhere he can go—and no sweat! You'll see!"

Slowly she stood up, smiling now. "Mr. Johnson, I'll be with you in the corridor in a few minutes."

Turning back to Art, she whispered, "Is that deluxe 'little girls' room' you inspected—farther down this corridor? I need to 'vanish' for a jiffy! Now—don't you run off too far!"

Hurrying into the surprisingly luxurious rest room, she hastily stripped off her cool mini-skirted dress and half slip, folded them neatly into her bag, and pulled out her crisp, rolled, blue jeans and a short-sleeved, blue-and-gray plaid, lumber-jack shirt. She had meant to file these at the office under "E" for "emergencies", but the first crisis had already arrived without warning. She felt much better now, after having used all the facilities in the quiet comfortable room. Then, slipping on her shirt and stepping into her blue jeans, she smoothed the snug-fitting material around her waist and hips and cinched up her shiny, black, leather belt with its chromed buckle. Twisting and looking back over her shoulder in the wall mirror, she patted her hips, wishing she could remold them ever so slightly. But, all in all, she felt quite trim and securely confident now, ready to leap over her next hurdle. She could appreciate the famous woman tennis champion who said all her victories were won in the dressing room *before* the match. Even Father might approve of her appearance now even though he frowned on most female figures in pants—because they appeared to be so obviously afflicted with "steatopygia" or "enlargement of the sitting muscles."

As she put on her hard hat and slung her bag over her shoulder, into the room swiveled a young, generously proportioned, plain-featured brunette, dressed in a diaphanous, sleeveless, white blouse over almost equally revealing, pajama-like, cerise slacks. Reflecting that this clerical worker's packed-in, bulging appearance was what Father had objected to—rather than her own modest attire, she quickly exchanged smiles with the girl and stepped into the corridor to face an impatiently pacing Art.

"Wow!", he exclaimed. "A fore-sighted, quick-change artiste! You look great! A real style show! But now you've sure out-foxed those wolves out there, boss lady! And here I was worrying about you all this time! We'll soon catch up with that leering crowd."

Walking briskly, they saw the last of the group entering the screen-well pump house at the waterfront. Everyone grinned good-naturedly as she smilingly ignored all the banter—like Ted Mohr's, "Joe, she's engineered her way out of that one O.K.!"

She was relieved that the guys didn't seem to resent her cheating them out of their anticipated peep show; rather, they appeared to appreciate her outsmarting them at their little joke.

Standing beside Mr. Johnson, she pointed up to the motor platform where four men chatted with lit cigarettes. "Looks like you were right! We'll not be delaying any work if we hurry. After you?"

Grinning sheepishly, he climbed the steel ladder slowly; and once on the platform, he grabbed the hand rail and extended his other hand firmly to help her up the last steps.

"Thanks, Joe," she whispered.

"You're welcome, Marion," he replied, puffing and blowing.

By their helmets now, she identified the four men as the vendor's service engineer, a contractor's-craft journeyman-electrician with his apprentice helper, and a Company test man, probably a relay technician. Soon Joe, George, Ted, and Art were all talking with these four original occupants of the platform as she surveyed the crowd gazing up from the floor far below her. At last Art and Joe turned to her; and the operating engineer said, "Marion, there's no use looking around up here; everything's pretty well buttoned up already. But you're right; in both cases, before any relaying or operator action could have occurred, the small lead quickly blew clear, removing the field short through the discharge resistor. The service engineer says he can check the factory engineers and arrange some relay tests here—with our relay fellows—to simulate various loss-of-field relaying cases. The guy says he'll send you a letter about how many hundreds of these 'black boxes' are out in the field—for the past dozen years—with only our two—and two previous failures,—each occurring within the first several days of service. The brief factory motor tests and 'black-box' vendor tests weed out almost all defective components in a combined equivalent of about four days, he recalls; but he'll put it all in his letter. Is that about the gist of it all, Art?"

"Yeh, that covers it, Joe. We'll keep after him—and the sales engineer—and check it all out, to wrap it up, put it all to bed."

Turning to her now, Art said, "Ready to descend, Marion? We'll let these guys finish up here so the testing can proceed."

Once more down on the concrete deck, Joe Johnson spoke to her quietly, "Well,—Marion, thanks for making me feel a little better about these fancy motors. But—see what you can do for us on that next River Shore job. O.K.?"

She smiled. "O.K., Joe. We'll study it—and keep in touch with you. But—don't forget that those big generators in there are also synchronous motors!"

SOLID STATE SNAFU   43

He grinned and shook his fist at her as she strode off triumphantly with the last word—as a lady should! As Art hurried her along, he said, "Now we've just barely got enough time to get rolling before the 800-man day shift pours out of here at four. Oh—oh!"

Now the public-address system was repeatedly blaring *her* name, "Marion Francis, please report to the Control Room."

Art groaned. "We could just duck out of here, anyway. It's just more trouble! What d'ya say, boss lady? That way we won't be so late getting home."

Art's urgent plea was very tempting, but she'd better not make a bad impression—on her first day here.

Wearily she replied, "I guess I'd better show. Art, please lead the way!"

The cavernous buildings were nearly vacant now; already the normally deliberate workers must have rushed outside to line up at the gates, poised for the race home. Although the big control room was very impressive with its horseshoe-shaped array of panels crowded with hundreds of instruments and controllers, her first impression was overwhelmingly olfactory. The sickening odor of rotten eggs pervaded the air, and a haze hung over a group of men huddled around a table. Then Mr. Roberts called over, "Oh, there you are! I was afraid you'd already gone! These two drawout annunciators have 'conked' out on us! We only put the system *in* service this morning, and it's *all out* now; we need all this stuff now for startup monitoring. So—what gives here? Oh, Ted, show her the mess!"

As the electrician handed her the foot-long drawn-out chassis, she asked, "Ted, have you got any wiring diagrams handy? And a good one to compare—from Unit 2? And—and an ohmmeter?"

That smell was solid-state, sulfur-family failure,—probably selenium.

"Here's an elementary I had for checking it out this morning," George Foray volunteered. "It's 'kinda' dirty and crumpled now from being in my pocket all day, Miss Francis."

Now Ted Mohr drew out a good unit from the other side of the room and announced, "Here's one from Unit 2,—and here's my ohmmeter."

Hastily probing with the leads as she desperately pored over the diagram, she fervently prayed for a quick-and-easy answer; for she was tiring fast now.

Art complained, "Where are all the relay and test guys? Have they dashed home already?"

Just as George grunted a gloomy assent, the light suddenly dawned on her,—happy day! The good unit had a tiny component that was missing from both faulty ones.

"Fellows, I think the trouble here is that the Unit 1 equipment doesn't have these little voltage suppressors, which are present in the Unit 2 ones. See this, Art? And on the diagram here? And—the ohmmeter shows the blocking diode has failed—due to D.C. switching transients probably—without the protection afforded by a voltage suppressor. Then—with this common bus—!"

Now Art, George, and Ted were all checking over the units with the print and ohmmeter. Ted was the first to murmur with flattering amazement, "Why,—she's right, damn it! Now—tonight—we'll have to move hundreds of these Unit 2 'animals' over here—and unplug these damned Unit 1 drawers!"

The Chief Engineer asked, "Ted, will that fix up the Unit 1 annunciator—just like that?"

"Sure looks like it should, Chief!" the electrician replied in apparent disbelief.

"Good! Let's get with it then!" Turning to her, Mr. Roberts asked fretfully, "Marion, will you please get after the factory about this rotten batch on Unit 1? How could those factory nuts do a thing like this to us? We've got enough trouble without this 'kinda' stupid stuff!"

She smiled and shrugged her shoulders. "I don't know,—Doug; but—everything seems to get past factory QC today! Even my new hair dryer had no heater connections! That was serious to *me*!"

As they all laughed, she said, "We'll get right on this for Unit 2. Well, keep things under control now, gentlemen! 'Bye now!"

As she turned away to pursue the disappearing Art, the Chief Engineer called after her, "Thanks for coming down here and helping us on your first day, Marion!"

Smiling, she waved to the little group of grinning men and ran to overtake her fast-vanishing guide-and-chauffeur.

"You wouldn't abandon me way down here, would you, Art?"

"Not a chance! I'm just trying to get you to hurry out of here before someone else nabs you, Marion! But—I couldn't blame them! You were great at putting out both 'brush fires' before they blew up into real front-office forest fires! They couldn't stump you, boss lady!"

"Thanks, Art! And I can count on you to follow through on them both now?"

"Yeah, sure thing!"

Suddenly she felt an invigorating surge of exhilaration, enabling her to match Art's swift pace without faltering in the stretch.

Fortunately, both troubles had involved solid state electronics, a field in which her master's R & D industry-fellowship program had given her some expertise. Too, she had Mr. Sellers and his cram course last week—to thank for her new-found familiarity with power equipment in the Company. Her study of Art's file hadn't hurt her either. Maybe it was partly beginner's luck; but, anyway, she hadn't struck out on her very first time at bat. However, she *may* have stuck her credibility neck out too far if the motor failures continue; but she'd cross that bridge—if she came to it.

"Marion, Bob Sellers told me that our I&C group had the board vendor buy that annunciator—without competition—because the operating people insisted. You noticed they didn't blame us for the annunciator *purchase*—as they did for the synchronous motors!"

Puzzled, she murmured, "I&C group?"

"Yeah, you know,—'Instrument and Control Group'. Didn't you have an I&C group up north?"

Oh, oh! Watch it, Marion! Don't relax too soon today! How to get out of this one now? Just keep quiet!

And Art merely continued—without even noticing her blank expression, she hoped, "Oh, I guess your group did all that electrical work, too,—just like Bob said we used to do—before the office reorganization several years ago. Now we don't have much 'say' in the engineering of it, but—we catch *all* the electrical troubles anyway! Well, the rat race is about over! These 800 jocks clear out of here like on the Indy Speedway. Those 25-MPH signs are a joke."

Rolling along the highway at last, she fell limply against the seat back.

"Art, I'm certainly glad you're driving—and not me! I'm beat! Is every day going to be this rugged?"

"Yeh, but soon you get so it all runs off like water off a duck's back."

Oh, oh! More of those clichés! Surely they must come with this job!

"Art, will we be very late?"

"An hour overtime pay for me—as an engineer; and they'll ask you to explain why!" He grinned.

"And,—for you,—a *senior* engineer,—zippo! Oh, say, I'll drive you home, boss lady! You ride the busses, don't you?"

"Not unless you'll stay long enough to meet my aunt!"

"Sorry, Marion, but I've got to get home for supper tonight."

"Well, anyway, Art, I do appreciate your thoughtful, kind offer very much; but—I'll catch a bus O.K."

Drowsily she studied his lean, handsome profile and wondered what sort of a timid woman his wife could be.

CHAPTER FOUR

Cliffside Encore

ALIGHTING NIMBLY from the bus, Marion walked briskly across the plaza with springy step. It was still delightfully cool at seven-thirty in the morning, but it would be another scorcher. There wasn't a cloud in the sky—nor any crowds on the streets. Clad jauntily in her summery navy-blue pantsuit, she felt fully recharged by her night's rest and ready to face any challenges on her first full day of work. A grinning young meter reader pushed the revolving door for her as she strode into the nearly empty lobby. Confidently flashing her new ID card, she at once caught an elevator held for her by three, laughing, male, meter readers, who were good-naturedly joshing an uncomplaining, cute, red-haired, girl, meter reader.

The eleventh floor corridor was deserted, and so was her long room. No,—there was the tall spare figure of Mr. Sellers, standing by his desk at the window at the far end of the aisle. He didn't hear her approach on the soft wall-to-wall carpet. Smiling, she greeted him brightly, "Good morning, Mr. Sellers! I see I'll have to get up early in the morning to get here ahead of you!"

Whirling about, he said with a grin that miraculously transformed his serious face, "Well, good morning, Marion! You look pretty as a picture—and ready for anything!"

She laughed. "I *do* feel that way! I really do! But I don't know how long this—feeling of euphoria will last—in my fool's paradise!"

He smiled. "You'll make it, Marion! You're doing fine! You were a real winner down there yesterday."

"I was?" She looked innocently surprised; seating herself beside his desk, she hoped he'd sit down, also. And he did so, smiling.

"Yes, indeed. In fact, I was kept long after quitting time listening to ecstatic eulogies about you,—your charm, modesty; and they couldn't get over a pretty blonde being so sharp in the gray-matter department."

She laughed gleefully. "Oh, pray tell me more, Mr. Sellers! My fragile feminine ego is wilting under the burden of a guilty inferiority complex here in this all-male environment. Who are my converted admirers?"

"Well, my phone was kept busy from four-thirty to five. The polite Doug Roberts;—gruff Joe Johnson, without whom our new plants would never start up!;—and earnest Ted Mohr. And, already this morning, George Foray. They were all enthusiastically emphatic—that, while they'd miss me, your presence would more than compensate for my departure!"

"Oh, Mr. Sellers, they were all just kidding!"

"Some, maybe. But not much! Marion, you really must have turned in a topnotch performance!"

"Beginner's luck! I lucked out that the troubles were about solid state electronics, a field I knew a little bit about, at least. And,—last but not least, I'd have struck out all around if I hadn't had last week to bone up on your correspondence course!"

"'Thanks—for those few kind words'—as my uncle used to tell me." The smile slowly faded away.

"Now, Marion, I'm glad you're rested and refreshed after yesterday's grueling first day—because you've got another one today. I know it isn't fair, but George Foray wants you back down there this morning; so—I took the liberty of signing up the car again—for Art—and you."

She smiled triumphantly. "Well, with my pantsuit, I'm dressed for the plant today! But yesterday I had my blue jeans in my bag, fortunately. I'll file them here now!"

"Good girl! I was worried about you down there yesterday. But don't ruin your suit today because you'll need it this evening! Midge asked me to come up to see Ken Blood at five."

"Oh, oh! About me?" she asked anxiously.

"Yes. Of all things, he wants you to attend the Green Knolls Woman's Club meeting tonight at eight; listen to a Health Department rep 'sic' all the good ladies on us electric company people as the black-hatted No. 1 villains who're polluting their air and water; and then, like a surprise bomb planted in the audience, you're to arise and defend us 'baddies'!"

She gasped in shocked amazement.

"Me? An electrical engineer! Just because I'm a woman? Why not someone from our Environmental Section?"

"Because they will all be at other similar meetings, including Ann Teach. Ken didn't seem to know much about the whole thing. Somehow, I suspect your cafeteria encounter with Mr. King! If so, this could be a great opportunity for you as you can imagine. Management exposure, you know. Ken had to come to us directly because your three supervisors, Howard, Joe, and Ben, are away at various industry society meetings, committees, or seminars—as usual. You'll find you'll be left largely on your own in this group! About the matter of attracting executive attention, we once had a Company manager who moved into an apartment in the same building as our Chief Executive Officer. He carried out the big man's garbage and did other chores and favors—until he became a vice president in no time at all!"

"But, Mr. Sellers, except for what you've told me—and what little I already knew, I'm pretty ignorant of the subject!"

She was glad she was seated because suddenly her knees felt trembly and rubbery as her mouth dried up alarmingly.

"Marion, you'll do fine—as usual. You'll come across refreshingly sincere and irresistibly persuasive, I'm sure! Here are some notes I got from Ann. Try to get back here as early as possible this afternoon—before three, so Ann can brief and rehearse you—before she has to leave for her earlier dinner meeting."

"Oh, Mr. Sellers, what have I done to deserve all this?" She drew a deep breath to compose herself.

"And, Mr. Sellers, were you able to learn what George Foray's latest troubles are today?"

"Yes, Marion, here are my notes on his phone call about his three problems. Right now, please excuse me for a minute—so I can intercept Art before he disappears somewhere. He should pick up the car tickets now, so the car won't be given to someone else who's 'rarin' to go somewhere!"

Hopelessly clutching the sheaf of papers, she managed to get to her swivel chair, but her poor brain was having great difficulty in concentrating objectively on the technical subject matter when her emotions subjectively wished to indulge in self-pity for her undeserved predicament on her first full day on the job. Sighing, as she resolutely forced herself to scan the well-organized sheets of information, she gradually became calmer and more confident. If Mr. Sellers had faith in her ability to swing it, then she mustn't let him down. He had assembled a separately clipped file on the background, both practical and theoretical, of each of George Foray's three problems—together with the answer in the transformer-cooler motor complaint, a suggested solution or cue for her to field-check about the generator differential relaying C.T. mystery, and an array of formulas and data to resolve the 13,000-volt-cable sheath-grounding questions. She could study all this information further during the long ride back to Cliffside. This last package included Ann Teach's tenth-floor room and phone numbers, a street map marked with the Green Knolls Woman's Club location, and some notes and articles on the pros and cons of the environmental issues.

"Mornin', Marion. Bob says we've got an encore,—a rerun—to make today! It's up-and-at-'em again! Are you ready to go another round? You look super, boss lady!"

"Thanks, Art! I guess I'm ready—if you are!"

"Well, then, let's hit the road. The sooner we go, the sooner we return."

"Right," she murmured as she stuffed all the papers in her bag. Turning to Mr. Sellers, she said, "Thanks for all the 'info.' I'll go over it on the way. Keep your fingers crossed for me now! I'll see you this afternoon, I hope."

"Just take it easy, Marion," he replied, smiling reassuringly.

Down in the basement garage as they seated themselves in their car, she noticed two unmarked cars just arriving at this late hour; and she recognized Mr. King and Mr. Blood as the chauffeurs. RHIP! Rank has its privileges, she mused. At least—unlike her—they were driving themselves.

As Art maneuvered through the heavy rush-hour traffic, she asked, "How often do you drive down to Cliffside, Art?"

"Oh, once a week last year, then twice a week this year,—and soon I'll have to get a room down there, I guess, like our test and relay fellows. Getting our first nuclear plant in operation is the Company's No. 1 job now to reduce costly, imported-oil consumption; to build up our generation reserves, now a negative one per cent; and to minimize consumer rate protests to the P.S.C."

Lapsing into silence while studying the papers, she suddenly was startled by her chauffeur's sharp voice, "Wake up, boss lady! We're here again! Up and at 'em! Give 'em hell!"

"Now, Art! You know I wasn't dozing!"

He laughed. "Just resting your eyes a moment? Come on now! Bob said we're to meet George at the Unit 1 generator step-up transformers at nine-thirty. This time we've parked up by the Construction Building, you see."

Nodding, she scrambled out of the car, donned her hard hat, and grabbed her bag as she stood, squinting in the bright sunlight. It was good to stretch her arms and legs and bask in the soft morning sunshine.

"Well, Art, even I can find our first destination! You can't miss those towering transformers over there, can you? And those two fellows standing beside them look like pygmies, don't they?"

He grunted and strode off along the dusty road. Stepping into the ditch as the big trucks rumbled past, she was glad no rain had converted the dust into mud—although she did have a pair of thin plastic overshoes in her bag. As Art exchanged salutations with the construction leader and the chief electrician, she now greeted them cheerily, "Morning, George! Ted! You've got another fine day for us down here!"

She wouldn't ask about annunciators or synchronous motors; bad news always travels fast enough.

George grinned and responded quietly, "Yes, Miss Francis. If only Ted here wouldn't keep spoiling all our days. Now then,—you know our motor 'specs' call for the new, industry-standard, 460-volt rating; but Ted noticed that these transformer-cooler oil *pumps* have motors with the old 440-volt name-plates. The *fan* motors are 460 volts alright. The transformer engineer thought the motors were O.K.—but offered no proof. What'll we do now?"

Ted added, "The bus runs up to 506 volts. That's the standard industry limit of 10% above 460 volts. O.K. But how about the 15% above the 440-volt nameplates? These new motors today can't stand much overexcitation without saturating, you know. And the bus might go higher when we're on the line."

She rummaged in her bag for the right papers.

"Well, gentlemen, our tap-and-regulation calculations indicate that a voltage of 506 is about our maximum at any time. And these vendor test sheets show that the motors are of the old-core, liberal design with an ample overexcitation ability. The guarantee is stated to be identical to a 460-volt rating, and everything has a one-year warranty *after* the unit goes into full-load commercial service. But,—just to satisfy ourselves *now*, can we run the pumps? It would do these de-energized transformers good to circulate the oil now. Then we could measure the case temperatures and use these factory-test relationships between coil-end and case values."

Ted and George accepted the test sheets she proffered and nodded in agreement as they scanned the data.

Now Art asked impatiently, "Well, fellows, what's the next 'gripe' this morning? Marion has to be back in the office for a meeting by two."

George looked questioningly at the electrician. "O.K., Ted? You'll let me know if you need me any more on this?"

"Yeah. Thanks a lot, Marion! Be seein' y'all."

Obviously pleased at getting rid of one of his three problems so easily, George walked towards the outdoor metalclad switchgear across the busy roadway. Opening clanging doors with his key, he announced, "You see this 13-kv cubicle is dead, tagged out—with locks on; and the grounding device is in place of the breaker. O.K.?"

CLIFFSIDE ENCORE

Art grunted, "So? What's the trouble here?"

The construction man pointed to the big cables emerging from the ducts in the concrete floor of the switchgear. "A craft journeyman asked me this morning if he should ground all those cable sheaths here. This is the copper ground bus,—and here you see the solder terminals of the sheaths—but no ground connections between bus and sheaths. His question seemed pretty sharp to me—if a little late—because most of these circuits are in service, you know. And usually these home-wiring electricians that the union hall sends us don't have any high tension 'savvy.' Even I don't know what to tell him, and Bob said you'd look into it."

Frowning, Art asked, "Is the other end of each of these single-conductor cable sheaths grounded now,—I hope?"

"Yep! Is that sufficient, Art?"

"Well, George, what did the consultant specify on his drawings?"

"Nothing at all! On either end! I asked the contractor's electrical foreman, who said a consultant electrical had told him it was a policy decision for the operating utility engineers."

In the ensuing silence, George added, "I'd like to know what to do now because very soon it'll be hard to get outages on these service circuits when the hot functional starts in earnest next week. Mr. Sellers promised you'd come up with the answer right away."

Pulling out of her bag Mr. Sellers' notes together with her log-log sliderule case, paper pad and pencils, Marion sat down on the edge of the concrete foundation.

"Well, Art, let's do some instant engineering here for George. Can you find room to sit beside me? See this logarithmic induction equation? Will you feed me the numbers to crank in—from these cable 'specs' and switchgear studies. You know,—the max. fault current—and the cable sheath radii—and run length. O.K., Art?"

"Yeh, I see. You're going to come up with the induced voltage during a through fault beyond the cable—to see if it's high enough to be dangerous to someone in contact then."

"Right", she murmured. "That's it; your numbers look good."

Shortly, she announced, "Oh,—oh! Nearly 800 volts. That'd be a bit unhealthy out here on a wet day! Now, Art, let's figure the annular area of the soft zinc sheath—and the sheath resistance—from the specific resistivity. Then we'll get the sheath current—if it's grounded at both ends. And, using this formula with these sheath data, we'll get the temperature rise over ambient at the relay-setting time. O.K.? Here we go!"

At last she smiled. "Nearly ten amps, and that's near the allowable limit per our numbers—although the vendor's interpolated data give almost fifteen. Anyway, the sheath can stand the fault current; so—let's ground both ends for optimum personnel safety and equipment damage control. Art, do you want to check my 'slip-stick' work now?"

Handing him her sliderule, she stood up and brushed the seat of her good pants with her hands. "Everything always seems to come out to make more work for you, doesn't it, George?"

He nodded. "That's O.K. We've got the time to do it now without delaying the startup. We'll start right away. For the record, can you get the consultant to specify this on the drawings now, Miss Francis?"

"O.K., George. You hear that, Art?"

"Uh—huh. Your numbers are close enough, Marion. But—what would we have done if the sheath couldn't stand the current? Add a resistor in one connection?"

"I guess so, Art! Good idea—for a compromise,—a half loaf!"

She glanced at the small circuit identification plates tied to the cables. "George, can the guys move those tags back off the dielectric leakage paths of the terminations to a harmless place over the sheath jacket? Even though the tags and ties may be good plastic insulators, they won't have compatible dielectric characteristics; and, anyway, the vendor's engineer won't back up his warranty if he sees that!"

George frowned. "Wow! I'll get after them at the same time. I'll check all cables."

Art stood up now, handing her the sliderule and papers. "Boss lady, where can I get one of your hand bags,—the grab bag that has everything an engineer needs?"

She laughed. "Now, Art, you know you wouldn't be caught dead with one of these feminine curiosities!"

And where was *she* going to find everything herself after Mr. Sellers left the office? Art had now turned to face the construction man. "Now, George, what's your third—and positively the last—trouble today?"

"Well, Art, let's all head for No. 1 generator. The 30,000- to 5-ampere differential C.T.'s were all checked uptown in the meter lab O.K.; but, in place down here, there's some inaccuracy on one phase—in the field tests—which might trip the unit off the line. The test fellows are puzzled. Ditto the vendor's engineers. I hope you can clear it up now—as easily as the first two items, Miss Francis."

Art laughed. "Hope that bag's got the answer again!"

Crossing her fingers, Marion fervently hoped so, too, as she mulled over Mr. Sellers' notes in her mind while she hurried after the two men, who were already striding towards the Turbine Building. This time they descended stairs into the bowels of the structure, and at last stood on a concrete floor looking up at the generator's belly where the busduct approached the bushings.

George asked anxiously, "Think you can make it up all those ladders and scaffolding, Miss Francis?"

It looked higher than her aunt's third floor attic above grade. Grimly she replied, "If all those *men* got up there, *I* can, too! But—I'll leave my bag down here by the ladder—where I can watch it. It'll be all I can do to get way up there by myself!"

Not looking down, at last she stood, panting, on the platform under the generator bushings and busduct. As usual, all the men eyed her curiously,—skeptically,—perhaps resentfully even—in this male domain. There was a profusion of test wiring, drop lights, and portable test equipment surrounding the huge, doughnut, current transformers above the massive cylindrical busducts, each phase well over a yard in diameter. Peering up at the confusing sight, she realized that another climb was necessary—up the small ladder tied against the nearest bus. She felt George's eyes hopefully, expectantly fixed upon her as she whispered to him, "Is it O.K. if I go up that ladder?"

"Yes, Miss Francis, but be careful—and hang on tight!"

Reaching the top rung, she now could see the small drain pipe that Mr. Sellers' notes had mentioned as a clue; it emerged from the lowest part of the generator shell, threaded its way through the doughnut C.T.'s, and then ran down the concrete haunch. And there was the red insulated joint in the pipe—to break the unwanted loop or "false turn" through the C.T.'s.

But there was no metal rat guard that might have shorted out the insulation as on another job Mr. Sellers had recalled. A plastic sign hung below the insulating pipe joint with its warning legend, "Do not short this insulation." Straining upwards, she managed to finger the ties lashing the plastic sign at each end to the pipe on each side of the insulating coupling. The wire was aluminum, and her trembling fingers excitedly felt behind the sign. The metallic tie was continuous between the two holes in the sign and so spanned across the insulating fitting. The other signs were all on the generator side of the couplings. With a sigh of thankful relief, she loosened the twisted wire, slid the sign past the coupling, and then re-tightened the tie. As everyone awaited her judgment, she carefully descended to join all the others on the platform.

Impatiently, Art asked, "Well? Do you need your bag hoisted up here, Marion?"

As everyone chuckled, she perversely turned to George.

"Can you ask the test fellows to try it again now? How long will it take?"

There was a hurried consultation, and then George whispered, "It will only take a few minutes to make another preliminary run on this set-up. I couldn't see what you did up there, Miss Francis."

Relenting, she murmured to George and Art, "I just moved that warning sign along the pipe away from the insulating joint. The aluminum lashing wire was shorting out the insulation,—just what the sign was warning against! I sure hope that fixes it! All the ties should be changed to plastic on all the signs—to prevent this happening in the future—if I'm right!"

"You'll see! I'm telling you;—the boss lady's always right!"

Now Art suddenly clasped his right arm firmly about her waist and exclaimed, "How do you do it, boss lady?"

"Oh, Art, stop it! Let me go!" she protested; but there was no space for her even to attempt to escape his enthusiastic embrace on the crowded scaffolding. Finding his grasping hug too powerful for her to break,—at least without an embarrassing struggle, she decided to relax and ignore Art—if such a feat were possible when she could hardly catch her breath now. Fortunately one of the test men announced in obvious amazement, "It looks like the readings will be all right now! What did she do, George?"

Now Art laughed, whirling her around to face him. "You tell 'em, George! What'd I tell you? How do you do it, boss lady?"

Glancing at her wrist watch, she tried to ask calmly—if a bit breathlessly, "George,—it's—almost noon. Is it—alright—if Art—and I—leave now?"

George grinned happily. "Sure thing, Miss Francis! Just be very careful on the ladders. We can't afford to lose you *and* Mr. Sellers!"

"George, Mr. Sellers told me that we just fix a few troubles; but *you* straighten out hundreds of messes down here—without our ever knowing about them uptown! I know he's right; and—I'm counting on you to help me the same way from here on in, George!"

"Thanks, Miss Francis! We'll keep on trying!"

By now the overly enthusiastic Art had released her; so, smiling, she backed over to the swaying ladder and cautiously started down with her eyes fixed on the rungs at her feet. Safely on terra firma again, she grabbed her bag and followed Art out through the labyrinth of stairs and elevations. She wondered how much longer it would take her to find her way around by herself.

Pausing before long rows of switchgear, Art said, "This is the upper

Unit 1 main switchgear room with 480-volt, 4-kv, and 13-kv switchgear and some 480-volt motor control centers. Hundreds of circuit breakers, millions of dollars, and billions of chances for troubles!"

Seated on boxes, craft electricians were slowly taping over the terminal lugs and bolting in dozens of compartments; but already some were standing up and stretching. With long pony-tails below their shoulders, many workers looked like girls—from behind; but, when they turned around, she could see they needed a good shave—and a haircut!

Now Art glanced at his watch. "Oh, oh! Only ten minutes to beat the noon lunch-whistle rush! Let's see if we can escape the stampede!"

At last, breathless but seated safely beside her chauffeur, she relaxed as Art drove out the mile-long access road through the deep forest to the state highway. Softly, she asked, "Have you ever seen deer along here, Art?"

"No, but George says he often sees them in the early morning. And 'coons and 'possum and squirrels—and skunks—and even foxes. And quail—and osprey—and turkey buzzards—and all kinds of birds. Are you one of those nature-ecology nuts, too, Marion?"

"Yes, Art. I guess I've always been one at heart. But—you make it all sound crazy; and, after tonight's environmental-pollution meeting, I'm afraid I'll react against all my old nature friends!"

"I heard about that! You're going to some 'confab' of dames tonight to argue them out of making us the ecological whipping boys for the far-out 'pushbutton Hiawathas'?"

She sighed. "I sure wish I could think of some good way to get out of going to that hassle! I'm afraid they'll tear my hair out by the roots—before they all get through with me for trying to throw a wet blanket on their fun hour!"

"I don't envy you on that caper, boss lady. But—you'll make out. You always do!"

"Thanks for your moral support, Art. I'll need it!"

It really was very soothing to her nerves—and ego—to have a handsome young man chauffeur her through this beautiful countryside on a fine midsummer day.

"Hungry, Marion? After all that hiking and climbing and mental gymnastics! You should be as ravenous—as you are ravishing, boss lady!"

"I guess I could be persuaded to sit up and take some nourishment at that, Art!", she murmured, slumped restfully in her seat.

"Fine! I generally eat with the uncouth horde of gorillas at a noisy greasy-spoon hash-house a mile south of the plant when I'm going back to the site afterwards. But here's the quiet spot I prefer—if it's O.K. with you."

"Anything you say, Art,—as long as it's dutch treat."

"Oh, I thought my well-heeled, *senior* engineer, boss lady would take *me,* her engineer slave, to lunch!"

"But, Art, our *principal* engineer, Mr. Sellers, didn't pay for *my* lunch at his cafeteria yesterday!"

"You twisted his arm, I'll bet! How'd you like his favorite spot? Alright, isn't it?"

"Yes, I could see why he eats there regularly. But, Art, this little place looks real nice! 'The Hearth Side in the Pines'! A quaint old converted farm house!"

No sooner had they entered the front door than a pleasant motherly woman greeted Art like a prodigal son, "Well, here's your table by the window! And where have you been for the past week, young man?"

"Oh, they've been keeping me too busy to get up here lately; and— I'm rushed for time today, too!"

"Well, now! I hope this pretty, young lady brings you back more often in the future!"

As they all smiled in unison, Marion sat down at the rustic oak table and scanned the tiny menu; almost at once she exclaimed, "Just what I wished! A bowl of home-made vegetable soup with cornbread muffins and milk!"

"My usual: hamburger, rare, with everything—and black coffee!"

By the time they had returned from the rest rooms, their food was on the table. Then for a few minutes both were busy until at last she broke the silence, "Everything's really very tasty, Art."

"Yeah, not too bad, boss lady," he grunted as he finished his hamburger.

"Art?"

"Yeh?"

The waitress had left the room, and no one sat near them—to overhear their conversation. She resolved to have it out—right now— once and for all.

"Art, would you please do me—and yourself—a favor—and let up on rubbing it in with that 'boss-lady' bit? It's embarrassing to me, especially in front of others. And it must be hard on you, too. You know, Mr. Sellers says I'm really not your boss. Mr. Board bosses us both—or he's *supposed* to be our supervisor."

She took a deep breath.

"Art, I know how you must feel—after working hard, only to have an outsider,—a woman, at that!—brought in to get the promotion. I'm sorry it was this way. What else can I say—or do? And I *am* counting on you to be on my side. It's going to be tough all around without Mr. Sellers. Please, Art?"

Slowly picking up her check, she at last dared to look across the table at him; but he was still staring gravely into his cup. There was only one other occupied table in the quiet room now with an elderly couple dawdling over coffee.

It was no use; he wasn't having any. Finally Art spoke with an obvious effort.

"I'll confess it hurt; and, that first Monday you dropped in, I did hope, and think, you couldn't 'cut the mustard!'"

He downed the last of the coffee and looked her in the eye. With a wry grin, he said, "It's a bit hard on my male chauvinism to admit it, but these past two days now you've made a believer out of me. You've got what it takes, which is more than I can claim for myself."

"Oh, now, Art! Please stop running yourself down. You *do* know your job, and I said I'm depending on you! Without your help, I can't make it! And yet I've just got to swing it somehow!"

At last he grinned. "You win, as usual, Marion! Shall we go now?"

He quickly snatched up his check without any banter. Outside again in the searing sun, she whispered, "Thanks—for everything, Art! I'm glad you brought me here, and I'd like to come again with you."

"Alright, Marion, we'll just do that!"

Marvelously, they smiled at each other as he unlocked the car door and closed it carefully behind her as she buckled up her safety belt, rolled down the window, and settled comfortably back in her seat.

They should arrive back in the office early enough for her to get in two frantic hours of environmental engineering coaching from Ann Teach and some more common-sense counsel from Mr. Sellers before quitting time. Then she would be on her own tonight, making her last stand at the Green Knolls, surrounded by hysterically militant club women, probably screaming for her scalp.

CHAPTER FIVE

Massacre at Green Knolls

LOCKING HER CAR door, she noted that only a dozen automobiles were scattered about the parking area; but then she was a full quarter hour early. The simply designed, ranch-style club house nestled beside a grove of maples, oaks, and elms; and somewhere a mockingbird was caroling away in the gloaming. Walking reluctantly towards the entrance, she had to admit the locale was ideal for a pep meeting to rally public opinion against the polluting power plants, which were threatening to suffocate everyone and bury these last green sanctuaries under a Pompeiian avalanche of flyash.

Although the sun had set, it was still sweltering hot and sticky without a breeze stirring even a leaf anywhere. As she cautiously stepped through the entry vestibule into the meeting room, she was thankful that at the last minute she had yielded to Aunt Dinah's suggestion to change from her pantsuit into this cool, flowered-print, cotton dress as being more disarmingly appealing to her potentially hostile critics.

Halting prudently at the rear of the rather small room to survey the battleground, she saw a slide projector and screen; so—she might be able to bring Ann's arsenal of slides to bear upon the foe. There were about fifty comfortably padded metal chairs, perhaps a third of them already occupied by club women, happily chatting together in little coveys. Now into the room strode an efficient-looking, bespectacled, young woman with raven-black hair, pulled back severely into a bun. No doubt a teacher by profession, the trim, pant-suited, little lady began fussing with the projector's plug-in cords, fan and light controls, and slide carrier. Fortunately, there was no formal rostrum or stage; down in front stood a table with three chairs and the usual water pitcher and glasses.

As Marion tried to plan her next move, a laughing group of middle-aged women entered the room; and the gray-haired one in a summery blue dress began shuffling papers at the table. On the assumption that the chairlady now had arrived, Marion forced herself to walk down the aisle. Her tactics took a lot of nerve right now, but she didn't like the idea of exploding her questions and spiel like bombs without warning from the midst of the audience after the guest speaker had finished. Apparently that had always been the Company's approved modus operandi on these uninvited forays into enemy territory, but Marion couldn't believe that such a brutal strategy could win any friends for an electric power company in these critical times.

Standing beside the generously proportioned woman now, Marion noted they both were of about the same height. With a questioning expression on her pleasant face, the tall woman at last looked up from the sheaf of papers. This was her cue. Diffidently Marion managed to say with a smile, "Good evening, ma'am! I am Miss Marion Francis. Are you the chairlady for this meeting?"

A nervous smile now relieved the obvious anxiety lining the clubwoman's round face.

"Why, yes, I am! That is, if Dr. Harrod ever shows up! I am Harriet Williams,—Mrs. Williams. Are you a—a reporter, Miss Francis?"

"No, Mrs. Williams. As you can see from my ID card here, I am an employee of the electric company—on my own time this evening! I'm the engineer responsible for the electrical engineering of our power plants. And I was wondering if I may join with Dr. Harrod in a question-and-answer panel session—with participation from the audience. This would be after the doctor's talk, of course! I realize this is short notice, but I just learned of your meeting today!"

"Oh, dear,—Miss Francis! You—you certainly don't look like one of those—hard hat power-plant engineers!"

Marion laughed as Mrs. Williams smiled tentatively in incredulous confusion.

"Yes, Mrs. Williams, I experience your reaction everywhere I go! But then, you know, the only way we women can beat the men at their own game—is to join them!"

As they both laughed now, Mrs. Williams exclaimed, "Why, of course, you're right, Miss Francis! We women must stick together! Well, I don't see why we can't do what you suggest! It should make the program more interesting! Let me talk to Dr. Harrod as soon as—Ah, here he comes now!"

As the man hurried towards them, Marion couldn't help experiencing a strange feeling of empathy with her antagonist; for his sensitive, good-looking features exhibited the same unmistakable signs of the nervousness and anxiety that were afflicting her. She couldn't decide whether he was ill at ease because, like her, he was apprehensive of his ability to deliver the goods in an unfamiliar situation—or whether his apparent foreboding stemmed from his being a lone male surrounded by so many appraising females. Perhaps he suffered from both conditions, Marion thought. Certainly his lean features and spare frame made her imagine that he wasn't being fed well at home. Nearly a head taller than she, he seemed to be about thirty years old. His rather tousled, brown, wavy hair, though trimmed short all around in the old-fashioned, conservative way, nevertheless had an unruly forelock that insisted on falling down onto his horn-rimmed glasses.

"Well, Dr. Harrod, I am Mrs. Harriet Williams. You are—right on time."

Shifting his bulging brief case to his left hand, he shook hands with the chairlady as he spoke softly with an apologetic grin, "I'm Dr. Frank Boone, ma'am; Dr. Harrod called in sick today. You know—'doctor, heal thyself!' I'd have gotten here earlier—except that it took me awhile to get all this together; and I got lost, too!"

"Well, Dr. Boone, we appreciate your stepping in at the last minute for us. This young lady is Miss Marion Francis,—Dr. Boone."

His nice brown eyes looked into hers as he clasped her hand firmly,— yet not painfully hard. Her own palm was perspiring so much that she couldn't discern whether his was, also.

"Doctor, Miss Francis is with the electric company; she's the engineer responsible for designing and building all those polluting power plants. In effect, she will be your adversary."

There was no use for her to try to explain that she was only the electrical engineer and not the mechanical, civil, nuclear, or environmental engineer—or the architect—and certainly not the project engineer. To these clubwomen she represented the whole ball of wax. As Marion smiled back at his surprised double-take of her role, Marion heard Mrs. Williams speaking even more enthusiastically now, "Doctor, as you were entering, Miss Francis and I were discussing a slight change in our program format. I hope you will concur since I think her suggestion should make the evening far more interesting and instructive. After your talk, then Miss Francis would like to speak—briefly, I think; finally, the three of us will sit at this table and conduct a sort of—talk panel. I'll try to moderate between you two experts. Our audience can even participate, also,—with questions and discussion from the floor. Doesn't that sound simply fascinating?"

"Why,—why, of course, Mrs. Williams!"

"Now, Doctor, please let me have your slides for our projector operator—in the proper order, of course."

This was Marion's chance.

"Oh, Mrs. Williams, here are several of mine, also."

"Fine!" the chairlady beamed.

Mrs. Williams vigorously pounded the table with a delicate little gavel to silence all the buzzing conversations amid the audience, which by now had almost filled the room to its seating capacity.

"Ladies, as we agreed at our last meeting, we shall dispense with the reading of the minutes tonight—and start right into our program. We are fortunate in having Dr. Frank Boone from our State Health Department—to speak to us on a very relevant subject these days, 'Pollution of Our Air and Water'. Then, after Dr. Boone's talk, Miss Marion Francis, here, will say a few words. She is from the electric company where, incredible as it may seem, she is the engineer responsible for designing and building all those power plants that Dr. Boone will be mentioning. Equal time, you know!"

There was considerable whispering with much eyebrow-raising in the audience at that point until the chairlady rapped the gavel for order. "Finally, I shall moderate a discussion panel, and all of you are encouraged to participate freely. Of course, after the formal meeting we'll have coffee and doughnuts with informal discussions. Now, without more ado,—may I present Dr. Boone."

Hesitantly the young doctor began his speech.

"Ladies, I shall show you how your Health Department—in concerted action with the EPA and other governmental and private nature agencies—has been working to prevent industries and especially the biggest polluter, the power industry, from choking us with sulfur dioxide, burying us under flyash and cinders, and thermally polluting our waters,—killing off our wildlife and vegetation. You have—in these past six years—directed your legislators to pass laws enabling us to force the electric power companies to burn cleaner fuel—and to take the flyash from their stacks—and to cease excessive thermal pollution of our waters. You'll see curves of six years of decreasing sulfur dioxide and flyash in the air we breathe. And you'll want to see this remarkable progress continue in the coming years."

Although Marion took notes as he plunged resolutely through his lecture, her precautionary efforts were unnecessary because Ann's briefing had covered everything very well, indeed. At last, obviously ad libbing at the end, he said, "As your chairlady said, it *is* unbelievable that this beautiful, fastidious, young woman would permit herself to be associated with such dirty work being perpetrated upon us all."

As the obviously relieved doctor sat down on the other side of Mrs. Williams in the center of the front row of seats, a polite wave of subdued clapping rippled over the room; and now the chairlady tapped Marion on the shoulder. Taking a deep breath, she stood up and smiled out at the suddenly attentive audience. Her voice sounded amazingly calm—in spite of her pounding heart and cotton-dry mouth—as she began to speak.

"Ladies—and—gentleman, let me begin by stating that I yield to no one—not even our crusading doctor here—in my love of Mother Nature and her children. To prove it, I have enough wildlife stamps to paper the walls of my house!"

Encouraged by the laughter, she spoke more easily now with the ice broken so early in her oratorical effort, "And, far from feeling any guilt over my employment by an electric company, I am proud to be a small part of the power industry, without which our civilization could not exist. Without electricity, we could not be a free nation in today's world—with the industrial and military sinews to defend and support ourselves—and our less fortunate fellow human beings. Our health and comfort are dependent on electric power for refrigeration of food and medicine, for hospitals and medical supplies, for air conditioning, for power to produce fertilizers and agricultural machinery and to operate our modern farms so that we can save millions of starving people in the world, for power to relieve drudgery everywhere, especially in the ghettos, for electricity to operate sewage disposal plants to clean up our major source of water pollution."

She smiled at Dr. Boone.

"Now let's do get back to nature as the good doctor ordered! He showed us a slide of hundreds of acres of forest denuded to provide a site for a power plant. But trees are raised as a crop to harvest for our use like wheat and corn."

She smiled at the teacher projector-operator now.

"Now, if I may have my first slide,—we'll see first a beautiful forest along a quiet road. That's a deer peeking out of the woods on the right! This view is only a small part of the hundreds and hundreds of acres of undisturbed Nature at our new nuclear power plant soon to be in service at Cliffside—to provide us with less expensive electricity and to release more scarce oil and gasoline for our use. And American nuclear plants are so *safe* that the probability of *any* substantial radiation release from our 100 plants in 1980 is less than once in over 2,000 years! And the sophisticated security of the plants with their fuel and wastes is now excellent!"

She nodded to the projector lady, who was smiling now.

"The next slide shows the visitors' overlook pavilion with its view of the attractive plant and surroundings; you are all welcome to be our guests there! Thousands do come!"

Again she looked at the teacher.

"This slide is of the waterfront at our River Shore Plant, which can burn either coal—if permitted by our doctor and his cohorts—or expensive oil. Here you can see swans, geese, and ducks—as well as boat loads of successful anglers,—a view repeated throughout the year.

"Dr. Boone showed us a slide with curves of how in the past six years his agency—with others—has been able to force our power company to comply with new anti-pollution laws, thereby lowering the concentrations of flyash—or particulates—and SO_2—sulfur dioxide—in our air—each year."

She now smiled again at her cooperative teacher.

"Now let's look at my last slide—of curves extending back not just 6 years—but 35 years ago—before World War II—and long before my mother had ever seen my father!"

She paused for the slide to be focused as the titters died away. "These two curves *descending* from left to right—like my utility stocks on Wall Street—show that the densities of flyash and SO_2 in the air we breathe—have been decreasing through the whole 35-year period—without any efforts paid for by our taxes—since there was no EPA then. But even back then, without any EPA or nudging by the Health Department, your electric company was spending millions of dollars installing precipitators to remove flyash from the coal flue gas. Now note the curve *rising* from left to right. This curve is the combined incidence rate of serious respiratory diseases,—such as TB and emphysema. Why has this curve been *rising* when the twin curves of flyash and sulfur-dioxide pollutants have been *falling*? It would seem that the medical community could spend more effort on this research question rather than on throwing brickbats at your electric company, owned by many thousands of our citizens!"

She glanced over her interested listeners now.

"We all desire even cleaner air and water than we have, but how much do we want to pay for each bit of improvement? How much do we dare to squander on ourselves—when there are millions of less fortunate people who need our resources of food and financial aid in *our* land—*and* in the world? And make no mistake about it,—we all must *pay* for all of this anti-pollution work in one way or another. Practically all of our coal-burning plants are now burning low-sulfur oil—to comply with these new air-quality laws. If our laws and regulations could be amended to allow industry to *return* to burning coal again, there would be no crushing energy crisis with its shortages of oil, gasoline and natural gas, causing balance-of-payments troubles—and inflation—and recession. Think of that! And the cost of our electric bills would drop dramatically—perhaps as much as 25%!"

She pointed to the stack of papers on the table.

"Our worthy doctor has a pile of sheets here listing your state and federal legislators—with their addresses. I suggest that we use *my* handout sheets—over here,—listing also, the laws—now in congressional or legislature committees or on the floor—that would let us proceed in a more orderly and reasonable manner in this whole matter—of burning coal when air quality permits—and switching briefly back to oil only as long as conditions require, of—strip-mining coal with reasonable safeguards and restoration, and of exploration and tax incentives for more oil and gas. I hope, in conclusion, that we all can work reasonably together to arrive at the most practical solutions year by year for all of our pollution problems. To that end,—that Dr. Boone's fraternity—and my colleagues,—instead of always confronting each other as adversaries, demanding equal rights and time,—can work together with you all in the best interests of everyone. Thank you!"

As she sat down with flushed cheeks, Marion was cheered by the impression that the applause was much louder than for her debating opponent. Now, Mrs. Williams was wielding the gavel with great gusto.

"Ladies! Ladies! We'll now begin our little talk panel. I'll recognize anyone from the floor. Come now, Dr. Boone, Miss Francis."

No sooner had they seated themselves at the table than the chairlady asked, "Doctor, what do you think of Miss Francis' suggestion—that we turn back the clock a couple of years and burn coal again,—that relatively cheap and dirty black stuff,—in the plants? I've read where we have five hundred years of coal, 'more than the Arabs have of oil,' their black gold! Yet *we* may have only twelve years of gas and oil, which now supply over three fourths of our energy needs!"

Dr. Boone squirmed in his chair as he stroked his forehead.

"Do we want to give up all we've gained recently, Mrs. Williams, and risk our health? Remember all those who died of smoke and smog at Donora? Yes, Miss Francis, what about that sad incident?"

"Those sixteen, critically ill, old folk whose premature deaths were attributed partially to smog at Donora? I guess maybe I *was* born then—or thereabouts! That *was* a tragedy! But—it hasn't happened since—anywhere. Last summer I drove by that little town—in the valley of the Monongahela,—an industrial region. I think it was a rare case of weather inversion, of many factories, and a mountainous topography. Like the Johnstown flood! Today monitoring systems would alert everyone, and the mills would either shut down or reduce operations or change fuels for a few days. Dr. Boone, I've read where the same scientists who set the maximum permissible ppm of sulfur dioxide now are backing down on their original claim of those SO_2 concentrations being harmful, anyway. Isn't that right?"

"I've read such reports, but I'm not familiar with the consensus on that subject today. But, Miss Francis, not being sure, I'd think your power plants should play it safe, and go along with the EPA, and install those SO_2 'scrubbers' to clean the stack gasses."

"Dr. Boone, you've read the famous 'ads', haven't you? None of those expensive, energy-consuming, long delivery contraptions has as yet *proved* to be reliable and practical for large, base-load plants in this part of the country. And you often trade air pollution for water pollution. Our industry is still conducting costly R & D on that—and, also, on cleaning coal before it burns. My company has just spent several millions of dollars on a prototype project for a scrubber which we had to abandon. To avoid unnecessary embarrassment of well-known corporations, I'll not name the participants in the unsuccessful venture. But let tax incentives encourage further industry research in all directions in the years ahead. Meanwhile, let's burn coal—to save gas and oil for their essential chemical and special combustion uses!"

At once a hand waved energetically from the audience.

Mrs. Williams called out, "Yes, Gladys?"

An excited young woman began talking urgently.

"Miss Francis, did you say your plants can switch back to coal right away? And then, if conditions get real stinking bad for a few days each year, you can switch them back to oil—temporarily?"

"Yes, ma'am. We have over two months of good coal in our stockpiles right now; but, unless we install costly, unproven, long delivery SO_2 'scrubbers', we can't burn it under present EPA and state regulations without a variance being granted—even though the FEA now is trying to force the EPA *and* us to go back to coal to save oil—at any cost—of 'scrubbers'!"

"Well, then, what are we waiting for? Our air and water are clean enough for my kids and me. We're not coughing—unless some inconsiderate so-and-so insists on smoking in my face! And we don't want to swim in the harbor with all those dirty ships! I'm a widow now; and I work hard on an assembly line,—which soon may shut down if this environmental, oil-crisis, inflation-recession goes on much longer. Now, due to this switch from coal to oil in the power plants, my electric bill has grown to be bigger than my mortgage payments;—and—I—may lose everything—any day now!

"Miss Francis, I'm going to distribute your sheets to everyone on the assembly line—and anywhere else I can,—and—and we're all going to write to our politicians, believe me! I say, 'Burn coal *now*—and strip-mine it!! Explore for oil off our Atlantic shore! Why should we expect those along the Gulf and West coasts to do it all for us? And—that was a crime for all those ecology nuts to delay the Alaska pipe line all those years! And—also your nuclear plant, too! Miss Francis, can I get more of your sheets?"

Marion smiled happily at her questioner. "Yes, ma'am. Our phone number to call is right on the bottom line. Meanwhile, I hope we'll all let our PSC, listed there, too, know that, if we want electricity, we'll all need to pay higher rates to cover increased labor and other inflationary costs—like we pay higher prices for everything else. Until the onslaught of these unreasonable environmental regulations, requiring us to burn costly oil, our electric rates had been decreasing for many years—while the cost-of-living index was rising with our persistent 'permissive' inflation since World War II. Even today our rates are still less than in the boom times of 1929. For lack of the necessary rate increases last year the utility stock prices dropped 50% so that it was not feasible to sell new stock—below book value—to provide funds for plant construction projects, which then had to be canceled—along with employee stock purchase plans."

Mrs. Williams looked serious. "Thank you, Gladys. We all know how *you* feel now! How about your reaction to consumer protests about inflationary costs, Dr. Boone? Isn't all this anti-pollution work inflationary?"

"Why—not altogether," he said. "I can't believe we want to throw away all our environmental gains—and progress—of the last several years. Miss Francis, surely your company doesn't advocate any such reactionary policy—or so-called 'environmental backlash'?"

As all eyes turned her way suddenly, Marion began slowly, "No, not at all! But burning coal *most* of the year will still permit us to maintain our air quality standards—as they now stand on the books; we won't lose that environmental gain! But let's proceed with further improvements only as fast as we can pay for them—and still meet our responsibilities in the 'real' world. And we can *all* try to help. The auto is the major urban air polluter today, so—we can car-pool. Or ride the bus downtown as I do. We must use more—not less electricity—in the future for heat pumps, mass transit, electric autos, and other uses—to save oil and gas for essential chemical processes, airplanes, and such. Today, less than half of our energy use is from electricity with only one sixth from coal.

"And just think! Only *one* nuclear generating unit can cut $100,000,000 off the fuel-rate part of our annual electric bills *and* save us over 600,000,000 gallons of oil a year! Our Project Independence can *use* that kind of help—since we're burning up twice as much 'Arab' oil *now* as *before* the embargo! Nearly half of the oil and gasoline we use today is 'Arab' import!"

"As for environmental progress, I have slides that show cattle grazing on restored pastures that were once coal-stripped, and slides of very slightly warmed water discharges from Florida plants helping to grow less expensive shrimp for us all. All that is necessary for us to succeed in all this—is for all of us to work together sensibly now. Doctor, can we shake on that?"

However, just at that critical moment, a kindly looking, white-haired, old woman raised her hand and at once spoke breathlessly, "Don't you think God wants us to—refrain from defiling His earth—with your dirty, smoky, power plants?"

Marion thought she should have brought along Aunt Dinah to talk with this nice old lady about religion,—a touchy subject here!

"I agree, ma'am! But the Bible says that God made and put all His creatures and plants on the earth to be under man's dominion. Like the Sabbath was made for man,—not man for the Sabbath; so the earth with all that's on it was made for man to use—wisely. And we should all pray for that wisdom. It is a matter of priorities—and hard choices. We've been cleaning dust from our flue gasses for a third of a century. How much should we spend—in hundreds of billions of consumer dollars—and fuel—and when—for sulfur removal? Sulfates? Or sulfites! Are the present, sulfur-dioxide, atmospheric concentrations harmful? Must we waste 50% more money on our power plants where the discharge water is only five or ten degrees warmer—like a teaspoon of warm water poured in a cold bathtub? Let us do our home work first,—more research at a reasonable rate! Let us try to gain more wisdom before we spend more of our resources on ourselves for 'super-clean' air and water!"

As the old woman smiled in apparent agreement, the slide-projection operator now spoke up intensely, "But, Miss Francis, surely we should all *conserve* electricity, so you won't have to *build* all those, costly, polluting plants!"

"Yes, indeed! I certainly agree! And you've been doing that, too,—because our loads dropped 1% last year, partly because of the inflation-recession, of course. But, nevertheless, even with maximum conservation and use of all other fuels and energy sources, the FEA estimates that we'll need twelve times as much nuclear power generation by the year 2000 as we have today. That means we need a new 1,000,000-kilowatt nuclear power plant put in service every 10 days to the year 2000! And, also, we must burn triple as much coal as we do now! And cut our energy-use growth rate in half! We should conserve electricity, and minerals, oil, natural gas, gasoline, automobiles, food, clothing,—everything! With our growing population and national maturity, we're fast becoming a 'have-not' country! We must not waste! 'Waste not;

want not!' The more we waste—or unwisely expend on unreasonable anti-pollution programs, the less energy, wealth, food, and military resources we'll have to help defend weak peoples against aggressors— and to continue feeding the world's starving millions. We now export three-fourths of the world's food contributions—and two-thirds of the world's poverty-relief monies.

"To do all this philanthropic work, we *do* need to use more power per person than other countries, which have not learned to use their resources yet—even with our technical assistance—and so cannot produce as we do. But we don't want to squander our resources to pamper ourselves on too much costly anti-pollution effort, do we? God made us adaptable; we can soil our hands while trying to relieve hunger, poverty, disease, drudgery—here and abroad—rather than wasting our resources on cleaning up our harbors so that we can swim in them—like a pool!

"Again, I—I hope we can all work together reasonably and wisely in making all these hard decisions. Doctor, again I say, 'Can we shake on that?'"

This time there were no interruptions,—just blessed spontaneous applause,—including the nice old lady and the projector operator. Now Mrs. Wiiliams assisted the doctor in achieving the handshaking as everyone arose at once.

"Thank you, Doctor Boone! Thank you, too, Miss Francis! We've all had a very exciting and thought-provoking evening! And now—we can continue our discussions informally—over coffee and doughnuts—on those tables in the rear of the room!"

Through it all Doctor Boone was still firmly holding her hand as they followed everyone towards the refreshments. Smiling in evident relief now, he said, "Miss Francis, you were wonderful!"

"Thank you, Dr. Boone," she murmured, smiling. "This is all out of my line though, you know. One of our environmental engineers, Ann Teach, spoon-fed me most of this only several hours ago—so that I wouldn't have time to forget it all!"

"Oh, you know Ann? A very competent biologist. I'm not a medical doctor. I'm a Ph.D. The State Health Department has retained me as one of their 'ology' consultants—from Less and Ladds."

"'Ology' consultant?' she asked blankly.

"Yes! Your company uses a lot of our kind, too,—for all the environmental-impact reports with cost-benefit studies, required by state and federal laws today—for just about any big project. We work both sides of the fence, government and private clients. We write shelves of encyclopedic ecology tomes—for each project—and check over the output of our brethren—for opposing clients!"

"What is an 'ology' though, Doctor Boone?" Marion questioned.

"Our people specialize—in various disciplines—as you engineers do! Ichthyology, hydrology, geology, and also meteorology, seismology, biology, ornithology—and so on! Mine is 'limnology', but I've expanded from freshwater lakes to the study of littoral—or shore ecology. And our 'ology' business is really mushrooming,—a plug for mycologists!—just booming—as the result of all the new laws."

He smiled at her obvious confusion. "I can see now you're a real electrical construction engineer—despite your deceptively demure and beautifully feminine appearance! You should have brought your hard hat along!"

"Why?" Marion asked softly, hurt by his sharp tone. "You heard me say I'm a born nature lover, didn't you?"

"Yes, I heard you, but you build power plants! That's your bread-and-butter! 'Damn the torpedoes! Full speed ahead!'"

"Now, Doctor Boone! You are jumping to unreasonable conclusions."

"Perhaps, Miss Francis. I'm sorry. May I get you some of those doughnuts—and coffee?"

"No, Doctor Boone. Thanks just the same! It's a matter of calories."

"Well, now, my friendly enemy, don't run away! I don't want to lose you in this hungry mob of women. And you said we should work together now. Look, your handouts are going like hot cakes, while my sheets look like they have leprosy. Miss Francis, you fascinate me—even though you *massacred* me,—clobbered me unmercifully before all these ladies!"

"Is your wife among them?"

"I don't happen to be married. Incidentally, you're a great speaker! You came across real sincere—and natural,—not canned and—stereotyped! That's mostly why you beat me. I should never forgive you!"

"Sorry about that! You weren't very easy on me either, Dr. Boone!"

She smiled as he turned away to thread his tortuous way through the pressing throng of ravenous females. For herself, she resolved to observe her diet by foregoing the doughnuts; and she really didn't like coffee, anyway. No sooner had he disappeared into the crowd than a short, plump, middle-aged woman approached her. Graying hair set in soft waves, the pleasantly self-assured lady smiled cordially.

"Oh, Miss Francis, you were just perfect for our program! Ed was right! Although he only saw you yesterday for a minute, he was sure you were the very one I was looking for! He'll be so pleased when I tell him all about you—and tonight! Oh, pardon me! I am Victoria King."

As they shook hands warmly, she was glad that the wife of her Company's Chief Executive Officer had not come forward *before* the meeting; no doubt the result would have been a terminal case of nervous prostration.

"Oh, Mrs. King, I was so nervous! And I'm afraid I showed it! I'm not used to this sort of thing! I'm an engineer, you know,—not an orator!"

"Oh, nonsense, my dear! You were marvelous! And engineers must be speakers today! Ed is an engineer, too; and he—knows his business! I'm really glad that he discovered you for my club's meeting tonight—to speak up for his side! Oh, you must excuse me! Harriet Williams is waving to me over there! 'Bye now!"

"Goodbye, Mrs. King! It was good to meet someone—of the Company here!"

Mr. Sellers was right. She wondered what this evening portended for the future. More such affairs? On the speakers' circuit—like Ann? Several women smiled at her, and one remarked, "I'm with *you*, Miss Francis! I'm satisfied with the air-and-water thing as it was! Let's burn coal in the plants—if that'll get us plenty of cheaper gasoline and house-heating oil—and reduce our electric bills—and high prices of things!"

As she nodded in smiling acknowledgment, a scholarly looking lady said, "I agree with you about Mother Nature! Man's puny pollution efforts are dwarfed by the effluents from volcanoes, salt springs, lightning, soil dust, forest effects, mineral leaching, and—even muddy rivers, which General Oglethorpe described in colonial Georgia,—and even continual natural oil seepage—now and long ago—in the Santa Barbara Channel. And all that stuff about aerosols destroying the ozone radiation shield! I've read where radiation forms that ozone in the first place! It's hard to get the right story!"

Still smiling, Marion glanced at her wrist watch as soon as she found herself alone at last; and she was shocked to see that it was nearly ten o'clock. There had been more talking than she had realized. She hoped that she hadn't rudely usurped Doctor Boone's speaking time. He seemed to be—a nice man; and then, also, he appeared to be—attracted to her in spite of their reluctant forensic duel. There was something so—so vulnerable about him. It would be impolite for her to run off now before he returned with the nourishment he so obviously needed, but she was Cinderella. After looking after Aunt Dinah and her own chores, she wouldn't get to sleep now until after midnight; then it would be five o'clock before she knew it—with breakfast to get, more chores to do, and her aunt to attend—before chasing the 6:45 bus for her third rugged day on the job. Her work might be exhausting—but certainly not dull, for she could never imagine what the next day might bring her way.

Picking up her slides, she slung her bag strap over her shoulder and slipped quietly out of the room full of milling women. Perhaps Frank Boone would get in touch with her through Ann—if he desired to fraternize with the enemy. Then she smiled at the comforting memory of that gold wedding ring she had noticed safely and snugly fitted on Ann's pretty left hand.

CHAPTER SIX

The Third Day's The Charm

AGAIN, AS YESTERDAY, she was happily reassured to find Mr. Sellers awaiting her at seven-thirty in the deserted office, which was still soothingly quiet.

"Oh, Mr. Sellers, you were right about the meeting! I met Mrs. King! She seemed pleased that her husband had 'volunteered' me for the extra 'soapbox' duty! And—she thought her fellow club members were now thoroughly 'brain-washed' in our favor by my amateurish rehash of whatever I had absorbed from Ann and you! I only hope this sort of thing doesn't get to be my regular job!"

He grinned sympathetically and then said reflectively, "Would it really be so bad, Marion? The Company really has fallen down on its public relations, and nothing is more vital today. Power companies used to keep out of trouble just by maintaining a low profile in public affairs—but not now! Our PSC is afraid to grant us the necessary rate increases to meet our inflation-boosted material and labor costs—because of protesting consumers, who have had *their* wage raises! And a few, hysterical, upper-class, idealistic, ecology-dabblers,—not the working class or the poor people,—make so much noise that our legislative and regulatory bodies are fearful of granting us the hundred licenses required to put a new plant in service. And, even though most people are familiar with how expensively and inefficiently our government operates anything—like the postal service, for example, yet some always wonder if their electric bills might be shared with other taxpayers—if the government took over all utilities. A *man* is now our public relations vice president, and our corporate image couldn't be worse! Maybe he should retire early—like me—and let a very attractively appealing, highly qualified, young woman engineer take over the job of winning citizens to our side!"

Sighing, she sat down by his table. "Oh, no! Let us not dream such nightmares on such a beautiful summer morning! My calendar promises today will be a nice, quiet one. With your counsel and advice, I can catch up with all those papers piled on my desk!"

"Well, not exactly, Marion! There's a note in my in-box this morning, left after quitting time by our Chief Mechanical Engineer, Harry Fisher, saying that a car load of our River Shore consultants will arrive at ten. Among them is our project's electrical chief, an Englishman,—John Winton. He's 'bumming' a ride with their civils and mechanicals so that he can discuss wiring systems in a preliminary way. Your list shows Tom Fields assigned to wiring. Since this will be his first meeting on the new fossil-unit project at River Shore, you'll probably want to sit in—at least for a while."

Now he grinned apologetically. "Then, also, you were so busy yesterday that I couldn't mention an anguished call I had from Joe Johnson after lunch. It was about Tom Fields continually 'bugging' both Doug Roberts and Ted Mohr about one of Tom's new batteries, which the Cliffside operators ruined one weekend several months ago,—by tagging the charger circuit out of service for maintenance but neglecting to transfer all load to another battery system. There was some mix-up with the contractor on that foul-up, I heard.

"Well, Tom won't let up on them. He wants them to try another 'umpteenth' round of equalizing charges—and tests—and so on and on even though both our own and the vendor's battery technicians say the battery's warranty is voided and its twenty-year life expectancy is halved. Tom naturally is reluctant to go through the embarrassment of ordering a replacement battery, costing many thousands of dollars, when the operating department is at fault. The operator did not even post a man in the control room that weekend,—and the annunciator was not in service. Of course, no tests or operations were scheduled for that weekend."

Mr. Sellers grinned wryly at her. "Now, can you hear Tom out on the matter and then decide if the time has finally come to persuade him to let up on the contrite operators now? Tom tends to be a bit on the obnoxiously defensive side all the time! Yet—he won't be of much use to you in the future if he gets permanently set in a locked-horns posture with the operating department."

Now his eyes met hers. "Marion, I think you can help Tom out of this impasse—without hurting him—or anybody. One way out may be a rumor you can check out with Ann Teach—when you chat with her about last night! I hear that *our* environmentalists will soon want us to get them a battery for their new 'temporary' test station at our proposed site for that next nuclear plant, even though indefinitely deferred—for lack of cash flow. O.K., Marion?"

She nodded, trying hard to smile. "But, otherwise, a nice, dull day at my cozy desk! Right?"

He laughed in obvious relief. "Good girl, Marion! You're ready to go it alone already! I may as well go up to Ken Blood's office *today*—and coast in! Why wait two more weeks to leave here?"

"Oh, no, Mr. Sellers! Not yet! Please don't! Uh—oh, yes! I wanted to ask you about something I saw at Cliffside yesterday morning. The workers were tediously taping all the 4-kv switchgear cable connections,—and there must be hundreds of cubicles to do. Yet I noticed the switchgear manufacturer didn't tape *his* bus connections; he used some kind of plastic boots. If the boots save the factory taping costs, why doesn't the vendor furnish us boots to put over the cable bolting on the job? Doesn't the vendor supply the bolting and connectors?"

Hesitating only a moment, he nodded in assent.

"A very good suggestion, Marion. The manufacturers used to tape their permanent bus connections, too. Why don't you get the order data from Art's files and write the local sales engineer about it? It's too late for Unit No. 1 but not for Unit No. 2. And then there'll be the River Shore bid specs. You could ask John Winton, too. Of course, the vendor will probably say that the customers' cable designs vary too much to allow a standard boot. We use from one to eight cables per phase—and from size 4/0 to 750 MCM. But still—with some ingenuity—certain standard boots could be offered or even some interphase-and-ground barriers—good for any layouts. However, I have a suspicion that in the end the vendor's prices will be 'functional',—that is, not so much based on his boot costs as on his idea of our taping savings! But I think you've made a sharp observation there, and you should pursue it! And to get credit for your idea, send copies of your correspondence to Joe Knight and Ben Board. That was very perceptive of you, while just passing by yesterday, Marion!"

By the brevity of his reflection after she had described her suggestion—and by the completeness of his reply, she felt sure that he had already tried this idea on at least one vendor at some time in the past; however, he must think that her brain child merited further action now.

"Thank you, Mr. Sellers. Here comes Tom now!"

As she arose, pleased and reassured by his praise, he commented brightly while standing up with her, "I like your flowery, summery dress, Marion!"

"Thanks again, kind sir! I wore it to the forensic duel last night, and—I overslept this morning—and had no time to select something different!"

Twirling about to cause her modestly short skirt to swirl upwards and outwards, she made like a model for his admiring gaze as she smilingly walked lightly to her desk to shuffle through her growing pile of papers while she considered her approach to Tom's problem.

THE THIRD DAY'S THE CHARM

At last, after phoning Ann, she hoped she was ready. Exchanging greetings with Art and Ed as she passed their desks, she sat down beside Tom's table and waited for him to get off the phone. His half of the conversation didn't sound too happy, and from the technical jargon she guessed the subject must be her problem. At last Tom slammed down the receiver as she smiled at him. "Good morning, Tom! Sounded like the new Cliffside battery that Operating ruined for us. Mr. Sellers was telling me about it just now."

"Mornin', Marion. Yep! Those jokers down there still want me to junk that new battery and buy 'em another one! Just like that! Thousands of dollars shot by their carelessness! Let 'em sweat over some more testing and re-charging! Why should I take the rap for 'em? What am I supposed to do with the battery,—and how am I to explain a new purchase already?"

"Yes, Tom. That's a tough one alright, but I know you'll come up with something to get them and us off the hook."

As Tom's phone rang again, she crossed her fingers fervently and listened closely to catch his salutation.

"Hello, Fields here."

There was a tense pause while she waited nervously.

"Ann Teach? Oh, yes! Down in Environmental! What can I 'do you for' this morning?"

Casually she returned to her desk to refresh her memory by glancing through the wiring section of Mr. Sellers' texts in preparation for the consultant meeting. Very shortly thereafter she became aware that Tom had sat down at her reference table. By his grin and jaunty appearance now, she was confident that Ann had come through for her just as Mr. Sellers had predicted. Now Tom was speaking in a carefully offhand manner, "Well, Marion, you won't have to worry about that battery. I've arranged with our Environmental Section to use this half-life battery in their five-year test station at the new site. I'm to work up a power layout for 'em. Now I can let up on Operating—and go out for bids through the purchasing guys on a replacement twenty-year battery. O.K.?"

She smiled. "Good! I knew you'd do it! I was counting on you, Tom!"

He grinned broadly. "You know I wouldn't let you down, Marion! Oh, yeah. Did Bob show you that note—on the consultant's wiring meeting at ten? Do you want to sit in with us? I've signed up the little 'B' cubbyhole,—the conference room over there. O.K.?"

"Yes, thanks, Tom. I'd like to get in on the ground floor of the wiring 'specs' for the new plant—with you—and Mr. Winton, I believe."

Suddenly Tom exclaimed, "Hey! You'll be interested in this one, Marion! It'll really grab ya! Some guy,—a consumer 'groupie',—buzzed my door last night to try an' get me to sign a petition an' ante up a buck to hire a 'legal eagle' to beat on the PSC to cut back our electric rates,—which have risen 40% in the past three years, he claimed."

Marion grinned. "Did he have any bright ideas we could use—on how to do it? How about his own wage increases—and the price hikes on oil, food, and so on? Our rates are up only 13% since 1940 compared to 300% for the Consumer Price Index!"

Tom scratched his head. "Yeh,—but—he said industries pay only 2¢ to our 6¢ per kilowatt-hour of electricity; so—let the big 'fat cat' corporations *pay* that can afford to,—not us peons! I—really couldn't answer him, but—I didn't sign—or pay up either!"

He paused. "But, Marion, you know, lucky guys like me,—who've almost got it made,—aren't like the *poor* blacks still in the slums,—who couldn't care less about all this conservation of the environment *and* energy—but only about gettin' some of that good life that the 'whiteys' have been enjoyin' all along,—that 'fair share' of cheap electricity that's due 'em!"

Ignoring his last remarks, she spoke slowly, "Well-l-l, how's this sound, Tom? If your door-to-door protester ran a delivery business, wouldn't he have to charge more to deliver a load of *thousands* of packages—each to a *different* address—than all to *one* location? *We* have similar costs to distribute, meter, and bill for electricity, you know!"

"But, Marion, he said electricity is a 'piddling' part of a factory's total expenses! Those big companies could easily subsidize *our* lower rates *and* a 'fair share' for minimum, necessary amounts of electricity for the poor people!"

She frowned. "I'd say industrial electric bills run from several per cent to over half of the total costs, depending on the industry. His idea could make companies noncompetitive and drive them out of town, costing our citizens a lot of jobs. And his 'fair share' scheme sounds like 'electric food stamps'! Sure! I'd like somebody paying *my* 'fair share', too! Who wouldn't?"

Tom smiled sheepishly. "Well, Marion, I dunno. I did ask him if he'd buy *my* utility stock! I predicted blackouts in the next decade for lack of rate *increases*—when he wanted the rates *cut*! I told him we had canceled power plants because investors were unwilling to put up their money when the PSC refused our fair rate requests two years ago. And this past year our residential load resumed its normal 6½% growth rate—with industrials not far behind! We'll have to *triple* our plant investment in the next ten years!"

"Right, Tom! Oh, there goes my phone, I think! Excuse me, Tom!"

It was the male lobby guard. "Miss Francis, Mrs. Art Core wants to talk to you."

Mrs. Core! Marion glanced over at Art's desk, but he wasn't there. She wondered why Art's wife wished to speak to *her!*

"Please put her on for a moment; I won't tie up your phone long."

"Yes 'm."

"Miss Francis?"

"Yes, ma'am."

"This is Jane Core,—Art's wife. I'm sorry to trouble you; I know you're very busy! But—Art's not at his desk right now, so—could you sign me in, please?"

"Why, of course, Mrs. Core! I'll be right down."

Taking her pass from her wallet in her bag, she hurried to Pat's desk, signed out for the lobby and noted that Art had not signed the log. Probably in the men's room. Walking towards the lobby desk after a fast elevator ride, she saw that Jane Core was an attractive pants-suited brunette of about her age, a couple of inches shorter—with a very curvy figure that was still a whistle-getter but now was obviously in need of some reducing around the waist and hips.

"Mrs. Core? Marion Francis. It's good to meet Art's wife!"

"Thank you, Miss Francis! And please call me 'Jane',—Marion!"

Jane's handshake was politely delicate.

"Well, Jane, I'll sign you in here; and we'll go right on up to Art's desk. He's probably there by now. He wasn't signed out anywhere. Maybe in 'the little boys' room!'"

As they laughed, she felt Jane's roving eyes appraising her warily.

"Marion, I'm sorry to take up your time like this, but I really *am* glad to meet you! Although Art's only known you several days, he's always praising all your—wonderful qualities—and—incredible capabilities! I—I just *had* to see you—for myself, Marion!"

"Oh, Jane, I'm afraid I can't live up to all that! And let me add, I don't know what I'd do around here without Art's engineering 'know-how'—to guide me! This is only my third day on the job, you know!"

"Yes, I know. This is my downtown shopping day, and I picked up some bargain frames—and put our pictures in them. I thought Art might like them on his desk. Would you—like to see them, Marion? Oh, here's our elevator."

"Oh, Jane! Such a cute boy,—so like Art! And a little girl—as pretty as you! How old are they? One and three? What are their names?"

"Jack—and Jill!" Jane laughed. "Art insisted on the names. I'm glad they'll not grow up as Army brats now! Marion, you're a good judge—of ages! And here's my wedding picture. I'm afraid—I've—let myself go—just a little—since then!"

"Now, Jane, we all have to watch our weight a little, don't we? My, Art's lucky to have such a lovely family! Here we are on the eleventh floor. Have you ever been up here before?"

"No, I never have, Marion."

Marion saw fear in the woman's eyes. She understood exactly why Jane felt compelled to come up; she had to see for herself the *woman*, the possible *rival*, as Jane saw it. Marion wanted to assure the wife that she had no intention whatever of intruding into a marriage,—*any* marriage; but what could she possibly say? Art might have deliberately stressed how *attractive* his new boss was. Rivalry between husband and wife—between *all* males and females—was constantly being played up in fiction.

Signing in, Marion noted that—as usual—Mr. Board was out of town for another industry-committee meeting at a convention. "Oh, Pat, this is Art's wife, Jane. Mrs. Pat Holder,—who struggles through our scribbling and dictating!"

As the two shook hands, she saw Art arriving at his desk from the other doorway to the adjacent system-relaying-protection offices. She also noted that Tom had now signed out to the "B" conference room; the consultant must have put in his appearance a little early.

"Jane, show Pat the photos. Pat has a picture of *her* cute little boy—there on her desk. And—Art has seen you—and is heading this way now!"

In that moment Jane's anxiously pleading eyes met hers, and the urgent message was clear and simple: "Please!"

She clasped Jane's perspiring palm again. "Jane, why don't you and Art go to lunch together today? I'd like to join you—some other day; I can't today—because I'm due at a meeting with a consultant now."

Now Art stood smiling beside them with his left arm around his wife's waist. "Well, Jane, this is a nice surprise! You two getting acquainted—with girl talk—and all?"

She laughed. "Art, I told Jane how lucky you are to have such a lovely family—and to have these pretty portraits for your desk! Also, that—I'd like to have lunch with her someday; but—I have that consultant in 'B' right now. So—I've got to run!"

Art's guarded eyes flicked across hers—as though in silent appreciation for her discreet restraint. As others in the office began to gather around this latest welcome diversion from work, Marion smilingly whispered, "'Bye now, Jane! Nice to have met you!"

Signing out for "B", she hurried down the aisle and into the conference room after a brief stop at her desk. She was disappointed not to find Mr. Sellers anywhere. Tom and the consultant were drinking coffee and discussing the hot spell as they awaited her arrival.

"Sorry to be five minutes late, gentlemen! Mr. Winton? I'm Miss Marion Francis."

His handshake was politely gentle for a man—even one of slight build, no taller than she. Prematurely white-haired in a distinguished way, he probably wasn't much over fifty; and he wore a wedding ring as all benedicts should!

"Why, this is a genuine pleasure, Miss Francis! In our offices we have women in the drafting rooms and clerical groups, but we haven't been able to find a female engineer as yet!"

She laughed. "Have you really looked hard, Mr. Winton? I hear you've conducted a successful 'brain drain' all over the world for *men*,—Turks, Hindus, Pakistanis, Filipinos, Germans, and—British! But—no *women*? There are thousands in the U.S.!"

He grinned. "Our firms have an anti-pirating agreement; otherwise, I'd steer our Personnel boss your way! From all the wonderful things Tom's been telling me about you, my supervisors would richly reward me for discovering such a prize as you, Miss Francis!"

She smiled demurely. "Thank you, gentlemen! Now—before you embarrass me any more, shall we get down to work?"

Since the two men were already stationed on opposite sides of the small table, she sat at the end near the door—for an easy escape! Mr. Winton sighed as he opened his bulging brief case. "Ah, a pity! 'All work and no play make Jack a dull boy.' Well, here are our tentative wire 'specs'—and tabulations—and some prototype cable-schedule computer printouts,—just formats,—and typical duct-and-tray layouts and 'specs', and some detail standards—and sketches our boys put together for me yesterday—to bring down for your comments today. How many sets of all this do you want? And may I call you 'Marion'?"

"Please do, John."

Today everyone seemed to use only given names; surnames were apparently a superfluous nuisance face to face. She looked at Tom, who was obviously overwhelmed by the instant mound of paper. She breathed deeply and said, "John, suppose you lead us through it all,—just hitting the high spots this time. Then Tom will distribute as many sets as you have here to our Test, Construction, and Operating Departments—as well as around here. For next time, Tom will give you our distribution requirements in advance. How soon will you need all our comments?"

"Well, Marion, two weeks will do very well on this—since we have a lot of other work to catch up on now. Well, then, we'll start with the general categories."

As John droned on, she often found it difficult to understand the Queen's English; but she made notes of several discussion points wherever she could recall discrepancies with previous Company practices as covered by Mr. Sellers' manual. When Tom opened a handbook of specifications of the Insulated Power Cable Engineers Association and pointed out numerous errors in the consultant's data, she added another note.

At last John laid down his papers. "Isn't it about time for me to take you to lunch over at the hotel? I had to move out this morning at seven,—and I'm famished now! Then, too, my bunch downstairs wants to leave at two!"

Smiling, she countered, "In that case, let's go now—dutch treat—to a fine cafeteria we know. That way we'll be back within the hour—instead of over two hours! It's eleven-thirty."

Also, the consultant couldn't charge our job with a lot of booze and stuff plus a 15% overhead surcharge. Although both men looked disappointed, neither cared to object. And so, even though she had unsuccessfully asked the Briton about the switchgear-boot idea, they were soon back at the table once again with an hour and a half to go. When the consultant had finished his presentation, she handed him a copy of her notes, which she summarized, "Gentlemen, my four suggestions are as follows:

"First, refer to the IPCEA standards wherever applicable;—but don't try to repeat the numbers. Then Tom—and others—won't find any errors!

"Second, get alternate bids for aluminum conductors in all the big—or circular mil sizes—to check the copper bids. Even considering the extra costs of raceway space and special connections, our Company has saved hundreds of thousands of dollars by using aluminum whenever prices dictated during the past twenty years—with good service, too.

"Third, study alternates for extending the use of silicone insulation from just the hottest areas to the turbine zones and firing aisles so that—after an oil-fire disaster—the wiring would be reusable in an emergency, per our tests, and others.

"Fourth,—and last, get labor estimates from your own construction people on the use of field installation of power cables in ducts and trays rather than vendors', special, bus-cable designs only.

"Then we'll discuss all these points—and any others that Tom may send you in the next two weeks. O.K.?"

THE THIRD DAY'S THE CHARM

John nodded wearily and then asked, "How are you all coming along with your review of our July 1 study of preliminary, auxiliary service, one-line, wiring diagrams—with the transformer reactances and other ratings—and the switchgear IC's and so on—and the motor-starting voltages—and system steady state regulations? I think your Art Core had promised comments before September 1. I know it's still early, but—"

"I don't know, John. Tom, if you want to escape now, could you send in Art—if he's available?"

After Tom had taken his leave of John and departed with the stack of 'specs', she stood up to collect her own papers and stretch her legs. John murmured, "Marion, I just can't get over—realizing that you,—a charming, young, American girl,—are an experienced electrical power engineer!"

"And you should see her trouble-shooting in the field, too! How are you, John?"

"Good afternoon, Art!"

As the two men shook hands, she asked, "Art, how are we coming along with the review of John's station-service studies? He says they are due by September 1; that still leaves us over a month yet, doesn't it?"

Art scratched his head. "Well, what with Cliffside—and everything else, I'm afraid we haven't gotten far enough this month yet—even to have any questions to ask John!"

She sighed. "Certainly the three days I've been on this job—we've been tied up on other matters. Art, I did glance at one of the single lines on your table. Let's study 13 kv for the largest motors—over 2,000 hp— to see if wiring and transformer savings will exceed the motor and switchgear premiums. And—why can't the ID-and-FD-fan motor pairs be started by one breaker instead of two? That's the way our diagrams are at the other older plants—per Mr. Sellers' reference guide. That should save thousands of dollars and prevent the furnace from exploding or imploding if the interlocks malfunction and so allow one fan to run without the other!"

Both John and Art made notes but offered no comments until at last the Briton remarked, "Well, we'll have to recheck the motor-starting dips, of course,—and the relaying problems of large-motor, thermal protection coordination with the fault settings. You know, our company policy is against the use of aluminum conductors inside power plants;— and we've never started pairs of fans on single breakers!"

She smiled wanly. "Well, John, please study it with our four cable suggestions—and check with your other client projects, also."

She decided not to inform him *now* that his firm had agreed with both practices for her Company during the past sixteen years—and that half of the clients *do* use aluminum *and* copper—although Mr. Sellers surely would have done so. She thought how he had told her that the Company—to save cash flow—was at last reversing a twenty-year trend towards more contracting of engineering, construction, line work, guard service, doctors, hauling, computers; and, Mr. Sellers had joked, he had feared for a while that there would be no Company employees at all— with a management-consultant firm even replacing the corporate officers and reporting directly to the executive committee of the Board of Directors.

She only added, "Now—have a good trip with your cohorts,—who'll be pleased to see that you're not going to keep them waiting until the rush-hour traffic! Call us, John!"

"Righto, Marion! And, Art! 'Bye now!"

Returning to their desks, she asked, "Art, is Ed helping you much these days?"

He frowned. "Well, I guess I should be using him more—on calculations—and checking stuff—and not only print handling—and filing— and errands—and clerical chores. I'll work on it more, Marion. We *are* getting snowed under lately, it seems; and Ed could help us more, I suppose."

Did he really mean that the work had been piling up ever since she had arrived to replace Mr. Sellers? Back at her cluttered desk, she squared her sagging shoulders and took a deep breath. As the steno-receptionist strolled casually past her desk, she asked softly, "Pat, could you please bring your pad and pencil? I have a letter and a memo I'd like to get out tomorrow."

Strangely, the girl looked pleased—and afterwards explained, "Marion, it was a relief to have you *dictate*! They say Mr. Sellers used to dictate a lot—but not since I've been here! Now the young fellows just scribble all their stuff. That way my shorthand gets rusty,—and I'll slip back to a 'typist' rating from 'steno'—and never qualify as a 'secretary',—a promotion I'd like to get some day—to work for some big-shot! Anyway, I could understand you, but these guys all mumble— and hem and haw—and reverse themselves—whenever they try to dictate! So—I discourage 'em!"

She smiled gratefully at Pat and then plunged into her pile of papers to assort them into an order of priorities. Especially she had to decide which items she should delegate to which of her three men,—and just how to accomplish each assignment—in the Tom Sawyer fence-painting tradition,—and which work she must do herself. And now at last, as her appointment notice was being read by more and more people all over the Company—and even made known to manufacturers on the outside, she was getting more frequent telephone calls from persons who introduced themselves and then dug right into their missions—and problems.

And some calls were real brow-wrinklers—like this one right now might be.

"Miss Francis?"

"Yes, sir."

"Sam Ready, customer service engineer. I've got an emergency on my hands! I've called Ben Board, Joe Knight and Howard Richards; but—they're all out of town. I phoned Midge Mitter just now, and she got Ken Blood's O.K. for me to dump my hot potato in your lap! O.K.?"

She laughed nervously. "I don't know! How hot and heavy is the spud? You've got me 'kinda' spooked right now! I'll sure try to help out, though!"

Now he laughed. "Midge says you're now the electrical engineer responsible for power plants. And power plants have hundreds and hundreds of motors! And my problem is motors. The county's chief engineer has just called and wants me to come out there at nine tomorrow morning to hear their 'gripes' on some rather new sewage pumping stations where for several years we've been giving them voltages nearly as high as 485 sometimes on their NEMA-frame-size, 440-volt, squirrel-cage motors. And Distribution says the transformers on their new 33-kv lines have no taps,—and the other substation loads on these lines require that high a voltage on the peaks."

He paused, but she just waited for him to continue.

"Uh,—anyway, the Test Department recorder showed the mean voltage is nearly half way between a maximum of 110.2% of motor rating and a minimum less than 91%. Therefore, the taps requested by the county engineer would be useless; and step-voltage regulators—or new line work would be prohibitively expensive—and a bad precedent. So— can I introduce you as our Company's engineering expert on motors, which they fear will burn up with this overvoltage? Can you quiet them down? They'll have their consultants as well as their own design and maintenance people at the meeting. I'll pick you up down in the lobby by the receptionist's desks—at eight. O.K.?"

"I'll be there."

"Fine! 'Bye now! Have a good night!"

"'Bye! Same to you!"

At least the meeting was not this evening; she had tonight to do her homework. From her planning work up north, she knew something of the line-correction costs and problems of Distribution. She would review the motor section in Mr. Sellers' manual. Then, if Mr. Sellers returned in time, she could get some advice before quitting time; anyway, she could rehearse her presentation with him tomorrow morning before eight.

As was now becoming a habit, she sighed and tried to relax in her swivel chair as she attempted to organize her conflicting thoughts. Well, with less than a half hour left now, it looked as though she might pull through her third day in fairly good shape. The third time's a charm, they say; and today must be the normal, "routine", office day,—Wednesday,—"hump day"—over the hump of her first week.

But, then, there was always tomorrow—to upset the apple cart.

CHAPTER SEVEN

Orpheus and Eurydice

As SAM READY and she entered the conference room at nine sharp, the six men set down their ubiquitous coffee cups and stood up to introduce themselves. There were the consultants for the pumping-station projects and various county office engineers and maintenance personnel as Sam had predicted, but she didn't get their names or positions straight. While the men resumed their baseball discussion, she assembled her papers from her bag and marshalled her thoughts. Apparently everyone was waiting for the Chief Engineer to put in his appearance.

Although the men stole furtively curious glances at her from the opposite side of the table, she was thankful no one was asking just what expertise or qualifications a young woman could have in this technical matter. She had worn her conservative navy-blue pantsuit instead of a dress in order to fit into this masculine scene with as much credibility and authority as she could muster.

"Well, good morning, Mr. Ready! Sorry to be late! Another meeting down the hall!"

"Good morning, Mr. Bowfroid. And this is our motor engineer, Miss Marion Francis." As they shook hands firmly, the tall, elderly, chief engineer smiled politely and, to her relief, did not comment on her sex and profession.

As they all sat down with Mr. Bowfroid at the far end of the table, Sam said briskly, "Gentlemen, I think I have your story over the phone. I have discussed the situation with our Distribution people, who say that our costs for any significant improvement in the voltage regulation would be prohibitively costly at these 33-kv locations. However, I am sure that our Miss Francis can relieve your concern over any injurious effect of the maximum voltages on your motors. She is our senior engineer responsible for all electrical engineering in our generating stations,—where we have thousands of motors. She is not only competent in this field in her own right, but she knows our considerable Company experience. Marion, the floor is yours!"

Before she could speak, Mr. Bowfroid quickly rose from the table, saying, "Please proceed with the meeting now. However, I must excuse myself for another session in my office; but—I shall return later."

He must be like a dentist, flitting from patient to patient—or a juggler keeping three balls in the air. Feeling somewhat slapped, Marion smiled, sweeping her glance up and down the row of six men seated opposite her. "Gentlemen, Mr. Ready tells me that the maximum voltage on your 440-volt motors is 485. Now, your concern naturally is that the 10.2% over-voltage is slightly beyond the 10% figure specified in industry standards. However, our long Company service record in power plants has been excellent at comparable overvoltages. We do avoid *under*voltages—below the 10% limit; but we *try* to operate our motors at *over*voltages, ranging usually from 5% to 11% on our plant busses. This is because motors of your type function better at these overvoltages than at rating."

She held up her pocket-sized G.E. technical data book. "I'm sure you have these handy annual booklets. I have enlarged the motor characteristic curves on page 68 and extended them by reference to the G.E. Industrial Power Systems Data curves from plus-and-minus 10% to 15% range. Now—I have a copy for each of you—and one for Mr. Bowfroid."

She passed out the curve sheets she had drawn last night and duplicated between seven-thirty and eight this morning.

"Now—you will note all the significant improvements at 10% overvoltage: 21% higher torques for starting and pullout, 2% better efficiency, 7% less full-load current, and 17% less slip. Also, the motors run correspondingly cooler. On the other hand, had the voltage been 10% below rating, all these same parameters would be worse by similar margins."

She paused as everyone pored over her handouts with flattering concentration. At last she continued, "Of course, the newer 460-volt motors with smaller frames are somewhat less generous in these respects,—especially as to the saturation point for the core, which I have shown on the curves as a broad band from 15% to 25% overvoltage, depending upon the standard design of the usual squirrel-cage motors. Special attention must be given to such unusual designs as multi-speed, ultra slow speed, jogging, and intermittent-duty types; but I understand yours are just rugged, standard, squirrel-cage, induction motors, which thrive on this overvoltage."

Now the six men began talking among themselves until at last one asked calmly of the others, "Well, fellows, do you all agree that the data presented here this morning by Miss Francis are reassuring enough for us to accept?"

They all nodded in silent agreement, but she wondered how the conference would end as several men arose to refill their coffee cups. It was now nearly ten o'clock since the session had not convened promptly at nine but rather closer to nine-thirty. Even though this was only her fourth day on the job, she began to worry again over the ever-growing mounds of papers and drawings on her desk and table back at the office.

At last Mr. Bowfroid strode into the room again and resumed his chairmanship of the meeting. She hoped he wouldn't ask for a repeat of her entire presentation as she handed him one of her sheets, saying casually, "Mr. Bowfroid, this is the set of standard motor curves we have been discussing. As you can see, the 10% overvoltage results in much better motor performance than at 100% rated voltage; and this is our Company's experience, also. Therefore, I believe all your men are now in agreement that there is no cause for concern over your motors at the pumping stations."

The chief engineer accepted the paper and then glanced along the ranks of his men. "Do you all concur with this recommendation now?"

Amid a mumbling chorus of "yes, sir" and the like, Mr. Bowfroid, in obvious relief over such a painless solution of this nuisance, looked first at Sam and then at her. "Mr. Ready, Miss Francis, I want to thank you both for taking the time to come out here and reassure us in this matter. And—we won't hold you any longer. I know you all are as busy as we are these days. It's been a pleasure to meet you, Miss Francis."

"Thank you, Mr. Bowfroid," she murmured as Sam led the way down the corridor and into a waiting elevator. In that moment the opposite elevator opened its door to disgorge its load of men with brief cases when she suddenly recognized Frank Boone in the midst of the group. For an instant their eyes met in startled surprise, and spontaneously their mouths opened as if to voice their greetings—just as her own elevator door automatically closed. There was a fleeting second when she almost lunged past Sam to push the door-opening button; but then the floor began to drop from under her, leaving her heart in her mouth. Somehow she was reminded of the poignant separation of the mythological Orpheus from his lost Eurydice, who was descending against her will into Hades while he remained upon the earth. However, she doubted that the image was valid. Frank Boone knew where to reach her, and she knew how to contact him. She was tempted to phone, but could not overcome the scruple that the man should make the first move. Since the meeting Frank had not yet phoned Ann, so there was no way to discern whether the feeling of attraction was truly mutual or not. Perhaps he was really not such a *friendly* enemy, after all.

Still stuffing her paper into his brief case, Sam had missed the flashing scene of drama. For that slight bit of good fortune she was thankful, for she didn't feel like explanations. Riding back to the office, she only half listened to Sam's profuse expressions of his appreciation for her surprisingly easy achievement this morning.

As they parted at last in the office elevator, he patted her on the shoulder. "Thanks again, Marion, for getting me—and the Company—out of that nasty one! 'Bye now! Have a good day!"

"Any time, Sam," she replied absently with a smile; and she was still thinking of Frank as she began once again to sort through the blizzard of papers on her desk. She simply must speed up the process of getting more stuff effectively transferred from her "in" tray to those of her three group members while at the same time learning what it was all about herself—and keeping up with the progress. Soon the hectic office emptied at lunch time, and her noisy phone at last subsided into blessed silence. As she began to make real progress with her paperwork, she appreciated Mr. Sellers' choice of a later lunch period. Time flew by until at last she saw Mr. Sellers returning to his desk.

Picking up an approval print of consultant's elementary wiring diagram for Cliffside Unit 2 on which he had red-penciled some comments last week, she approached his reference table.

"Mr. Sellers, may I interrupt you—to bother you some more?"

He smiled as she quickly sat down before he could arise.

"Sure thing, Marion. That's my only job now: to offer any advice I can to my successor! I'm just 'signing-off' these engineering magazines—to keep them circulating! You know,—I'll leave no skid marks when I stop my career here! How did the meeting go with the politicos?"

"Alright,—thanks to you! If you like, I'll give you a blow-by-blow account at lunch—if you can go with me today?"

He smilingly nodded in assent as he took the print from her hands, laying it out flat on the table. "Marion, I'd give this to Ed Eager—to consolidate my notes with any returned directly to him from the relaying fellows and the operating people. Can you read my comments?"

She stroked her forehead. "Yes, but—how do you spot all these errors? A missing control ground. That interlock discrepancy with the logic diagram. The fuse on the high side instead of on the low side of the starter control transformer. And so on—"

He grinned. "Just practice—at detecting repetitive mistakes."

"But—why are there so many foul-ups on our consultants' drawings? Especially after all the years of our being their clients!"

Now his grin had a wry quirk. "You sound like a boss now! Well, Marion, maybe *you* can straighten them all out now. You know,—'the new broom sweeps clean'! Sometimes I think the consultants figure to make a better man-hour project record with our management—by depending on us to do a lot of their checking work for them—and to educate and train their newly hired novices for them! You could try sending back some prints without any marked comments; just hold your corrections here. Then, when the consultant issues the prints for construction—without making any revisions, confront him with your comments in a meeting—with your supervisor present—and demand better design and checking effort."

"But, Mr. Sellers,—you've tried that tactic, haven't you?"

"Yes, Marion, but—not for several years. And—with the consultants' turnover—their crews are all new now! And I've given up on these fresh ones, I guess!"

She laughed. "And you think I should take up the cudgel now? Alright, I'll try to shame them! Now,—isn't it about time for our quiet haven of respite from all the world's clamors—at our window table—high above all the confusion of the bustling city far below? How does that sound?"

"Fine! Especially with the attractive company I'll have! Just a minute—until I find out in this magazine—just how that 'ole' sea-going engineer, Marmy, gets out of this 'doozy' of a problem!"

"Mr. Sellers, already this week you've even got me hooked on those true, salty tales! They're real epics!"

All too soon their half-hour luncheon date was over, and she knew that the quiet, cozy, little table would soon be a lonesome place—after his retirement—without his sympathetic and wise counsel.

Passing Ed Eager's desk, she saw him intently working on his calculus. The open textbook and his scrawled integral signs all over the pads would betray him to the most casual passerby,—like one of *her* supervisor bosses.

She might not be his official supervisor, but at least she could give him some "technical direction". Seating herself beside his desk, she spoke in her most conciliatory tone, "Ed, can't you do your homework on your own time? Art says he's asked you to work on some calculations for him. After all, the Company *is* paying your tuition at night school—in winter and summer sessions. Is it fair for you to 'dog it' this way,—really now?"

Ed grinned sheepishly as he stared at his papers.

"But, Marion, that's just the trouble! I simply *can't* get this damned integral calculus all by myself! And, if I flunk out, the Company won't pay for the tuition,—and the Company will never get my services as an engineer, will they?"

He looked up at her triumphantly and added appealingly, "Marion, you have a master's degree—with honors and all—and were a graduate instructor in college! Will—you tutor me?"

Well, she had only herself to blame; she had stepped into this one—but good!

"Alright, Ed! I'll grant that integral calculus is something of an arcane art, whereas differential calculus is a beautifully pure science! Let's try this! You come in fifteen minutes early in the morning instead of on the dot or a minute or so late. And—cut your lunch time to half an hour as I do instead of an hour and a half or more now. That way we'll have a 'legal' half hour a day to work on your troubles. But you'll have to work harder at home, too! We'll see to that! Agreed?"

Ed grinned ruefully. "O.K., Marion, but—you sure drive a hard bargain. Do you electrical engineers really ever use calculus, anyway,—with computers and all today?"

She had to think a little on that one before replying.

"Ed, you'll never graduate—and you'll never be a good engineer until you grasp this concept. You may not work often on differential equations, but without that knowledge you'll never understand the engineering principles—of transients, for instance. Mr. Sellers was telling me only today how he had once used calculus to determine that a boost or buck position of $8\frac{1}{4}\%$ gave the worst short-circuit rotary force to deform induction-regulator-coil end turns. When the vendor's engineer corroborated his calculations, they were then inspired to redesign the equipment to increase its fault strength. Anyway, all the technical literature is full of calculus; how can you read it all and thereby keep on learning after you graduate—and so not become obsolete? Believe me, Ed, you'll need to know your calculus!"

"You win, Marion,—as usual!"

Art must have talked to Ed because now neither one was calling her "boss lady" anymore.

As she prepared to stand up, he exclaimed, "Oh, please don't leave yet, Marion! I was waiting for you to return from lunch—so I could ask you—if you would play tennis with me this evening? You do play, don't you?"

Oh, oh! What was he drawing her into now? "Well, Ed, I did play some in college, but I—I haven't played much since! But is it fair for a big, tall, muscular guy like you to pick on a little girl like me? I'm afraid I couldn't give you much competition!"

"Oh, I didn't say you would play *against* me! You'd play *with me*—and *against* a couple of bums in Distribution Engineering. You see, our group has a tennis team,—Art and me! Bob and Tom don't play tennis. We play one doubles and two singles, best two of three sets—with game tie breakers—but the old deuce stuff in points. And the tie breaker's just the thirteenth game, unlucky for the one who's not serving 'cause we don't bother with all that nine-point, changing-serve-every-other-serve stuff! Like World Team Tennis, the team with the most games wins! But Art says his wife just phoned; they have to go over to her parents' tonight. So, Marion, *your* group's team will have to forfeit tonight—unless you'll help out! And we've got a perfect 3-0 record so far! It'd be a shame to ruin it now—by a forfeit! Please, Marion!"

She had been hard on him just now—about doing his school homework on Company time; and so she ought to be a good sport about this "esprit-de-corps" group-activity—if she were going to succeed at being their first woman leader. And she really did need this exercise—if it could lead into a continuing, regular program. She wouldn't arouse Ed's hopes unduly by telling him how she had captained the women's varsity tennis team in college—and quite often had played in practice matches against the men's team members—though seldom with much success.

Beyond a bit of company competition, she had to avoid a Jane Core repetition. She did not know whether Ed was married or not, but he invariably had that sly look in his eyes which seemed to say, "I'm attractive to women, and I'll play it for all it's worth." This bothered Marion. She had enough to do without inviting emotional complications, ... but she considered herself sufficiently resourceful to handle *any* situation.

"Alright, Ed, I'll go quietly. You twisted my arm, but don't expect any miracles from little me!"

"Wonderful, Marion! I told Art you'd come through for us! I'll give you this street map, marked with the public park location. Matches start at seven-thirty; but, if you can come half an hour early, maybe we can get in a little warm-up practice. The courts have lighting, of course. O.K., Marion?"

She smiled gamely. "I'll try my best, Ed."

"Great, Marion! See you at seven, then!"

Back at her desk, she hoped her tennis racquets didn't both need restringing, and that she could find a clean, pressed, tennis dress and all the other togs, and that they would still fit her.

As she tried to concentrate on her desk work between numerous phone calls and visits from Company people and vendor sales engineers, she couldn't help hearing a lot of chatter all around the office concerning her local tennis debut this evening—to uphold the athletic honor of her generation electrical engineering group.

All in all, it made for a long, nerve-wracking afternoon; but, at least, her busy mind had little time to dwell on her fleeting vision of Frank in the elevator this morning.

At last it was quitting time, and for once she rushed out of the office in the vanguard of the minute men. Fortunately she succeeded in catching the early express bus, which was, wonder of wonders, equipped with an air-conditioning system that actually worked. And, last but not least, for a change, she found a vacant seat and so could rest in relative comfort to conserve her meager strength for the ordeal which lay ahead for her this sweltering evening.

CHAPTER EIGHT

Lose Every Battle,—
But Win the War!

HURRYING THROUGH A skimpy supper, Marion spent an agonizing half hour frantically searching for all her tennis gear and at last triumphantly zipping herself up snugly in her blue-trimmed, white, flared-skirt, sleeveless, tennis dress over modestly plain white underpants. Slipping into a light, blue, warm-up sweater, she told her aunt not to worry, picked up her bag and racquets, and drove off towards the city after a quick study of the street map. Traffic kept her mind off her tennis qualms until she parked beside the row of clay courts and recognized among the gathering crowd of spectators many of the transmission-substation engineers from the other end of the room. Slowly she locked the car.

Picking up her racquets and slinging her bag strap over her shoulder, she hesitantly walked towards the nearest court. Suddenly she was overwhelmed with misgivings about making a fool of herself before all these fellow employees as well as letting down her own group. Then suddenly from nowhere Ed's handsome figure towered over her; somehow, he seemed even taller—and, well, more "physical" in his navy-blue, T-shirt, jersey top and matching shorts.

Grinning appreciatively at her, he exclaimed, "Beautiful! Those guys won't be able to keep their eyes on the ball! So we've got it made!"

Hugging her reassuringly around her waist, he hurried her towards the benches behind the umpire's chair. "Marion, it's already ten after seven, but those Distribution jokers aren't here yet. They've got a perfect 4-0 record, I hear; but I don't know 'em. Anyway,—we'll warm up ten minutes; and then let them have ten. C'm'on now!"

As they strolled onto the court amid a raucous cacophony of whistles and cheers, she forced herself to smile gamely at the enthusiastic spectators. Ed was whispering in her ear, "Marion, we've never had *any* gallery before! Even Tom and Pat are here—with their families! We never have any 'ump' or linesmen, just the honor-and-argue system.

But this time we'll have the works—with ball boys yet! Let's each serve a dozen at each other first. Then we'll each volley a few. O.K.? Do you want me to serve to you first?"

She nodded and took up her usual position three paces behind the base line as she swung her racquet to limber her arm and also flexed her knees.

"Ready, Marion?"

Springing up and down on her toes now, she answered, "Right, Ed."

His first big serve hit the cord, but his second was a cannon ball that she was lucky to get her racquet on at all as she lunged to her forehand side and netted her return. Now he netted another fast one, but the following hard one she managed to return with a deep forehand drive that overshot the baseline. Retreating another pace behind her baseline, she was forced to take his next boomer on her backhand, which failed to keep her return within the side line. Then she had to let him ace her— in her far forehand corner as she watched helplessly, calling, "Nice shot, Ed!" Finally she drove a respectable forehand return deep into his backhand corner, thereby restoring a little of her fast-ebbing confidence. After succeeding in returning his next serve deep to his backhand, she then attempted a high lob, which overshot his baseline by several yards. After netting a hard one, he cannon-balled one far too deep for her service court. Scoring another ace on her, he called, "I'll quit while I'm ahead; now you try a dozen, Marion!"

Scooping up two loose balls with her racquet, she carefully served an accurate but softly looping ball, which he returned whistling into her far forehand corner—but just outside the baseline. With each successive serve, she gradually increased the severity of her strokes until she at last netted the sixth one. Then she began alternating her soft loopers with her fast serves until she felt reasonably satisfied on her twelfth try—even though Ed seemed to be having little trouble returning her best efforts. After they had each practiced some mediocre volleying and a few dubious lobs and smashes, she noted from her wrist watch that it was now seven-twenty; and she was beginning to perspire freely under her warm-up sweater.

"Enough, Ed?" She didn't want to leave what little game she had on the practice court this sweltering hot, humid evening with not a breath of air stirring in the bordering trees.

Just then four men in shorts trotted onto the court; and, after some hasty introductions and explanations, she could only recall that Ed as her No. 1 would first play Tim, their equally tall No. 1. Then Herb and Bill would play them in doubles. With a sinking feeling, she learned that she would have to meet Steve in a third and final night-cap match to decide the outcome of the evening's encounter—unless either team by that time had gained a run-away lead of more than twelve points. Since that optimistic eventuality,—of either winning or losing big, probably was mostly wishful thinking—even with her dragging Ed down in the doubles, she studied Steve. Her opponent would be fresh and rarin' to have at her when she would be limp and exhausted right after her doubles match with those two Tarzans, both about Ed's size. Fortunately, Steve was no taller than she, but he was the quick, muscular, tireless, wiry type of masculine athlete who could make a female player look bad in any sport.

Watching the four practice together, she was fascinated by the sinewy Steve's, fast, cat-like movements, his springy step, his bounding leaps, and his sharp volleys, interspersed with towering lobs and competent ground strokes. His serves varied from fast shots to deceptive loopers. Seated on a bench beside Ed, she whispered, "They all four look like 'bad news'!"

Ed shrugged, muttering, "We'll see soon enough, Marion."

At seven-thirty he arose and strode out onto the court to begin the first match. Exactly an hour later, after some exciting serve-and-volley tennis, he returned—all sweaty and crestfallen. Sitting down heavily beside her as he wiped his dripping face and neck with his towel, he grumbled, "Well, I blew the first one after all—6-3, 4-6, 6-7."

She laughed nervously. "But—the score is 16-16—or still 0 to 0! Now, when do we have to start our doubles,—the best chance for girl versus boy!"

Gloomily he mumbled, "Let's not hurry! Let Bill and Herb come out first. I need to catch my breath!"

Sympathetically she said, "Just relax! I'll rub you down!"

"Thanks, Marion!" he whispered as he sat limply while she mopped his arms and legs. Then all too soon Herb yelled, "Come on now! It's getting late, and we've got to beat that big thunderstorm. Let's cut out the practice!"

Glancing over at the dark clouds, she hoped the storm might save her.

Ed whispered, "Marion, you always win! You spin the racquet!"

She did and—to her surprise—won. Ed elected to serve first—to gain the advantage of jumping into the lead at once while his aim was still in the groove from his last match. His first serve was a good cannonball, which Herb netted; but Bill connected solidly with the next one, which she barely had time to duck at the net, allowing it to whizz harmlessly over her head and on past the baseline. Then Ed succeeded in scoring a back-hand-corner ace on Herb, and she grinned at Ed as she moved across court. It was 40-love, and she hadn't even had to hit at the ball yet! Of course, their opponents weren't warmed up yet like Ed, but still she felt encouraged that he might be able to carry her part of the match.

Just then Bill's return cracked right towards her breast. There was no time to duck the blurred-white bullet; only her instinctive reflex action moved her racquet very slightly upwards to defend herself. At once the gallery cheered as the speeding ball rebounded off her weakly held backhand stop to slither over the cords for a cross-court double bounce before Herb could even get started. It was pure dumb luck on her part, but Ed had carried his first serve with a morale-building love game. As they walked over to the bench to change courts, she patted Ed's sweaty right shoulder. "A super start, Ed! Let's hope we can keep it rolling now!"

He grinned happily as he hugged her around the waist.

"Right on! But they're getting tuned up now! And watch out for Bill! You sure pulled a miracle stop on his last one there, Marion! Now let's hold this lead! Even Bill should be a little rusty on his first serves, at least."

Stripping off her warm-up sweater to get ready for real action now, she smiled at the approving wolf whistles—and some girl-watcher, urging her to "take it off". Apprehensively taking up her position four paces behind the base line, she danced lightly on her toes as Bill slammed a hard one into the net. His next shot was only slightly less severe, and she was scarcely able even to get her racquet on the ball, which returned weakly into Bill's forecourt. Since Bill had rushed towards the net following his fast serve, the big guy had no trouble smashing his volley right back to score a neat crosscourt placement on her.

Although in his first turn Ed got his return back nicely, again Bill intercepted the ball at the net, driving it deep at her backhand. Anticipating his move, she ran over and lunged at the bouncing ball, sending it back over Bill's head in a deep lob to the back court where Herb caught it squarely after the first bounce, driving it deep in her forehand corner. It was a perfect placement, which her racquet just missed after her all-out race. She had known they would be picking on her, but the question now was what could she do about their predictable tactics.

Retreating twelve feet behind the baseline this time and moving over several paces to limit her backhand exposure, she was able to get off a respectably deep forehand return of Bill's booming serve; and it raised her drooping spirit to watch her two hulking opponents crash their racquets together as the ball escaped unscathed from their uncoordinated efforts to earn a point at last.

On the next serve Ed cannily returned the ball to Herb, who volleyed it her way, of course. Although the ensuing rally was a prolonged affair, in the end Bill forced her into an error as she netted one of his deep, booming, power drives. Now she had to save this game and their slim one-game lead as Bill tossed up the ball to serve to her again. She was proud that her low lob fell accurately behind Herb, but the relentless Bill ran over and smashed a hard placement down the line past her vainly outstretched forehand lunge. Well, she had let Ed down and lost his hard-earned one-game lead. It was now one-all, and she had to serve.

Evidently the relaxed Herb had the usual masculine contempt for the potency of feminine serves, for he was standing casually a full pace inside the baseline. Serving her hardest top-spin, she was pleasantly surprised to see the chalk fly for a close one as her fast ball took a crazy bounce that caught his racquet rim. As her tricky ball glanced past the overconfident Herb, she was heartened by the encouraging cheers of her partisans—as well as by one Distribution rooter's sarcastic exhortation, "Hey, Herb! Keep your eye on the ball—not on the 'broad'!"

As she moved over to serve Bill, Ed called back from the net, "Nice one, Marion! You've got 'em on the run now!"

Apparently granting her serve a little more respect after witnessing his partner's fate, Bill was crouching a full pace behind the baseline. Carefully she served her softest "pitty-pat" looper, which fortunately just cleared the cords to bounce feebly in the clay dust. To his credit, the alert Bill roused his massive frame from his braced posture behind the baseline and raced forward, scooping up the slithering ball, which dropped in deadly isolation in her own forecourt. To her heartfelt relief, the welcome call rang out, "Not up!" Her change of pace had worked, and she was half way there already!

This time the nonplussed Herb was crouching tensely right on the baseline. However, to her dismay, she netted her first hard serve; and now the grinning Herb moved several steps towards her. Easing up only slightly on her serve, she happily watched her fast ball come off Herb's racquet in an easy drive for her forehand to return right back to him. The rally was long and hectic, but at last she sighed thankfully as Ed intercepted one of Herb's weaker volleys to score a neat crosscourt placement.

Bill was ready for her soft looper serve and returned it high above Ed's leap. Running hard, she barely succeeded in returning the lob to Herb, who,—overeager to kill her soft ball for an easy point,—instead smashed it into the net to give her a love game on her first serve, matching Ed's achievement. As they walked over to the bench once more, Ed hugged her enthusiastically. "Hey! How about that? You're a whizz, Marion! Now we're ahead again 2 to 1! And—poor 'ole' Herb has to serve next! We'll clobber him! Let's break him—but good now!"

Really creaky on his swing, Herb first helped their cause along by double-faulting to her and then sending a weak second serve to Ed, who made a clean placement on his return, hard and deep to the far corner. Her next return developed into a vicious two-on-one attack until her anxious partner at last was able to come to her rescue by intercepting one of Herb's shots for an untouchable, crosscourt, volleyed smash. Finally, Ed drove a deep return to Herb's backhand, which resulted in a fast drive to her own backhand. Taking a long chance in letting the hard ball whistle past her, she was overjoyed to hear the linesman's "out" call, followed by the umpire's professionally intoned "Game to Miss Francis; they lead three games to one, first set." Another love game!

Rolling along now on their winning momentum, Ed carried his service handily with only a few assists from her as he gallantly succeeded in shielding her from most of the hard-to-handle returns. Towelling off below the umpire's chair, Ed exulted, "Just think, Marion! We've got 'em on the run now at 4 to 1! It's a real rout for sure!"

No sooner had she permitted herself the luxury of smiling back at her partner than she was again facing Bill's cannonball service. Unerringly his first sizzling serve kicked up too high, hard, and fast for her backhand to handle; and she ignominiously netted her poor return. Ed did get his return back alright, but at once Bill forced her into another irritating error as her backhand overdrove his baseline by yards. Shifting to her left now, she was able to get off a clean, deep, forehand return of his next big serve; but relentlessly Bill nagged at her inadequate backhand with another booming drive. With Bill already rushing to the net, she desperately attempted a lob,—which sailed far over his baseline. She was almost relieved when Ed netted his next return of service to end the debacle of Bill's second service win—at love this time!

As she grimly prepared to serve, Ed ran back to her and whispered, "Don't worry, Marion! Just give 'em your baffling change of pace—like last time, and you'll carry your serve again! No sweat!"

But—it didn't work out that way. Now Herb was not only solving her change-up serves but also was tagging her woefully failing backhand with discouraging regularity. Even with Ed's desperate attempts to shield her by heroic interventions, her two powerful opponents were wearing her down. It was deuce again, but she couldn't recall how often she had heard that call. Wearily she tapped her softest serve to Herb even though he was standing far inside the baseline. This time the dusty bounce was so low that Herb could only shovel the ball over the net for Ed to make a neat crosscourt point. Now, with "add-in" comfortably in her hot grasp again, she must somehow win her service to the formidable Bill, who now was also crowding contemptuously up on her. Unleashing her fastest service, she cautiously remained near the center of the baseline. This time, as she had anticipated, his deep return came squarely to her forehand; and she connected solidly with all her might. Predictably Herb ducked her fast one, and even Bill's great strides and long reach failed to spoil her winning placement.

"Game to Miss Francis; she leads five games to two, first set."

Seated at the bench again, she listened with quiet satisfaction as Ed exuberantly patted her on the back again, exulting, "You were 'super' again, Marion! All we have to do is break 'ole' Herb again, and we've got it made for a 6-2 first set! A rout!"

But evidently "ole Herb" wasn't about to cooperate this time. The two giants were really humbling her in this game despite Ed's best efforts to save her from further humiliation at their hands. It was that old deuce again. Gritting her teeth, she awaited Herb's serve once more. With the ball coming on her forehand side, she gave it all she had and watched, panting, as her fast drive cleanly passed Bill at the net and then caught Herb a little off balance on his far backhand. Although his hasty return boomed menacingly at her, she daringly let it whizz by her backhand side to overshoot the baseline by inches. She only hoped that Ed could handle this last point all by himself. But he had nothing to do after all because—incredibly—the over-anxious Herb proceeded to double-fault in an anti-climax. "Game to Miss Francis; she wins the first set six games to two."

Now, above the wild cheering and applause, Ed spoke into her ear as he squeezed the breath out of her. "We've got the first set under our belts with four points to spare! Great, Marion! We can't lose now!"

But, somehow, they did manage to lose the second set at 6-7; perversely she was relieved that it was Ed—and not she—who had suffered the only loss of service—and that in the crucial tie breaker. And they also lost the close third set the same way at 6-7, this time without anyone having a service break. Seated at the bench again, Ed said, "Well, our team may have lost the first two matches; but we're still ahead by two points, anyway. Now, all you have to do in your singles match is not to lose to that little runt, Steve, by more than one tie-breaker point—so that our team will maintain its unbroken winning streak—and louse up theirs!"

His obvious relief at being "home free" somehow aroused her frustrated anger now. "Ed, it's alright for *you* to say that, but *I'm* the one who has to come through all by myself now! And—I'm exhausted after this three-setter with those two monsters both picking on me all the time!"

Suddenly alarmed now by visions of ultimate defeat, Ed began speaking very solicitously, "You just rest now, Marion. Let me help you on with your sweater. That's it! Don't chill or cramp your muscles! Here's a sip of cool water. Not too much now! Oh! I'll towel off your legs."

She sighed deeply. "Ed, it's no use! I can't do anything against Steve—even if I were in condition,—which I'm not;—and even if my game were tuned up,—which it's not;—and even if I weren't 'bushed',—which I am!"

Now Ed tried to reassure her. "That shrimp, Steve? He won't give you any trouble—after the way you handled those *big* guys!"

Hopelessly she watched Steve's swift feline movements as he began to warm up against Tim. Following her gaze, Ed exclaimed, "Hey, he's not supposed to practice any more! Marion, it would be best for you to go right out there—and dust him off now—while he's still rusty—and you're still warmed up, sharp-like! Here! Let me help you up! I'll get your racquet."

Taking her hand, he pulled her up; and she could only groan in protest while following him reluctantly out onto the court again. Ed yelled, "O.K., you guys! Knock off that practicing! Marion's ready to play right now."

With crossed fingers, she twirled her racquet, but her luck had run out. And so it was that she found herself all alone behind the baseline when Steve's surprisingly severe first serve slammed into the net. Ed was right; Steve's service was not zeroed in yet. His second safe serve was softer and easier to handle, and her all-out forehand drive was satisfyingly speedy and deep,—far to the right. Incredibly her lithe quick-footed opponent bounded over and snared her should-be winner with a snappy crosscourt return to her backhand forecourt. Fortunately she had recklessly rushed the net behind her promising drive so that she was in position to make a running drop shot, which even his awesomely fast foot-work could not catch.

Next, in his desire to crush her with an overpowering, masculine, big serve that was not yet in tune, he double-faulted to her profound relief. However, his following first ball bounced so high and hard to her weak backhand that she could return only an easy shot, which he put away neatly as he rushed the net. She was luckier on his next serve's softer second ball as her best "go-for-broke" forehand drive just passed him at the net for a clean winner down along the side line.

Then, just as she felt a little confidence flowing back into her exhausted spirit, she had to watch helplessly as his booming serve aced her deep in her overextended forehand corner with a little chalk kicked up by the ball. "Perfect!" she cried out.

As she heard the call, "30-40", renewed fears gripped her. Worn out, she had to break his first serve or lose everything; but—that ace meant that his serve was no longer rusty.

However, he did net his next fast ball and she was able to convert his softer second serve into a creditable lob that dropped just inside the baseline. She moved cautiously towards the net as he raced back after the high-bouncing ball. Unbelievably he lofted a towering lob back over her own head. Running back in her turn, she frantically tried to locate the ball; but it was lost in the lighting glare. After what seemed like an eternity of waiting, she heard the heart-warming cries, "Out" and "Game to Miss Francis; she leads one game to love, first set." It was only then that she really saw the ball bouncing behind her backhand baseline corner.

Panting heavily already, she walked slowly back to the umpire's chair; she still couldn't believe that she had actually broken Steve's first service—until Ed again hugged her tightly.

"Wonderful, Marion! I told you—you'd beat him!"

She smiled wanly. "Oh, Ed! Come now!" she protested feebly.

She took a fleeting second to think of something other than the game. It was the third or fourth time that Ed had hugged her—much too exuberantly for comfort. There had been that gleam in his eyes. Once the game was over, she would again have to be her cool, poised self; friendly, but in a way which could permit no misunderstandings.

As she removed her sweater again, Marion was pleased to hear once more the same appreciative whistles and calls. Her thoughts reverted to the game.

Since Steve was respectfully awaiting her serve just behind the baseline, she delivered her softest "powder-puff" floater, which did barely clear the cords without arousing any call of "Let". Springing forward quickly even while her tell-tale, slow-motion-serve wind-up was still evolving, her nimble adversary was there ready to pounce on her "junk" ball's minimum upward bounce. Hurriedly pulling herself out of her post-delivery contortions, she daringly ran forward far enough to forestall a dropshot—yet not too far, she hoped, to be invitingly vulnerable to passing shots or lobs.

Outmaneuvered, her foe had to make a snap decision with the slow ball already falling again far below net-cord height. As the resultant lob exploded just over her head, she back-pedaled, allowing the ball to descend from the lighting glare and bounce up and back down almost shoulder high before she risked everything on her hardest overhand smash. By fast foot-work and a quick lunge, he did get his racquet on her fastest ball; but she happily heard the welcome sound of the net snaring his return.

Because Steve now had moved up inside the baseline, she served with all her remaining strength; and,—miraculously,—her speediest ball bounced right at him so that he had to defend himself awkwardly. Rushing boldly to the net behind her most powerful serve, she was in a perfect position to kill his weak return with a strong crosscourt volley.

On her next serve, she netted her first fast one; and he moved up on her. Not trusting herself to fire another hard one, she had to loop him an easy one, which he drove deep to her backhand. Running all-out, she launched a high lob as he waited at the net to kill her usual groundstroke backhand return. Undaunted, he retreated cooly to the baseline as her ball fell just inside; and, waiting until the ball began falling from the bounce, he fired a smashing overhand shot right back to her far backhand corner, which she had just deserted in favor of a midcourt position. Racing over again, she lunged futilely as the fast ball deflected from her racquet.

Discouraged by her wasted expenditure of scarce energy, she could only deliver another soft serve, which he drove again deep to her backhand corner. Managing to raise yet another lob to his baseline, she was disheartened to hear the dismal cry of "Out". Now she summoned all her ebbing resources and served a clean fast one, which he drove deep to her forehand corner—because she was haunting her backhand side now. Watching motionlessly with affected calmness, she saw no chalk fly up—but was much relieved to hear the linesman yell, "Out", nevertheless.

Biting her lip, she knew she couldn't afford to lose this vital point now because she would surely wilt if he dragged her through "deuce" and the elusive "add-in" and "game" ordeal. With all the strength she could muster, she not only hit her first serve much harder than she had ever dared; but, also, she rushed madly to the net without weighing the consequences. As she ran forward, she saw him drive his return towards his favorite target,—her backhand corner. Having accurately foreseen this move, she was in a good position to intercept the whizzing ball as it cleared the net. Skidding to a dusty halt on the clay surface, she seized her racquet with both hands and obliquely stopped the speeding ball, which obediently rebounded off the taut strings back over the cords to fall crosscourt just beyond his racing lunge. Amid all the cheers and clapping, she smiled gratefully as Steve grunted, "Great play!"

As she listened to the comforting announcement of "Game to Miss

Francis; she leads two games to love, first set," she wearily plodded back to the baseline to face his sharpened serves now.

His first booming serve fortunately roared at her forehand side, and she leaned on it with all her might. Hers was a good return, but the ball zoomed right back on her wrong side this time. Nailed behind her baseline by his powerful drives, she had to content herself with just getting the ball back over the net. Unable to advance towards the net herself, she watched helplessly as he moved up on her fastest returns until at last he was able to end the long rally with a briskly authoritative crosscourt volley at the net. As this deadly pattern continued to submerge her best efforts beneath his overpowering serves and fast following returns, she subtly yielded to the inevitable to conserve her waning strength. At last she was almost relieved when he had held his serve at love; at least, with the score still 2–1 in her favor, she could return to her bench to rest for a moment on the old pretext of re-tying her shoelaces. Ed tried to comfort her by saying, "Let him carry his serves, Marion. You just keep on holding yours,—and you'll win the set. It's a sure thing for you!"

Doggedly she made his words come true, but it was torture. Even using all her change-of-pace in serving, her growing reliance on lobs, her emphasis on her forehand drives, and every "junk-shot" trick she knew, she found it harder and harder to hold each succeeding deuced service while he was now breezing through his services at love on the merit of his overpowering stroking, his uncanny aces and placements, and his unflagging mobility over the court.

As she prepared to serve the tenth game with the score now 5–4 in her favor still, she knew she had to carry her service or collapse. Amazingly there had been no more breaks since she had luckily broken his rusty service in that first game. But now she wondered if she could swing it just once more. Desperately she started off with her fastest serve, but then the interminable rallies resumed their inexorably exhausting course. With perspiration blinding her eyes, she struggled on through never-ending "deuce-cycles" until at last she heard a linesman call "Out" on a high-velocity return she had let whistle past her fatigue-anchored feet. Waiting incredulously, she listened to the gladdening words, "Game to Miss Francis; she wins the first set, 6 games to 4."

But her moment of triumph was brief and fleeting without even the respite of a restful visit to the haven of her bench. All too soon, as Steve's cannon-ball serves pounded her unmercifully, she heard the umpire's melancholy call, "Game to Mr. Ball; he leads one game to love, second set."

Now the pattern of the first set carried over relentlessly into the second—only with ever-increasing difficulty in holding her service. At last, with no service breaks thus far, the score stood 4 to 5 against her, and she must carry her service once more or lose the second set. But try as she might, her weakening backhand cost her more and more points until at long last, as she frustratingly netted another hard one, the umpire finally called mournfully, "Mr. Ball wins the second set, 6 games to 4; the sets are now 2 all."

Her increasingly aggressive antagonist had now caught up with her, evening up their grueling match; he had even paid her back for breaking his opening service by crushing her last feeble service. And, worst of all, by now Steve must know that he had run her ragged; he had sweated all the zip out of her. Even now he was ready to serve to her as she was still wearily trudging towards the umpire's chair for what she had hoped to be a rejuvenating ten-minute rest period. But forlornly she realized that this was not a women's match; and there would be no hard-earned, desperately needed respite.

As her watchful rival eyed her appraisingly, she panted, "Steve,—may I have a couple of minutes—to change my sox? They're wrinkling on me—and starting blisters!"

He grinned triumphantly. "Sure thing, Marion! I could use a short breather myself!"

As she wearily changed her sopping wet sox and wrist band, Ed was cheerily inflicting a pep talk upon her inattentive ears, "You're doing great, Marion! You've got it made! Now you can let down a little in this last set. Take it easy and coast from here on in! Don't kill yourself out there! Let him win this set and the match. Don't wear yourself out trying to do anything with his services! Just be sure to carry all your *own* services up to the 6-6 tie. Then let him break you—and see if we care then! We'll still win tonight by one point—50 to 49! We can lose all our three battles—but still win the war! Oh, hi, there, Bob! Isn't she magnificent? She's coming through for us in fine style! We've got a real Chris Evert on our team!"

"Marion certainly is giving us all an exciting evening of topnotch tennis alright, but I'm afraid she's going to hurt herself out there now—or make herself sick!"

At the sound of his voice, she looked up in amazement. "Oh, hello, Mr. Sellers! I didn't see you here!"

"Well, I didn't arrive until you had begun your doubles match; and, well,—you've been kept pretty busy since then!"

She was surprised that she could still laugh. "Yes, I've had all I could handle out there! That's for sure!"

She had never seen him before without coat and tie; now he looked years younger in an open-collar white shirt and gray work trousers. "Mr. Sellers, what's with that pad and pencil? Keeping score on me? I sure could use some of your analytical advice right about now!"

He grinned deprecatingly. "Well, I'm a non-playing armchair critic! Of course, you know that he's making most of his points by firing forehand shots at your backhand."

She nodded gloomily. "Yep. He's really nagging at my pitiful backhand."

"And you must see that most of *your* winners are off your forehand to *his* backhand. But—have you realized that he's a southpaw? His backhand side is opposite to where you'd expect it to be!"

She frowned—and grinned ruefully. "I—I hate to admit this, but I'm so befuddled by now—that I—don't know! I'll try to—put my attention to it this next set, though! Any other pointers, Mr. Sellers?"

"No-o-o. I think the variety—of your strokes and tactics—has been very successful;—*and* your 'big' all-court game—of rushing the net with volleys behind your hard serve—with baffling change-of-pace soft serves and deep baseline rallies, interspersed with your deceptive lobs—The only thing is,—your stamina, amazing as it is, has its limit! And I'm afraid you'll overdo yourself out there now and collapse from sheer heat prostration! Do you need salt tablets in water?"

"You know, somehow, I think I may just make it now! Salt tablets make me ill! I had plenty of salt—and water—with my supper. I—I'd better get up now before I get too stiff to straighten my weary knees!"

Mr. Sellers said solicitously, "At least, let me pull you up! And don't hurt yourself out there, Marion!"

Out on the court again—where Steve had been patiently awaiting her arrival, she was pleasantly surprised to find she could still dance on her toes as he wound up to serve. To conserve her precious energy, she didn't try to fight his powerful serves nor did she attempt to extend the rallies against his deep fast drives. But she did pick up some easy points off his backhand so that at least he was not able to carry his service at love. Changing courts this time, she rested only briefly to towel off before returning to the fray.

Although her first hard serve was an overlong fault, she eased off only a little on her next fast ball, which kicked up chalk as it bounced high to his backhand. Rushing the net boldly, she had to leap high to snare his lobbed passing attempt. Her smartly executed overhead smash rewarded her all-out daring attack by crosscourting him neatly, leaving him flatfooted at the baseline. However, when she again rushed the net after her "pitty-pat" serve, Steve succeeded in lobbing just within her backhand corner. Racing back, she barely got her racquet on the ball's down bounce, lobbing it towards his backhand corner. As she slowly repositioned herself while it was Steve's turn to scramble madly for his far baseline, she thought the ball nicked the chalk line and bounced on beyond his racquet. Thankfully she heard no "out", and she decided to try her "big" game again. This time her first fast one caught his backhand awkwardly high, and she could have spared herself the breathtaking dash to the net as his smashing return thudded into the net band.

Seeing Steve crowding towards her in anticipation of her next soft serve, she resolved to fool him by trying another "big" one. But her best wasn't good enough, for he got off an unusual two-handed backhand return, which overpowered her own instantly improvised backhand at the net with the ball glancing crazily off court. Still advancing beyond the baseline, Steve was forcing her into a "big game" to expend her fast-ebbing strength. Grimly, with straining muscles, she put everything she had into her next fast serve and recklessly rushed to the net. His resounding backhand return flashed far beyond her all-out backhand stab. Skidding to a flat-footed halt, she glanced hopelessly back to her baseline, but she was too late to see if the ball had been in or out. At long last the linesman yelled, "Out"; and she thankfully hit her spare ball over to the scowling Steve. Evidently her rush to the net had caused him to make a backhand aiming error in a vain attempt to pass her.

However, his booming serves soon wreaked their vengeance upon her as he easily carried his service at love. And so it was that his services were all won effortlessly while each of her hard-earned wins became an exhausting escalation of nerve-wracking cliff-hangers. In fact, she had carried this last tortuous ordeal only after at least six agonizing "deuced" crises of threatening "add-outs" that had brought hot tears of nervous exhaustion welling up in her dimming eyes. But at least she had escaped any service break, and now the score was a 6-6 tie; of course, now Steve would have precious little trouble carrying his tie-breaking service to defeat her 4-6, 6-4, 7-6—even if,—for once, she made a "go-for-broke," "last-ditch" effort to break him. But still her group's team would win 50-49 and so preserve its perfect record.

Nevertheless, she'd hate to lose her own singles match after all her struggles. Panting heavily with the sweat running down in rivers all over her weary body, she used her racquet as a two-handed crutch to reinforce her rubbery knees as she awaited his serve. But, instead of serving, Steve now trotted over to talk to the umpire, who smilingly announced in very unprofessional language, "Steve says we all had better run for our cars if we don't want to be among the hundreds of lightning victims of this year—or be drowned in this cloudburst in the next minute or two! There's a big storm on the system alright,—and it's about here! Oh, yes! Steve says to record this evening's meet as lost by his Distribution Engineers to Ed Eager's Electrical Generation Engineers by a score of 50-48,—a real squeaker! Also, Steve wants to let this match with Marion Francis hang all even at 6-4, 4-6, 6-6, called on account of rain. And now, folks, we'd better all run like hell!"

She felt wonderfully light-hearted all at once—as if a millstone yoke had been lifted off her neck. Straightening up slowly, she called to Steve as he walked towards her, "Thanks, Steve! You're very kind! You know you really won our match alright! You're much too powerful for me! You've certainly blasted the zip out of me!"

It really was nice of him not to humiliate her unnecessarily by insisting on beating her in the last game instead of giving her a draw.

Steve shook hands and smilingly said, "You must be one of those women 'pro' ringers. *You* played a better game than any *guy* I've met all summer, Marion!"

Then Ed shouted, "Great playing, Marion! I told you—you'd do it for us all!"

Just then a deafening clap of thunder practically coincided with a blinding lightning flash over in the grove of maples, and everyone began running in all directions.

No sooner had she flopped in her car's front seat with her sweater around her shoulders and her bag and racquets beside her than the black heavens let down sheets of water, obscuring her vision even after she had started her engine and turned on the windshield wipers and headlights. Relaxing comfortably at last, she'd just rest quietly here awhile until the storm let up a little.

Though utterly drained physically and emotionally, she still basked in a happy glow of success. Athletically speaking, she *had* saved the day for Ed and her group; and her tennis had really not been at all bad, considering her being out of training and without recent practice. In college, no doubt, she had beaten some male players as good as Steve; but then she had been in the pink of condition with her game fine-tuned by her coach. It was flattering of Ed—even in jest—to compare her to Chris Evert, but she had never identified herself with that young champion, no longer called the "hitless-wonder". For just one thing, she lacked the necessary, patient, accurate, baseline game with that famous, dependable, two-handed backhand. And she was not nearly tall and strong enough to dream of herself ever becoming a Margaret Court. Neither did she possess the combative spirit and tactical versatility of Billie Jean King or the cannon-ball-serve-and-volley game of Virginia Wade, or the graceful cat-like movements and shot repertoire of Evonne Goolagong,—now Mrs. Cawley.

Of the world's top half-dozen stars today, the attractive Kerry Melville was the spirited champion Marion had always admired and emulated ever since, as a brand-new college student in 1966, she herself had watched the thrilling spectacle of her then-unknown fellow teenager from Down Under upsetting the top-seeded Mrs. King in straight un-deuced sets in the second round at Forest Hills. There had been no resisting Kerry's aggressive, well-rounded, all-court game,—those fast, well-placed, deep, forehand drives, "big" serves, and the killing volleys at the net. From that triumphant day to this, by indomitable spirit and talented effort, Kerry had fought successfully for a decade to stay near the top of the heap and always on the world's ten-best player lists. The scrappy Aussie's victims included Margaret Court, Chris Evert, Billie Jean King,—all peers on the courts. Only in March of 1974 Marion had seen in a paper where Kerry had been top-seeded on the professional women's tour—for the first quarter of last year.

And so it was that she had been saddened to read a sports dispatch in the paper early this year about how an unknown, powerful, Czech, teen-aged, southpaw, Martina Navratilova, had upset the gallant Kerry in the championship final match of a professional tournament near Washington. The article had reported that this sensational new star had continually rushed to the net behind overpowering serves and drives to force repeated errors off Kerry's racquet. Apparently, in losing by straight un-deuced sets, the overwhelmed Miss Melville had been unable to break any of her opponent's services and had succeeded in carrying only half of her own. Characteristically, Kerry had offered no alibi for the shocking upset—but had simply credited her conqueror with being "just too good." Of course, no matter how stunning an upset, that was just one match; everyone has "off" days. But, somehow, this surprising upset of her long-time favorite by some up-and-coming youngster had made Marion feel a little older and had stolen the zest from her day. But, even with the upset, Kerry had picked up an $8,500, runner-up, prize check; no doubt, her tennis heroine won more money in several years than she herself would ever earn in her entire career as an electrical engineer. Of course, the pretty, graceful, Melbourne secretary,—now Mrs. Reid,—could make the same observation of her own prospects had she remained in her original clerical vocation.

Like *Kerry's* success at *tennis, she* fought for *Marion Francis* to win big in *engineering*. For Marion, the tennis stars she admired—and who *won* had always inspired her to wage *her* fight more strongly, to win in *her* field; and she *was*, in her modest way, successful. A "champ" of sorts. She *had* to stay on her perch, lead a fight for other women to take up engineering. Once again she thought of Ed Eager, and how ardently he had embraced her. Would he be apt to grin knowingly when she saw him at the office? Sharply, she formed a picture of Frank Boone and wished that she had played with him.

Now at last the torrential downpour had slackened enough for her to brave the hazards of the road. As it was, she couldn't get home before eleven-thirty. Aunt Dinah would be worrying about her wandering niece out in the dark and the storm and all. And, like Cinderella, she just had to get a hot shower and hit the sack before midnight or she'd be simply dead on her feet at the office tomorrow. Charitably, she supposed Ed couldn't have reserved a court for the more popular weekend hours. At least she was thankful that tomorrow was Friday.

CHAPTER NINE

Her First T.G.I.F.

MUSTERING A WRY grin, she exclaimed, "Why, Mr. Sellers, I had no idea I'd be so stiff this morning! Every muscle in my whole body is sore! Even my bones ache! I'm uncomfortable if I sit still, but I hurt more if I move! I feel simply miserable all over! I'm glad today is Friday, but it's going to be a long one! Still, I know I'll make it!"

Turning, she saw Ed Eager and said, "Oh! Ed has arrived 15 minutes early—at 7:45, just as he promised! Now I've got to tutor him in his integral calculus 'til eight—and again after his *half*-hour lunch! Woe is me!"

Arising gingerly, she limped slowly over to Ed's table and eased herself as gently as possible into his side chair. In the hope of achieving a minimum of bodily discomfort in the chill of the air-conditioned office this morning, she had elected to wear a conservatively-tailored pair of navy-blue worsted slacks with a trim, long-sleeved, soft, white shirt under a light-blue cashmere sweater thrown over her aching shoulders. If she had worn her favorite mini-skirt, modesty would have impelled her often to suffer the unnecessary muscular pain of holding her knees together; whereas in these slacks, she could always let her tortured legs relax into their most comfortable positions. She still thought women looked better in skirts than pants, and in summer she usually favored mini-skirts for their cool comfort and freedom of movement. Although Aunt Dinah didn't always agree, she herself really didn't think *hers* were true *mini*-skirts because her hem lines were never more than four inches above the knee. Here in this building, she had seen girls with skirts nearly up to their hips, revealing briefs skimpier than bikinis.

"Good morning, Champ! You look 'chipper' this morning! Wasn't that 'super' for us to win last night?"

As he began to pat her shoulder, she protested sharply, "Don't touch me, Ed! We're in the office now—and not on the tennis court! And I'm sore all over! Besides,—you know we lost all three of our matches; and it was only by your crazy rules that we 'skinned' by!"

"Aw, Marion, you really were perfect last night! Say, can you make it again tonight? Those substation guys have challenged us!"

As she flashed him a quick look of sheer horror, he was instantly all contrite sympathy.

"I was only kidding, Marion! Even *I*'m stiff,—and I've been playing all summer!"

"Alright, Ed! We've got only twelve minutes now, so let's get with it pronto!"

Dragging out his text and scribble pad, he groaned. "I can't get these 'integration-by-parts' problems! And I don't 'savvy' this whole chapter! And there's a quizz Tuesday!"

Almost immediately she had gotten so engrossed in her tutorial role that the ringing phone startled her painfully; glancing at her wristwatch, she was shocked to see that it was already 8:15. Ed had no sooner hung up the phone than it jingled again. Then, at the third time, Ed's replies became a bit short with more than a trace of irritation. Softly, she asked, "Weren't you 'kinda' hard on that last one? Who are they all—so early?"

"Oh, the copy center wants me to drop everything and hurry down to pick up my memos I left yesterday morning. Ditto for the print room on my last batch of Cliffside construction sepias and whites. And that last joker is in the Mechanical Section. He wants our marked River Shore turbine-generator electrical outline prints right away—even though he got 'em to us a week late. Now here comes another of those damned Robinson Crusoes!"

Looking up with an excruciatingly painful effort of her neck muscles, she said, "Morning, Art! How's the family?"

"Mornin', Marion! All O.K., thanks! I hear you didn't miss me on the tennis court last night!"

Although he was grinning, she couldn't tell if he was ribbing her or not; so—she answered him straight, "Well, by your league's weird method of figuring, we did win—though we lost all three of our matches! But don't you dare 'rope' me in on that sort of torture again!"

Turning back to Ed, she asked, "What's with your Robinson Crusoe bit?"

Ed smiled sheepishly. "Oh, you know—that 'oldie' about how,—after 'goofing' off all week,—everybody wants to get all his work done by Friday, but—"

She laughed and volunteered, "—But only Robinson Crusoe ever could get all his work done by his man, Friday! Alright! And, Art, what do you need today from our poor overworked Ed here?"

He grinned, saying offhandedly, "Oh, you remember those instant sliderule calculations you 'zipped' out on that 13-kv-cable-shielding question at Cliffside Tuesday?"

Rather than nodding her head painfully, she whispered, "Yes, I remember, Art."

But Tuesday seemed ages ago today—on Friday.

"Well, Marion, Wednesday I asked Ed to check over the calculations—and write 'em up for distribution and file—by yesterday! That way,—if he should find some error, we could make a 'fix' before the field had gone too far down the wrong road. And now it's Friday,—not Thursday!"

Again, she spoke softly, "Well, Ed,—it looks like you're gonna be real busy today!"

At once Ed complained, "Can't we get one of those pocket computers to do this sort of thing? The relaying guys are always 'hogging' the desk calculator!"

Smiling, she replied, "Oh, come now, Ed! I see you have a good 'log-log' sliderule that can handle all the exponentials and log functions you'll need for the accuracy required for this problem. I—"

Art interrupted now, "Marion, your phone's ringing. Do you want me to get it for you?"

"Please do, Art," she answered gratefully. Now *that* was really very considerate of him. Did he suspect how sore and stiff she was? By the time she had painfully reached her desk, Art said excitedly, "Can you hold on, George? Marion is here now. Let me talk to her."

But—Mr. Sellers was not in the room now.

"Marion, the North 13-kv outdoor metalclad switchgear bus has tripped; and—the South switchgear is out for maintenance. Only the local construction feeder and two diesels are available for power at Cliffside, and they can't handle the startup and test loads. George Foray says they'll be able to get the South bus back in service within several hours, but the test and relay guys can't locate the breakdown exactly in the North bus supply cubicle because of the low fault current causing so little damage. You know,—resistance neutral grounding and sensitive ground relays. Ted Mohr thinks the switchgear is O.K.—and the trouble must be in the 13-kv cables. He wants to disconnect them and cut into the shielding terminations right away. Doug Roberts is after him to rush the job now. After last night's cold front system, this morning's warm humid air condensed all over the switchgear. George says it's all dripping wet. Shall we tell him to cut up the cable like Ted says? Or shall we drive down there before we decide? But they want the answer *now*! What do you think, Marion?"

Very slowly she eased herself down into her swivel chair.

"Art, I doubt if we can see anything that all those test, relay, construction, and operating fellows overlooked. It'll just delay them. I suggest they leave all those taped shielding terminations alone—and start untaping and inspecting the switchgear bus supports above the cables. And you could hurry the switchgear service engineer down there to air-ship in any parts we'll need—if I'm right! What do you think, Art?"

"And don't mess with the cables, Marion? Alright! Let me try to convince 'em!"

Quickly she added, "And ask George please to have Ted call me if he needs some of my persuasive words! And I'll just cross my fingers!"

Remarkably soon Art slammed down the receiver and said, "George convinced Ted to go along—as soon as he told him that *you* suggested it! You've sure built up a good 'rep' down there this week! But—aren't *you* sticking your neck out pretty far on this one, Marion? Wouldn't it be safer to tell 'em to disconnect and untape everything—and 'hi-pot' and examine all the switch-gear cubicle *and* the cables—regardless of any wasted time? Why are you so sure it's the switchgear—and not the cables?

"Because Mr. Sellers' write-ups show that no power-plant cables of that type have ever been faulty, whereas there have been several recent moisture-failures in the outdoor metalclad busses of gas-turbine packages. To speed up the restoration time and save a lot of money, I hope! I'm just playing the percentages this time, Art! So wish me luck!"

As Art shook his head, she grinned.

"But, Art, please try to get me some word as soon as you can to see if my head is going to the chopping block or not!"

"Will do, Marie Antoinette! Oh, yes!—George said the operators had shut off the heater circuits—to save energy, like we do up here with part of our lighting—since they thought the heating was only necessary in winter! Well, you know, those ex-Navy 'nukes' never had any *outdoor* 13-kv switchgear aboard ship!"

Slowly, she said, "Well, Art, it won't help us any to rub that into the operators—or, for that matter, into our consultants, who engineered it that way—instead of following our recommended, standard, *indoor* practice—per Mr. Sellers' manual. We'll catch it, anyway, for our electrical equipment failures. And we still have to work with our consultants and operators, but we'll keep it all in mind for the future."

Now Art sat down at her table.

"Marion, you've been going over my comment notes on the studies by the consultants for the auxiliary services for the new River Shore job. What did you mean by your suggestion to investigate the use of nonstandard reactances for the service transformers? Isn't that going to cost more than standard values?"

"Yes, but the special transformer price premiums could save even more money elsewhere. Higher transformer reactances might permit lower IC switchgear. Or—lower transformer reactances might save transformer kva—or motor premiums—if regulation—and motor dips—are the problem. I'm just saying—we shouldn't let the consultant do it the easy way—by always in each case selecting the standard transformer x. Do you agree, Art?"

"Yeah, I guess so, Marion. But, uh—can I—get Ed to—help me—with all this detail stuff? It'll take more time, you know; and we're going to run out of that—on this study, I'm afraid,—at the rate we're going now—"

She smiled faintly. "I doubt if Ed will welcome any more Robinson Crusoes *today*! He's already suffering from the T.G.I.F. syndrome this morning! Say, Art, if you'll excuse me now, I'd better get up front with the bad news about our 13-kv blackout at Cliffside—before they all hear about it from others!"

Halfway down the aisle, she saw Mr. Sellers signing in—and Mr. Board's empty office. Slowly she approached Pat's desk.

"Oh, Marion," he said grinning. "I've signed you out first for Joe's office and next for the Board Room. He and Ben are awaiting you—in Joe's office. They want you to accompany them to the Board Room right away—for another Cliffside progress meeting. And—don't worry about reporting that 13-kv trouble; they know about it. It was Doug Roberts to Wayne Landfall to Ken Blood to Howard Richards to Joe Knight to Ben Board to Bob Sellers, who's just called George Foray. You had already given him the same answer I did!"

Now Mr. Sellers must have seen the look of utter consternation on her face. "Yes, Marion—Mr. Ed King and two dozen of his top brass will be there. And—you'll not only be the only woman—but, also, the first—at any such high-echelon meetings. And,—no matter how you may *feel*, you *look* great! And, if anything electrical comes up, you'll know more about it than any of 'em all! As for the short notice, it's better this way—because you'll have no time to stew over it! It'll all be another good side show!"

She attempted a game smile, but suddenly her heart was pounding like an air hammer.

"Thanks, Mr. Sellers,—if you say so!"

As she entered the Chief Electrical Engineer's office, both men looked up from their papers on the table and smiled at her. Smiling in return, she said cheerfully, "Good morning, gentlemen! Mr. Sellers said you wanted to see me."

"Good morning, Marion. Yes, Ben and I asked Bob to get you. First,—can you return here at two o'clock?"

"Yes, sir,—as far as I know now!"

"Good! We want to review your first week with you then—and plan ahead—a little bit. But our second subject comes first—like right now! We want you to go with us now up to the 19th floor to the Board Room for another Cliffside meeting. You'll get used to 'em, and you might as well start now. Anyway, we want you with us in case some electrical question comes up; but—generally it's all about the AEC,—I mean,—what's the new name?"

"NRC,—Nuclear Regulatory Commission," she murmured.

"Right. Well, it's generally all about delays waiting for another meeting—or another decision or ruling from the AEC,—I mean, NRC. Or—it's 'griping' about the low productivity of the union crafts on the job,— 'the human statues'! Or it's QA-QC squabbling or paper work. Or—inflationary cost overruns. Or— All set, Marion?"

"Yes, sir."

No one spoke again on the upward trek, and soon they entered the dark-wood-paneled room with the super-long mahogany table and double rows of heavy wood chairs, leather-upholstered. She had never before even seen a board room anywhere. There was a tremendous oriental rug, genteely shabby; and, from the gloomy walls, paintings of the former Chiefs looked down sternly upon her—as though to challenge the temerity of any overambitious female presuming to intrude upon this masculine sanctum sanctorum. Pads of white paper and yellow pencils lay in precise positions before each chair along the shiny polished table top. As she gazed up at all the somber portraits once more, she tried to recall if it was Napoleon who told his troops in Egypt that thirty—or was it forty?—centuries of the Pyramids looked down upon them.

Recognizing her departmental manager, she said, "Good morning, Mr. Richards!" as he smiled his greeting.

Dave McLeod, the Chief Nuclear Engineer, was fiddling with a slide projector; and then she saw Joe Johnson, seated beside an elderly man who was either dozing or resting his eyes. She smiled across the table at Joe, who at once said with a wry grin, "Mornin',—Marion! I hope you're right—as usual this week—about that blackout trouble at Cliffside being in the switchgear—and not in your sacred cables! Otherwise we've lost a lot of time! Anyway, the switchgear service engineer is on his way by helicopter right now! I really thought you'd be down there to see for yourself, Marion! But then we can't be in two places at once, can we? My boss-and-manager here,—Will Cellarsly, swears it's your damned cables!"

She kept on smiling as she murmured, "I hope he's wrong, Joe! Of course, someone *could* have *sabotaged* the cables!"

But Mr. Cellarsly still slept on peacefully oblivious to it all. Ben said, "Let's grab our chairs down at this end before the mob shows. Dave's projector is here, and the screen is way down there behind Ed King's chair. He'll have to move for the pictures!"

No sooner had they taken their front seats in the double row of chairs along the table than the room began filling up fast as the big mantelpiece clock approached nine-thirty. Except for Mr. Blood—and her department's Chief Mechanical, Civil, and Environmental Engineers she didn't know any of the last minute crowd. But she wished she had chosen a less conspicuous seat in the back now by a door where she could slip out unnoticed,—maybe during the slide-show! However, it was too late for such timid ideas because now she was locked in tightly by the table and chairs surrounding her. All around her there was the usual loud buzzing sound of male chatter—about everything from baseball to the woman who used to be the AEC chieftain.

Suddenly—at 9:45—a silence fell upon the room. Peeking around Mr. Knight's nose, she saw Mr. King enter from his adjacent office.

"Sorry to keep you all waiting, gentlemen—" At once his somber look of preoccupation lit up as a broad smile spread across his face. "—And lady! Good morning, Miss Francis!"

To her exasperation she felt herself blush as all eyes turned towards her in unison, frankly forsaking the former furtive glances of natural curiosity. Although her small voice seemed lost in the large room, she managed to say, "Good morning, Mr. King!"

Now Mr. Blood smiled faintly and said, "I didn't know you had met our first woman engineer! This is her first week with us."

"Oh, yes, Ken! We not only met by chance at lunch Monday, but I've had a good report of how effectively she represented us at one of those women's-club air-pollution meetings Tuesday night. Excellent job! She even turned the environmental session into a persuasive plea for government permission to burn coal, you know, to save everyone's dollars on electric bills—and conserve gas, oil, and gasoline for all of us! Ken, I'll want to talk to you about how we can use this young lady's many talents even more fully."

Mr. Blood nodded gravely. "Yes, sir, of course, sir."

Just then Mr. Cellarsly must have awakened because she saw his lips growl, "Well, Mr. King, I hope her 'many talents' can be used to rush the replacement of her no-good cable that's blacked-out our Cliffside test operations this morning."

As she felt everyone staring at her again, she heard Joe Johnson remonstrating with his superior, "Now, boss, we don't know for sure whether it's the switchgear or the cables."

She leaned forward to meet Mr. King's keenly inquiring gaze, which was now fixed firmly upon her. "Miss Francis, *you do* have good reason to think that the trouble is with the switchgear—and not the cables?"

She took a deep breath and answered emphatically, "Yes, sir! And we are now proceeding on that basis; the switchgear service engineer should be with our people at the site within the hour, Mr. King."

Nodding, he said only, "Very good, Miss Francis." Quickly then, he turned to the Chief Nuclear Engineer.

"Dave, the meeting is all yours now. I hope you can make up the half-hour delay—and still let me out of here by eleven-thirty—since I have a luncheon meeting."

Dave grinned.

"Yes, sir. I think we can streamline the agenda enough to do that, Mr. King."

To her, a newcomer, the ensuing presentation of the construction photographs, especially of the Unit 2 job, together with all the commentary, was very interesting and enlightening; but she supposed that Mr. Knight's prediction of the program content was also largely correct. Anyway, Mr. Cellarsly slept peacefully on throughout the meeting. Just as the session was ending on a sour note of projected costs now amounting to over twice the original estimate due to the inflationary delaying effects of all the environmental groups' protests and legal actions and the governmental regulatory delays and rule changes as well as the crafts' poor productivity, a secretary brought a note to Joe Johnson, who quickly left the room.

Now Dave announced proudly, "Well, that's it! And it's now just 11:30!"

Before Mr. Cellarsly was thoroughly reawakened by the commotion of everyone trying to move the massive chairs, Joe Johnson reappeared and said a little sheepishly, "Well, she was right as usual all week! They've located the failure: leakage tracking paths in the switchgear,— the bus sleeves and C.T. supports. Already the switchgear service engineer has phoned the factory and will meet the plane this afternoon to pick up the new C.T.'s, insulation, and taping kits to repair the stuff tonight, working gangs around the clock. Hats off to you again, Marion!"

"Thanks for 'those few kind words', Joe!," she replied grinning happily. Then Mr. King's smiling eyes met hers for a moment before he turned away to leave the room, and she was glad she had remained seated so that he couldn't see her slacks. Somehow she thought that he and his wife liked women in skirts; today he had on a conventional gray suit and an old-style white shirt with an old-fashioned, solid-color-blue, narrow tie. Also, she recalled that his wife had worn a dress Tuesday night.

At last she arose gingerly; and, smilingly acknowledging several introductions, including Mr. Wayne Landfall's, she slowly made her way out of her first Board-Room meeting with a profound feeling of relief. After making a bee-line for the ladies' room, she was sorely tempted to stretch her protesting body out on the comfortable sofa for an extended lunch break; but her "Company-girl" executive resolve was reinforced by the bouncy, gushing Pat's inopportune entrance into her rest haven. Back in the now-empty office at her cluttered desk, which,—Robinson Crusoe or not,—she was determined to straighten up this afternoon, she was relieved to see the reassuring figure of Mr. Sellers, tossing piles of magazines, prints, and papers into the waste basket.

"Why, Mr. Sellers, is this House-cleaning Day as well as 'Thank-God-it's-Friday' and Robinson Crusoe Day?"

He laughed. "More like Moving Day! I've just been told to spend my remaining weeks as a supernumerary up in the rarefied ivory-tower levels from which you have just descended! How was your first elbow-rubbing with the top brass?"

"Oh, I'm just bursting to tell you everything at lunch! B-b-but I-I thought it was agreed—that you'd be with me three weeks, not just one!"

Stunned by this latest blow, she sat down abruptly with predictably painful results.

"Marion, women aren't the only privileged ones who are permitted to change their minds! A V.P. can, too! You'll get the official word from Joe and Ben at two."

All at once she didn't feel much like tidying up her desk, but she saw that Mr. Sellers did have forty years of accumulated stuff to throw away—or save—in the next several hours.

"At least, Mr. Sellers, they're not going to keep us from having lunch together today, are they?"

"No, Marion. And I'm sure we can sometimes get together for lunch in the next month."

Nevertheless, at their one o'clock lunch it was only with an heroic effort that she was able to rise occasionally above her gloom to smile at Mr. Sellers' dry humor and light conversation. And, later, as she listened to Mr. Knight's words at the two o'clock conference, she made no attempt to conceal her disconsolate spirits.

"Well, Marion, from Ed King's remarks this morning, it looks like you'll be 'roped' into the luncheon-and-supper 'spiel' circuit! How did you ever get tapped for that Tuesday appearance? Our environmental people—and Dave McLeod—do a lot of 'chit-chatting' at those hen parties. I don't know what good it does. Anyway, that's just some extracurricular stunts you've gotten yourself in for somehow. Now Ken Blood wants Bob to come up on the 20th floor as an extra handyman for his last five weeks, starting Monday at eight. Bob's told us some of the things you've been doing all week. Sounds like you've taken hold of the job 'pretty good' already. So—Ben and I couldn't put up much of an argument with Ken about Bob leaving you after only one week instead of three. Of course, Ben and I don't follow much of the work your group does. As you must know, you're more or less on your own back there—unless something comes up. Well, that's about it. You got anything to add, Ben?"

"No, that about covers it, I guess."

Then Mr. Knight snapped his fingers.

"Oh, yes, Ben. There *is* something else I wanted to say,—actually the *main* reason for this meeting. I've been getting some disturbing reports this week that the work is piling up in your group now, Marion. Studies. Vendor and consultant drawing comments. Purchase analyses and recommendations. Correspondence. Field—and consultant decisions. Work with the Mechanical Section,—civils,—'nukes'. I realize you've been very hard pressed to take it all over in just one week, but we electricals can't hold up any projects. Then *I* get the blame! And Ben here, too! Right, Ben?"

"Yeah, Joe. That's the way it goes."

"So, Marion, you'll just have to get on top of things—and stay on top! And keep your three guys 'humping' back there! Don't let 'em 'goof-off' on you just because you're a woman! You can't be a 'softie' and let 'em get away with anything! Like long lunches, lateness, or early getaways,—or socializing during working hours! We electricals don't want to take the rap for *any* of the delays in these power-plant projects. We don't have delays in our substation jobs. We never have been blamed for any plant-schedule troubles, so let's not start now! And don't let those operating guys or the mechanicals and civils and 'nukes' get away with anything or put anything over on you either! You've just got to turn out the work—on time—with the quantity and quality required by the job! That's why our management people had to go outside the Company to hire *you* as an experienced, qualified engineer who could quickly and smoothly replace Bob. You don't want to fall down on the job now—after all this buildup, do you, Marion?"

Mr. Board stared down at his pad and doodled with his ballpoint as Mr. Knight looked at her without smiling.

Suddenly a hot flush of resentful anger submerged her former gloom.

"Mr. Knight, as far as I am aware my group is on schedule with every job and is not holding up anything on any part of any project—as of today. We have a big work load for such a small group,—a huge backlog; but none of it is overdue—yet!"

She was surprised by the fiery temper showing in her voice as she paused to look at each of her bosses. Mr. Knight was staring at his calendar, and Mr. Board now was toying with his sliderule. Taking a deep breath, she rushed on, "But it's not going to be fair—to the job—or to me,—at least during the next two weeks, to remove Mr. Sellers from his originally-agreed-upon advisory position for me—and at the same time load me up right now with all these time-consuming, nonproductive things, which could—and should—be deferred—or I could even be excused for now, I should think!"

At last Mr. Knight asked, "And what are all these things, Marion?"

"Well, Monday morning there's my new-employees' orientation session with Personnel. In the afternoon there is our departmental United Appeal meeting. Most of Tuesday I'll spend at the fire-fighting school. All day Wednesday Transportation gives me my driver-training course. Thursday morning there is the annual Management session for supervisory and key employees. Next Friday morning I'm to give blood,—and our departmental coordinator tells me he's short on his quota—and can't find anyone to take my place. There's more on my calendar on my desk, and none of this is the productive work output you're asking me to handle. Also, sometime,—I forget when, I'm scheduled for a computer project-management application course. There's a day for some outside-consultant's seminar—on how to write English that anyone can understand—with no 'gobble-de-gook'!. Then there's the radiation-access training day for me at Cliffside—and another day for QA-QC procedure review—by the 'nukes'. And the departmental semiannual personnel meeting—and a relaying seminar, in-house, and another nuclear course—and—But the toughest timing is the week after next, my all-day, all-week supervisory training course in Personnel. Can anything be done about any of this stuff now?"

Mr. Knight squirmed in his chair and laughed mirthlessly. "Well,

Marion we all have *that* sort of thing—all the time. You may have noticed that Ben and I are often out of town—on industry-committee meetings—and engineering conventions, for instance. Everyone must cope with all that—and still do his work. Maybe you've noticed us carrying brief cases home each night. And, you know, those brief cases don't just contain lunch bags and dirty clothes—like in those jokes! Somehow, we monthly-salaried people are expected to take everything in our stride. If you think it's bad now, it will get worse later—after the next nuclear project is re-activated—too late! You'll have to work 'for free' at night—and on weekends—and go on trips to consultants, to factories, and to industry meetings to give papers,—speeches, too. We just *have* to take it all—and come right back swinging; but, most of all, stay on top of the job! Don't let it get you down, Marion! You *can* handle the job, can't you, Marion?"

"Yes, sir."

She gritted her teeth for one more try. "But can't I borrow an associate engineer or even a technician from the substation groups for a while? There seems to be some slack there—right now, at least."

Mr. Board spoke up at once. "Well, Marion, they're going to load up again—real soon, maybe next month or so. Anyway, by the time you broke them into your power-plant work, they'd have to get back into substation engineering again. Really, I don't think it would work out, Marion."

Mr. Knight leaned back in his chair. "Well, I guess we've covered it all *now,* eh, Ben? If there's anything we can do to help you, or if you have any questions, just call on us. But don't let it get away from you! Keep on top of it all, Marion!"

"Yes, sir."

Well, that was the old brush-off alright; there'd be no help for her here. After painfully arising from her chair, she was slowly walking towards the door when Mr. Knight called out, "You look like you're 'kinda' 'crickety' there, Marion! You're much too young for that! Oh, yes! I heard about your taking on all those big boys in tennis last night! Just remember that the Company doesn't pay us to be heroic athletes; so don't get all crippled up playing 'gung-ho' games now! You've got a job to do here; so take care of yourself, Marion!"

She managed to grin back at them.

"I'll live through it!"

Back at her desk, for the next couple of hours she struggled through a week's-end barrage of phone calls, visitors, and paper work that left her numb when everyone left on the dot at quitting time.

At last Mr. Sellers smiled and said, "We'll make it to lunch together sometimes. And, if you ever have any questions in the next month, I'll usually only be a phone call away—or an elevator trip, Marion!"

She nodded gently; but, as she stared at his clean desk and table beside hers piled high with papers, she knew this office would never be the same again for her—not next week or next month or ever again.

But, as for her first week on the job,—all she could think of at the moment was just—T.G.I.F.

CHAPTER TEN

Tough Day for Any Principal Engineer

THANKS TO A LOT of welcome assistance from her sympathetic friend on the 20th floor, those two worrisome weeks passed for Marion. Then three more weeks. As Mr. Knight had promised, by now every week seemed just as "challenging",—to use the bosses' euphemistic cliché for "nerve-jangling". She worked early and late at the office and even took some papers home at night. However, this Thursday in late August should be a bit of a breather; Mr. Board had asked her to get her group to a cable manufacturer's all-day exhibit at a posh motel. Marion had decided that Ed and she would go for a couple of hours in the morning, while Art and Tom would look in on the affair in the afternoon. That way someone would always be "minding the store", and yet all could take in any lunch that a "live one" might offer. Mr. Sellers was going to drop by around four to say goodbye; he was determined to slip away quietly without any retirement party or reception or dinner or departmental gift collections.

At last she forced herself to concentrate on the regulation problem spread out before her on the desk. Adjusting the sliderule with her right hand and noting the product on her calculation sheet, she mechanically lifted the ringing phone to her ear and absently answered the call while placing the decimal point, "Hello,—Marion Francis."

"Marion,—Midge. The boss has just left for Mr. Knight's office with your River Shore Plant wire study,—and he doesn't look too happy! Thought you'd better know *now*—to get yourself together—so early this morning! Good luck! And have a nice day!"

She laughed. "Thanks for the warning, Midge! I'll try to shift my poor brain into high gear—and pass the alert along to my troops at once! I haven't looked at the report since it left here early last week. 'Bye now."

Grabbing her wire-file folder from on top of her "hot" pile on her table as she replaced the phone, she had swiveled her chair around to face Tom Fields, who luckily was still poring over battery-capacity computer print-outs.

"Tom, are we all set to defend our silicone-wire selection for those River Shore controls—like right now? You have all of Ed's input, don't you? Mr. Blood's coming down pronto!"

Grinning in obvious anticipation at the exciting prospect of doing battle for his recommendation, Tom replied jauntily, "Sure thing, Marion! I'm more than ready to go to the mat with our V.P. Where will the rumble be? Right here?"

"Probably in Mr. Knight's office. Did you get John Winton's approval yet? We'd like the consultants on our side on this one especially—where *we*'re the big spenders for a change!"

"Yeah. I called their office yesterday afternoon, and John had come around to our way of thinking at last. They're all really with us for once!"

"Good! Now let's see if Art's ready . . . Art?"

Turning around at his desk, Art smilingly replied, "All set, Marion! I want nothing but the best and most expensive wire for my turbines—and steam-generator oil burners!"

Picking up her jingling phone again, she at once heard Joe Knight's urgent voice, "Marion?"

"Yes, sir." She felt confidently forearmed and prepared for anything.

"Mr. Blood wants to see you here in my office—right *now*! About your silicone-rubber wire report. And bring along Art and Tom."

"Be right with you, Mr. Knight." Carefully setting down the phone once more, she calmly announced, "Well, this is it! C'm'on, gang! Let's close ranks and move out!"

From the log sheet she noted that Ben Board was in another meeting. Leading the way down the hall, she paused at the open door of the Chief Electrical Engineer's office until her two bosses looked up in apparent amazement at her speedy arrival.

Smiling briefly, her V.P. murmured, "Good morning"; and Joe impatiently waved an arm toward three empty chairs, placed in a row on the opposite side of the table from where the two executives sat so grimly now. As pleasantly as she could under the strained circumstances, she said, "Good morning, gentlemen. Come in, Art—and Tom."

While they were still seating themselves with her in the middle, Joe fixed his stern gaze upon her. "Marion, Mr. Blood wants to know why we electricals want to spend a lot of extra dough 'gold-plating' your power-plant wire while everyone else is trying to *cut* expenditures of hard-to-get cash these days! You've got to stand up to those operating people! I've told you this many times, but you don't 'listen good'! Don't *always* give 'em *everything* they 'holler' for—just because that's the easy way out for you!"

She recalled that neither boss had backed Mr. Sellers and her when each in turn had fought in vain against a $150,000, emergency, diesel generator for "safe shutdown" of the plant during a system blackout when a "black-start" peaking gas turbine was already on the property— with many more available on transmission tie lines. Quietly she responded, "I don't think that's a fair accusation. We electricals have persuaded the operators to go along with us on most major issues— like—synchronous versus squirrel-cage 'circ' motors,—by correcting the initial troubles at Cliffside; and on large aluminum conductors instead of copper,—by citing our good twenty-year experience with the proper compression connections;—and on three-phase instead of single-phase, EHV, step-up transformers,—by proving the forced-outage probability economics,—just to mention three of our big victories, saving two million dollars in all. In return, we're only agreeing with the operators on this control-wire item with a first cost premium of only several per cent of our two-million-dollar saving. As our report justifies by overall economics, we're only using the silicone-insulated wire at the head ends of the turbines—and at the oil burners of the steam generators—instead of generally—as at Cliffside."

She looked directly at Mr. Blood, who had been listening intently and now at last spoke, "Marion, our fire tests have proved it's good wire alright—with the silicone burning to sand, held concentric to the conductor by asbestos jackets—so it can perform O.K. even after a severe oil fire. That's why we're using it at our very important installation at Cliffside. But—at a *fossil*-fired plant?"

At once she replied, "River Shore will be a base-load job, too,—with the two units nearly as big as at Cliffside. Our probability-cost study— in the report—does justify the very modest capital premium, Mr. Blood."

Frowning, the vice president turned now to Tom. "*You* also worked on this report, didn't you, Tom?"

"Yes, I did."

Already Tom sounded far too abrasively belligerent—and pugnaciously combative.

"Then do you still agree we should spend these extra thousands of dollars?"

"I do, indeed! I don't sign papers I don't approve, Mr. Blood!"

"Do our consultants concur in this recommendation—when we're so hard up for cash now?"

"Yes, sir! John Winton and his guys all have agreed that this was the way for us to go here."

Now Mr. Blood looked like the proverbial feline with the ingested canary.

"Now that's odd! Mr. Winton was put on the phone with his vice president and me only a half hour ago. He explained that this is *not* their corporate policy, but he had acceded only reluctantly to our insistent request and would prefer being released from our special requirement—to return to their own economical standard practice."

In the ensuing awkward silence, she could only imagine how the ever-obliging Winton's arms had been twisted unmercifully by the two V.P.'s to secure this recantation. Nevertheless, her opinion of the pleasant Briton fell precipitately; she couldn't stand a deserter who,—under fire,—left his comrades in the lurch—to save his own hide when the going got rough.

Next Mr. Blood swiftly directed his unsmiling attention to Art on her left flank. "We haven't heard from you, Art. Are your turbines and boilers going to be engineered so that they *can't* have any disastrous oil fires that would require this high-priced, fireproof, 'wonder' wire?"

As all eyes aimed at him now, Art squirmed in his chair. "Well, sir,—I'm certainly going to see that we get good oil-and-fire barriers in the tray runs near the oil-exposure areas—with adequate spacing—and—uh—the best fire-protection applied to the adjacent cables. And—and I'll make sure the mechanicals use guarded piping there—"

Smiling at last, Mr. Blood beamed at his Chief Electrical Engineer. "Joe, your man here is making sense now! How about getting *him* to rewrite this report? Art can call on Winton for help—to turn out the revised study now—by the first of next week."

Her eyes questioned Art's as she thought bitterly, "You, too, Brutus?" Under the table she laid a gently restraining hand on Tom's left knee; she sensed that the infuriated black was about to explode in some regrettable verbal fireworks against the critic.

Just then Art recovered his voice. "I—I hadn't finished my remarks, sir. While ensuring that all prudent precautions will be taken, I cannot conceive of *anyone*—uh—actually *guaranteeing* immunity from an oil-fire disaster. I hear *we've had* an oil-burner wiring fire, and others have had some 'whoppers'. Therefore, I did—and I still do—approve this report—as it stands."

Patting Art's right knee approvingly now—instead of being about to kick his shin, she spoke softly as she glanced at the glumly silent v.p., "I must say, Mr. Blood, that *my* initial reaction—like yours—was to save the money—as usual. Even after the dozen bad fires in those other plants across the country, I still thought that 'it couldn't happen here'—until Mr. Sellers told me how lucky we've been! For instance, that welder who blithely started a cable fire by splattering molten metal on a tray with covers removed for maintenance—and *then* burning a hole in a water pipe, thereby extinguishing the blaze! Two wrongs made a right! And through it all he was blissfully unaware of anything but his welding! But how lucky can we be? *That* made a believer of me! That's how—at last—I came to the conclusion set forth in this report—and agreed to by all concerned in its preparation. Over $130,000 a day for replacement, purchased, power-and-energy charges—from the interconnection pool—for unit down-time for weeks of rewiring after an oil fire over the summer peak—can be a most compelling reason,—especially when one is trying to fall asleep at night after wrestling with this sticky problem!"

Observing that Mr. Blood was still scowling, she reluctantly added in a quietly subdued tone, "Yesterday Joe Johnson assured me that Mr. Landfall is determined to carry the operators' case all the way to Mr. King if necessary. And John Winton insists *he* needs our decision *this* week to keep the project on schedule now. Therefore, I—hope we can have this report approved—at this meeting."

Despite Mr. Sellers' tactical advice, she hated being forced into playing her ace cards in a power play; it smacked too much of brute-force blackmail. But—the stakes were high, and she wasn't about to give in now. For what seemed ages, the Vice President of Engineering and Construction stared impassively over her head at the wall calendar as Joe doodled on his pad with a ballpoint pen. Finally Mr. Blood smiled faintly. "Marion, you've convinced me—as usual! And the old jingle, 'A man convinced against his will is of the same opinion still',—doesn't apply to me! Please accept my apologies for bearing down so hard on you all here this morning, but *I*'ve just endured a rough conference phone session with the Chief and his Board Finance Committee Chairman,—dragging me over the hot coals *again* about inflation-cost overruns on our power-plant estimates. Here—I've initialed your report, Marion. Now, if you three will excuse us, Joe and I will resume our discussion here. Thank you, Marion,—Tom,—and Art."

Smiling sweetly as she accepted the papers from his outstretched hand, she responded with a cheerful "Thank you—and good morning, gentlemen" as she arose quickly and led her victorious battle-scarred cohorts into the corridor. At the drinking fountain outside their office, Tom exclaimed fiercely, "That British traitor! Wait'l I get him on the phone now! 'Copping out' on us behind our backs that way!"

She grinned, saying soothingly, "Now, Tom,—easy does it! Cool it today—and talk to John first thing tomorrow—about the decision we've won this morning. Here's the report; send up a copy by the 11:30 courier run now. O.K.?"

Tom smiled at last. "O.K. it is, Marion! I'll go easy on the 'limey'!"

After Tom had disappeared into the "little boys' room", Art spoke up hesitantly, "Marion,—I hope you didn't think I was—uh—about to desert the sinking ship—and welsh on you under pressure in there—just to climb up on the winning band wagon? Did you, Marion?"

As their eyes met, she replied evenly, "Art, after just hearing of John's defection—and betrayal of us—under double vice-presidential fire, I—must confess—the thought did cross my mind—briefly. It—must have been a real temptation for you,—and it took a lot of loyalty and—guts—to stick up for me in there—all the way—even in what seemed to be a *lost* cause for *me*—when *you* might as well have *won*—the easy way! And—I appreciate it, Art,—more than I can say now! I'm very grateful to you!"

"Thanks, Marion!" With an obviously relieved expression on his face now, Art followed Tom into the male sanctuary, leaving her alone at last.

Sipping the refreshingly cool water, she reflected that once again Mr. Sellers' sage counsel had brought her unscathed through another threatening crisis—so that now she had survived to fight again the next time. And—for the first time—she really felt sure that her two graduate engineers had placed themselves firmly on her side—instead of being potential rivals for the leadership of her group. She even dared to hope that her determination to stand up for what she thought was right—even if unpopular—had earned her some degree of new respect from her vice president—and perhaps from the Chief Electrical Engineer as well.

Logging in again, she knew there was precious little time for her to scan the latest mail and clean up her desk and table before she'd have to leave with Ed Eager for the cable show. In fact, the time had already come.

Now Ed was enthusiastically rushing her along to pick up the car he had reserved at the main garage so that they'd be sure to get to the motel early enough to have lunch and also get back by three and yet spend time with the vendor "reps". Later, as Ed drove expertly through the traffic, she had to admit that he was fun to be with on the tennis court after a tense day at the office. They had played tennis once a week, and she had lost the five pounds—much to her delight. Their matches invariably ended in ties. She suspected that he allowed her to struggle through to a hard-earned, multi-deuced victory in the first set only to crush her easily with his overpowering big game as she tired in the second set. And he never insisted on a deciding third set to humble her when she was exhausted.

Yielding to his pleas, she had even played once for his Generation-and-Transmission Unit's soft ball team; when his pitcher then had become ill, she had reluctantly agreed to substitute for him. Though she had pitched her sorority team to a collegiate pan-Hellenic championship, her performance in this men's game left much to be desired. Her change-up pitches did baffle some of the office athletes; and, though she only hit about 0.100, she actually did slide home for the winning run when the catcher failed to stoop to tag her because he couldn't believe that a girl would "hit the dirt". With all this regular sporting exercise now she did feel better—physically.

At the motel the show proved to be very engrossing as she discussed the various cable make-ups with the vendor engineers in the constant search for the optimum balance between cost, flame resistance, reliability, size, and other performance and installation parameters for each application in a plant. Lunch was excellent. Before long she discovered Ed already leaving the lobby for the car.

Lost in revery about the retirement of Mr. Sellers, she slid into her seat.

"Thanks for making an early break," she said. "I have to see Joe Knight at three, you know." Grunting noncommittally, Ed tooled the car into the highway.

Shortly thereafter, on a secluded road, Ed rolled up to a shoulder and stopped. She was shocked to hear his slurred speech.

"I been thinkin' all the way in—how you've never even kished me all theesh nights! Jush hit the tennish bawl at me! Now—I'm not goin' on until you give me a keesh—an a hug—an—Aw, come on, Franches Mareyon, you pretty li'l swamp fox! Pleash, Mareyon!"

"Ed, you're drunk!," she exclaimed incredulously. "We've got to get some coffee in you—and cold water on your face—and walk this off—before you return to the office! Before you get in trouble! You're sick, Ed!"

"Naw! Ed can hole hish licker. I jush needed a few drinksh—to work up my nerve to keesh you, thash all! C'mon, Mareyon, pleash! Lesh have a l'il lovin'—while we have thish chanch! Lesh keesh!"

She had known from his breath that he had been drinking—probably at the bar with that red-haired, young, cable "rep"; but she hadn't realized that he was drunk. In despair she looked hastily around her, hoping she could spot some sort of a diner where she could get black coffee. Or tomato juice. She saw nothing. She was afraid to stop a passing car for fear she'd have to identify herself. She made a desperate try.

"Ed, can I get through to you?" she said sharply.

"Shure, Mareyon."

"Let me drive. You get in the back and try to sleep it off."

"Naw, I can drive—drunk or shober."

"If we're stopped, Ed, it will mean big trouble for us both."

"I won't give no cop a chance to tag me. See! I'll show yuh!" He put the car into motion and drove quite well, Marion thought. She opened widely the windows within reach, hoping the cool air might work.

Twice she saw restaurants, and asked him to stop; but he ignored her. Aside from that she had nothing to say, but prayed silently that he'd snap out of it before they returned. At last the car was spiraling up several levels of the garage ramps and finally eased behind a row of other cars to come to rest in its numbered space.

"Thanks for the ride, Ed," she murmured. "I've already copied down the odometer reading on the car ticket. The only trouble is I can't open my door; you've parked too close to this column. So—I'll have to slide over and out your door—after you. And let's hurry a little; it's 2:40,—getting along towards my three o'clock meeting with Mr. Knight."

"Aw, ole Joe can wait a few minutes." Ed grabbed her tightly, gently but irresistibly pressing her body down flat on the seat, *her* legs now forced outside his open door under *his* and her arms helplessly pinioned beneath her by his overpowering weight. Softly Ed began to caress her cheeks.

She cried out sharply, "Ed, stop it! Let me up! You're still so drunk you don't know what you're doing!"

"Aw, Mareyon, pleash don't fight it! You know we love each other and theesh is our chanch—right here now! Pleash!"

Now he was kissing her so closely that she couldn't even fully open her mouth, and she was having trouble breathing.

"Ed,—please—get off—m-me!", she pleaded frantically. Futile as it was, she redoubled her vain efforts to free her immobilized arms from underneath her—but his two-hundred-pound weight and her awkward position were too much for her. Her shoes had fallen off in her struggles, and now his knees were hurting her spread legs. His cold clammy hands were fumbling against her thighs, forcing her mini-skirt and slip up above her hips amid the sound of ripping fabric.

Tears of angry frustration welled up in her eyes as her frantic mind refused to believe that everything she had worked for so hard was now being ruined. She had once read where the dampening ridicule of a derisive laugh was a girl's best defense in such sexual emergencies; but, with his hard-pressed kiss still tightly muffling her mouth, she doubted if her hysterical efforts would be effective here.

Just then she heard a car, and she couldn't decide whether she wanted the driver to stop and discover them in this utterly compromising position or to drive on. After the car had squealed on around the spiral ramp, she knew that she had to act fast. Silently, she prayed: "Lord, if it be Thy will, deliver me from this evil."

It was then she succeeded in biting his lip, and Ed yelled out in pain as he jerked his head back with a thud against the roof. By using his arms to support himself above her in this reflex reaction, he had unwittingly released her. Swiftly freeing both arms from beneath her, she quickly drove a hard left punch to his chin and at the same time with all her strength shoved against his left shoulder with her right hand. Since his feet were now touching the concrete floor, he slid limply down along her body as on an inclined plane until his knees hit the deck. Drawing up her legs until her feet were upon his shoulders, she gently kicked him out of the car until at last only his head rested on the seat cushion between her thighs. Now she slid over him and at last stood erect upon the concrete.

Quickly she slipped her feet into her shoes and deftly rearranged her dishevelled clothing. There was an opened seam in her slip, but it wouldn't show. Lifting out her bag, she looked in her compact mirror and smoothed her rumpled hair. Now she wondered what she could do for her once-formidable, now-limp technician. On a sudden inspiration, she rummaged in her bag and produced a vial of ammonia spirits, which she held under his nose.

Sitting up instantly as if stuck by a pin, Ed yelled, "Hey! What are you doing to me?"

Firmly now, in her most authoritative instructor's tones, she said, "Can you stand up now? Here—I'll give you my hand."

"Sure. I can stand up O.K."

But he did accept the help of both of her hands.

"See? I'm alright! For a girl, you've got a fair left jab, but I'm tough—except for a touch of a glass jaw. But I come back fast; I can take it!"

He rubbed his jaw and said ruefully, "I sure hope you didn't hurt your knuckles on my jaw!"

Now he fingered his upper lip and exclaimed, "My,—what big teeth you have! Ouch!"

However, she noticed that she hadn't bitten hard enough to draw blood,—at least any visible externally. Quietly she asked, "So—you're O.K. now, but why did you scare me—by lying there—so limp? I was afraid you were going to ruin the Company's safety record with an on-the-job lost-time accident! And that would have been worse than what you were trying to do!"

Mr. Sellers had told her that a substation operator with multiple arm-and-leg breaks from a fall had been carried from his home to his desk for weeks—to answer an office phone—and thereby save the all-important safety record.

"Because—I was trying to think of—how I was going to—to face you now."

Miraculously, they both looked normal enough now. Ed had now fixed up his trousers and shirt. His slur was gone. It was almost as if nothing had happened. Could she,—should she—just ignore everything? After all, no harm had been done. Again in silence, she prayed, "Thank You, Lord. And now please give me wisdom and compassion—for whatever lies ahead."

At last she whispered, "Oh, Ed, do you realize what would have happened if that car had stopped back here? Or someone might have gotten off the elevator and seen us!"

"What can I say, Marion? I'll have to make it up to you, and some day I will, by God."

She recalled a story she wanted to relate to Ed.

"Ann Teach's father worked in the Company some years ago, and he told Ann that a couple was caught in the same circumstances as this—right here in this very garage, in broad daylight, on Company time, in a Company car, on Company property! The woman was fired, while the man was only reprimanded. Would you have wanted a scandal?"

Staring at the floor, he at last mumbled, "I didn't think I was quite all that drunk—really. I just thought—after all the fun we've been having playing tennis and all—that we must love each other; but—we just needed something like this—as an opportunity—to break the ice, to give us the nerve to 'make it'. You—you did let me hug and pet you—on the public tennis courts, but we were never alone together—where we could really get cozy. You always drove your own car to meet me for our tennis dates. So—I thought—I just had to make a try."

Blushing in spite of herself, she exclaimed; "Granted you misconstrued those tennis court hugs, is this the way you show your love for a girl? Is this the way you make love? In a car? I can understand it from a teenager—but a mature man!"

He groaned. "I'm ashamed to admit it now, but I have 'made it' before—in my car—on lovers' lanes. But the girls were always cooperative—and—uh—'liberated'. With the 'new morality' and 'the pill'—and all, I thought it was no big thing today. I assumed all girls now were sophisticated—that way."

So it had indeed been her own naive blindness not to have seen this coming, and to have controlled it prior to this crisis. If she couldn't even handle this "extracurricular" sort of thing, how was she ever going to lead her group?

Now Ed walked away—steadily enough—for a few paces before returning to face her gravely.

"Marion, I know *now*—what kind of a good 'ole-fashioned' girl you really are—behind all your modern engineering and athletic accomplishments—and mini-skirts! But—too late! I 'blew it'! So,—what is left now, Marion? If I may still call you by your first name?"

It was very quiet in the cavernous multi-story garage in mid-afternoon, but soon all the hundreds of cars would be returning to their stalls.

"Yes, you may, Ed. But I think we'd better not see each other anymore off the job. And here on the job we must remember and be careful of each other. And—never, never tell *anyone* about this! And—you and I—will never speak of this again. And, Ed, please, no more drinking on the job! And try not to drink—anytime! Shall we shake on it?"

"Thank you, Marion. I—I don't really deserve any such treatment from you now, but I—I do appreciate it. And—I'll try to live up to it."

They shook hands firmly, and she thought he was blinking back tears—just as she was furiously trying to do.

"Ed, do you think you can get through the next two hours back in the office—or do you want to go home—sick? I could try to 'swing it' as an emergency here without going to the Company doctor or Mr. Board now."

He frowned. "Thanks, again, Marion. But I'm really not all that drunk now. I think I can make it without getting into any more trouble! And I'd like to see Bob Sellers before he leaves us—for good."

She nodded. "Alright. I'm going to try to compose myself—and for the same reason; I want to say goodbye to Bob, too. Shall we go now? And, Ed, I've thanked God for sparing us today from some grave trouble."

They were silent all the way back to the office, and she left him at the office door as she slipped into her rest room to pull herself together a little more for her meeting with Mr. Knight. Since no one was in the room, she even used her needle and thread from her hand bag to tack up the rip in her slip seam. After one final turning look in the mirror, she straightened her shoulders and walked to the log sheet to sign out for

Mr. Knight's office since it was now three o'clock on the dot. As she entered the room, she said casually, "Good afternoon, gentlemen!" to Mr. Knight and Mr. Board, who were already seated.

The Chief Electrical Engineer said quickly, "You're two minutes late, Marion. But this won't take long, anyway. As you know, Bob is retiring this afternoon. And—Ken Blood says that Ed King thinks you ought to have Bob's title and grade of principal engineer now. Something about being more effective and impressive on your speaking tours. You know, introductions and correspondence. But you're like Bob has been lately, aren't you? Not much on letters, mostly verbal communications and written 'speed memos'! Right? And getting your group and consultants to write what you want written?"

She grinned happily. "Yes, sir. Saves my time! Well, I'm sort of overwhelmed—at the welcome news! . . ."

Mr. Knight interrupted her, "I was too,—frankly! After all, you've only been here a little over a month;—and here you get a promotion already—to a grade Bob had with over forty years of experience. But Ed King's the boss! I only hope he knows what he's doing! Let's see. You have been getting $20,000 a year, but now you'll have a 25% raise to a $25,000 annual salary. That's really unbelievable! Congratulations! It'll really be a tough job for you to justify this unprecedented confidence the Company has placed in you so quickly, Marion!"

She recalled then how Mr. Sellers had told her about Mr. Knight's jumping from senior engineer through principal engineer to supervising engineer in a month—and then on to Chief Electrical Engineer of the Company in a year or so!

"Yes, sir! Thank you! I'm really going to try to—earn that confidence. And—I certainly do appreciate it, gentlemen!"

$25,000! She had actually been getting only $15,000 up north before the promotion that coincided with her discharge. It did seem unfair for her to come in from the outside with a planning-department title of associate engineer—since she'd never worked as an engineer grade—and within a month or so rise three grades to principal engineer, leading the Generation Electrical Engineering Group. But now it was up to her to live up to Mr. King's trust in her—and without Mr. Sellers' help.

"Alright, Marion. Congratulations again—and good luck—to you—and us!"

Both of her supervisors grinned as she smilingly left the room for her office. She was glad that Art and Tom didn't arrive until after Ed and she had returned; now her group appeared to be back to normal again. Ed looked alright over at his desk as he sorted and folded file prints and transmittal memos. That was certainly the best kind of routine task for him to tackle after his excessive drinking at lunch. Actually, she only trusted herself to do such jobs as reorganizing her desk papers and sending file stuff and technical magazines on their way; for her poor mind was still whirling around in orbit with thoughts of her narrow escape, followed by her fabulous promotion, and then all too soon—the sad retirement of Mr. Sellers.

As it was, Bob Sellers surprised her by entering from the relaying engineers' offices. Stopping to shake hands at each desk on his last rounds, he finally came to where she was standing by her table.

"Well, Marion, here is the shiny pewter platter you'll get after forty years!"

Fingering the polished surface, she murmured, "It's beautiful, Mr. Sellers."

What could she say at a time like this? It seemed unreal somehow that she had met him less than two months ago.

"Joe told me of your promotion, Marion. You're worth it! The Company is the lucky one! Congratulations, and many more promotions to come—real soon!"

"Thank you! And, you know, I wouldn't still be here today—without all your help, Mr. Sellers. I—I only hope I can make good—somehow—after today."

"You'll make it O.K., Marion."

As they walked together down the aisle for the last time, she still clung to his handshake, reluctant to let him go. At the reception desk, before the entire office, on a sudden impulse—she kissed him lightly on his cheek. Amid wolf whistles and kindred exclamations from the spectators, his little-boy grin lit up his face for her for the last time in the office as she watched, smiling resolutely, through tear-dimmed eyes.

It seemed that his eyes were glistening, too, for a few seconds before he waved farewell to everyone and was gone, the door closing behind him with the solid sound of finality.

Yet, in that moment of sadness, she resolved that he would not simply walk out of her life—as he apparently had just done. Not if she could help it!

CHAPTER ELEVEN

Frank Frightens a Supervising Engineer

ENTERING HER DESERTED office with a light bouncy step on this perfect Indian summer morning in early October, Marion felt better even on this Blue Monday—than she ever had since that sad retirement day over a month ago. At last she was really "getting on top of her job"—as Mr. Knight was always urging her to do. And despite the tight corporate cash-flow situation, she had succeeded in getting Art promoted to senior engineer and Tom to engineer with even Ed getting a nice merit increase on his technician's work output. With her "troops" in better spirits through her suggestions to Mr. Board concerning their performance-standards appraisals, their leader was happier, too. Also, her several appearances at club functions around town had seemed to be increasingly successful in arousing sympathetic responses from her audiences.

Walking briskly down the aisle, she suddenly halted in amazement. There were her desk, table, chairs, and file cabinet in the corner of the building alright; but now they were enclosed in the same type of glassed-in partitions as surrounded Mr. Board's desk at the opposite end of the aisle. She noticed, too, that nothing,—not even a paper, cluttered the smooth surfaces of her familiar furniture. Staring in open-mouthed bewilderment at the closed door, she saw a cardboard sign with the inscription reading, "Office for Rent—Former Occupant Evicted for Breach of Contract." Trying the door knob, she found it to be locked. What kind of a joke was this?

Just then, hearing slight sounds of subdued merriment behind her, she whirled around to see all three of her men emerging from behind the relay-room partition. Grinning broadly, Art said, "Let me unlock your door, boss! And you shouldn't mind being called 'boss' now—because you *are*!"

As they all entered the little room on an "inspection tour", she asked, "Art, what do you mean?"

"You haven't read the bulletin board yet? You're now Supervising

FRANK FRIGHTENS A SUPERVISING ENGINEER

Engineer for the Generation Electrical Engineering *Unit*, not *Group*,—effective as of today!"

At that all three shook hands with her, offering enthusiastic congratulations. Still incredulous, she exclaimed, "I—I can't believe all this—anymore than I can believe that you three pranksters—came in at half past seven—just to behold my bewilderment!"

As they all laughed heartily, she suddenly said, "Oh! Good morning, Mr. King! This is my morning for surprises, it seems!"

Horrified, she heard Ed guffaw, "Now who's kiddin'? You won't get *me* to turn around to gawk at nothin'! 'Cause I know *he* doesn't show for another hour! This ain't April Fool today either!"

Embarrassed, she managed to say, "Mr. King, these are my unit members, Art Core, Tom Fields, and Ed Eager. They came in early to—witness my surprise over all this!"

After Mr. King had shaken hands with Art and Tom, he said, "Turn around young man. Don't I know you? Ah, yes! Last spring—at the Company dinner dance! You were rather confused; and, mistaking me for a waiter who was a little slow in serving you, I believe,—you collared me and tried—unsuccessfully—to get *me* to bring you your roast-beef platter before the other tables were served. Well, Marion, I'm glad *you*'re his supervisor—because I believe you're just the one who can straighten him out for us! Is he the joker who authored this sign here? How is he doing on the job now, Marion?"

She had never heard that one! If someone had only told her about *that* inebriated caper, she would have been forewarned enough to have escaped exposure to her harrowing cliff-hanger.

"Well, sir, he has just earned a very good performance appraisal and merit raise based on his fine technical work in this office lately. And he is keeping up with his engineering college courses at night, too."

Mr. King nodded. "I thought *you* could handle him, Marion,—if anyone could! Young man, you're fortunate to have Miss Francis as your boss."

At last Ed managed to respond gravely, "Yes, sir, I now realize that. I surely do, sir."

Turning back to her, Mr. King, said, "Well, Marion, I just thought I'd come in early and stop off on my way up to see you. I had asked Ken to arrange all this—as a surprise for you."

She smiled. "Well, Mr. King, I *was,* and I *am* certainly surprised alright! And very appreciative!"

Now he smiled. "Marion, I decided that your important contributions to our corporate, grass-roots, public-relations image—as well as to the competent engineering of our economic, efficient, and reliable power plants,—by far our largest and most important projects today—and tomorrow,—all justified your promotion. We want to maximize your opportunity, your freedom, your independent environment for further achievement in these most important areas, so vital to our hard-pressed Company in these critical times. I'm counting on you—not only to continue the excellent performance you have displayed these past several months—but even to surpass your fine record in the coming months!"

Daring to smile, she said brightly—like a true Company woman, "Thank you, Mr. King. And you can be sure that I'll do my utmost to deserve the confidence you've placed in me."

"I'm betting you'll come through with flying colors, Marion. Oh, yes! I've asked Ken to reassign any manpower as may be required by you—to reinforce your important efforts here in your unit. Good morning, now, Marion."

"Thank you, Mr. King," she murmured. As the Chief Executive Officer strode down the aisle, Art said, "Boss, can I touch you again? Something might just rub off on me! And, boy, oh, boy, you sure saved Ed here from a well-deserved fate!"

She grinned. "Alright, fellows! It's now eight o'clock. Let's all get down to work—like the Chief said! You all don't want to see me fall on my face now, do you? Oh, Ed,—do you have any urgent homework question this morning—or did our Friday session clear your weekend work O.K.?"

Ed murmured, "I'll be alright for tonight's class. Thank you, Marion!"

She sighed. "Well, Friday—before I knew I'd be a big-shot today—I signed up for a car to go over some things with George Foray—that he had requested for today. I hope I'll be back by three. Ed, can you straighten up my things here, please? You've hidden all my junk! My desk is clear as the C.E.O.'s!"

She hoped Mr. King wasn't too shocked by her pantsuit. Anyway, she was ready to take off for Cliffside. She noted from the log sheet that Joe and Ben were both out of town at committee meetings as usual.

The drive was unusually pleasant, and George's questions proved to be not too baffling for a freshly commissioned supervising engineer. It was nice, also, to have George, Ted, and even Doug, among the others, all congratulating her; for the notices were already posted at the plant, concerning her promotion and the "liberation" and independence of her generation unit from the substation unit.

Emerging from the Service Building at the lunch break, she

sauntered over to the Intake Structure and leaned against the piperail, lazily watching the graceful, white swans gliding among the Canada geese. It was delightfully soothing to relax here in the warm sunshine where the engineer's best efforts to employ natural resources to ease the crushing work burdens of mankind were truly in tune with Mother Nature.

"Well,—eureka! Supervising Engineer Marion Francis, I presume!"

At the sound of that still familiar voice, she turned around to see Frank Boone smiling as he walked towards her across the concrete deck.

"Frank Boone! Good morning to you!" She smiled and asked, "And how is my long-lost friendly enemy this fine day?"

"Great, Marion! And is this how the grasping, monopolistic, overcharging, power company's super-high-salaried supervising engineer labors to provide economical electricity for all of its slaving customers?"

She laughed lightly. "Frank, you know it's lunch time! And what are my hard-earned tax dollars producing for poor little me from our illustrious 'ology' Ph.D. just now?"

"Touché! But—I—I really did hope to find you here today! Ann gave me some encouragement—after checking your signout log! So—I—sort of 'engineered' this trip today—just to see you!"

"Ah, hah! I see! I was beginning to wonder if clairvoyance were one of your 'ologies', Frank! But then Ann also told you of my promotion this morning!"

"Yes, Marion. And many congratulations to you! Let me shake your hand!"

It felt good to feel his firm but somehow tenderly caressing fingers clasping hers as they stood smiling at each other in the noonday sun. "But, Frank, where have you—looked for me—all these many weeks,—*months*?"

Frank spoke again, "When you and I were in separate elevators that day, I was being assigned to—or banished to—an out-of-town job away from this area. And all the previous day I spent with clients till late at night. Today is my very first day back; I called Ann bright and early! And—being with you now—at last—is my delightful reward for my unflagging search for you today! Like the Mounties, I always get my—*woman*!"

They laughed gaily—at nothing, really,—just in the sheer enjoyment of being together once again after their involuntary separation for so long. "Frank, it truly is a heavenly day!"

"Yes, Marion, I believe God grants us such perfect days to enjoy—as well as the rainy ones—to ponder. Even your whistling swans and

Canada geese are on parade out there—just as you told the good ladies that night, Marion! And—they look well fed. Which reminds me. Do lady supervising engineers eat lunch?"

"This one does."

"Where? Not at that greasy spoon down the road, I hope?"

"Sometimes—if I have to come back here afterwards. But now I'm heading back to my office. May I lead the way in my Company car—to a charming little place, Frank? Or—do you have to return here?"

"I'm with you! I'm letting nothing separate us this time! You shall not escape me, fair lady! Lead on, Lady MacDuff!"

Keeping Frank's car in her rear-view mirror all the way, she was soon sitting opposite him at her favorite little table by the window. "Say, Marion, this is a real 'ecology' spot,—a cozy hideaway in the woods! You've even arranged for a cardinal and a mockingbird to sing us a duet of melodies—right outside our window here! But, Marion, don't you feel the least teeny-weeny bit guilty—of fraternizing with your corporate foe?"

She laughed. "Oh, not at all, Frank! I'm being paid to convert you to my side!"

"Oh, 'it's a shame to take the money'! Because—nothing's going to keep me from your side—from now on, 'my best beloved!'" He grinned. "And, Marion, you've already converted me to your ideology! I no longer cringe at the thought of us Americans being only 6% of the world's population and yet consuming nearly 40% of the energy and other resources of our planet. Because, as you said, who else is now able to convert it all into useful items, including food, wealth, and manufactured goods, which our unprecedented national generosity has bestowed so liberally on the needy around the earth? And to be able to keep up the good work, we mustn't squander all our wherewithal on idealistic extremes—but rather temper our conservation efforts with realistic moderation—and common sense! So—you see that you've already converted me, Marion!"

She grinned. "I'm glad, Frank! But now the solicitous lady standing at your elbow wants to find out how much *you* intend to consume—from that tempting menu before you!"

And so it was that, despite their gay chatter throughout the meal, all too soon their attentive waitress brought the checks. Grabbing hers, she asked, "Well, Frank, how did you like my 'Hearth Side in the Pines'?"

"Why, Marion, it's incomparably fine,—real restful! But, then,—it could be the charming company!"

"Thank you, Frank! I really enjoyed it! We must—do it again—real soon. But now—this slave girl of the grasping corporation must hurry back to her salt mine. Do you go on with your biota check-sampling now—or return to your lab for analysis?"

"Back to the paper mill at the office for now!"

He hesitated as they stood beside their cars beneath Longfellow's "murmuring pines."

"Marion, you said that you ride those 'ecology-energy-saving' busses, packed in with all that gasping humanity. This evening—could I pick you up—in my car—on the corner—in the inset below your main office door—at 4:50? We'd make a car-pool, wouldn't we?"

"That—would be very nice, Frank!"

"Good! 'Til then, Marion!"

With Frank to look forward to at the door, she made it back to her new office in good spirits and had just seated herself in exalted seclusion within her private domain when the office boy brought her a three-o'clock phone-message slip, marked, "urgent—Joe Johnson."

Dialing the unfamiliar number, she asked the female voice for Mr. Johnson. A long minute later, his deep resonant query sounded loud and clear, "That you, Marion?"

"Yes, sir. Just got in from the Cliffs. Where are you, Joe?"

"Gold St. That pleasant voice you heard first was our new girl clerk, who brightens up this old dungeon down here. We've just had a hydrogen explosion at the busduct on Unit No. 3. It's a shambles! Fortunately no one was hurt, but that was only because nobody was under the generator at the time. The unit had come back on line from overhaul this morning, and the guys were on deck using their fancy sniffer box, trying to locate a hydrogen leak that was causing excessive gas consumption from the bottles—when the 'cannon' blew! With so many Interconnection units off early for fall maintenance now, we need this old 'baby' back on line—at least in a couple of days. We got it back this morning three days ahead of schedule. But this mess looks like six months to our people down here. Can you slip down here right away, Marion?"

Art had told her that he was supposed to take his wife and children over to his in-laws' home for the father's birthday party tonight. And Tom had said that he was to meet his wife to look at a new house. Even Ed had night classes. Anyway, Joe was asking for *her*. The relentless telephone had penetrated her isolation cell, that status symbol of a supervisor; apparently her promotion to the executive ranks could not spare her from such hard demands.

"Alright, Joe. I'll be there within half an hour—by four-thirty. O.K.?"

"Thanks, Marion. I'll see you."

She'd call Ann and also leave a message with the lobby guards,—and at the departmental reception center,—and at her own log desk. Frank had given her no phone number; probably he was still making some lab rounds prior to returning to his office. Phoning the dispatcher, she caught her car before it could be reassigned and then dashed out the door, trying to figure out the best way to get to Gold St. in rush-hour traffic,—especially since she had never been there,—only seeing its stacks from afar.

She did come close the first time but had to retrace her route to the boulevard to get on the right side of the railroad yards. Finding a parking space between two other Company cars beside the tracks, she strode towards the ubiquitous little guard house, squatting incongruously before tall, ornamental wrought-iron gates reminiscent of an earlier more elegant era. Glancing up at the stack plumes, she noted that, while the big Unit No. 3 was down, the two, older, smaller units were on the line this warm afternoon. Since the guard told her that a mob of guys was under Unit 3 generator, she headed in that general direction, wondering just what, if any, contribution she could make to alleviate this latest disaster area.

Looking up from the railroad siding inside the turbine building, she was pleased to see that here she could walk sedately—like a lady—up steel stairs to a concrete deck just beneath the generator bushings. As she at last stepped onto the concrete floor behind a crowd of men, she stood there quietly while she caught her breath and surveyed the scene. The line, B-phase, generator-bushing porcelain was obviously badly cracked at the flange with large hunks missing across the entire leakage path. The other two line bushings had some small, white, porcelain areas showing in several spots where the glaze had been chipped off by a short circuit, no doubt.

Recognizing a test man, she learned that a three-phase ground fault had developed at the bushings after the B-phase gas explosion, set off apparently by a static discharge. During the overhaul, the flange gasket of B-phase bushing had been re-installed incorrectly, causing the massive undetected leak, which the rather small venting area could not handle adequately. She recalled that Mr. Sellers had told her about how the isolated-phase-bus hydrogen-seal bushings had originally been deleted from the order to save several thousands of dollars at the vice-president's direction, but later the seals were re-instated when Mr. Sellers had reported on a case of gas leakage on another utility system. The vice president had claimed that the operators could always "sniff" for any gas leaks—before any explosion could occur. It was fortunate that the seal bushings had been in service here to prevent the light hydrogen from filling the entire bus run outdoors to the transformer—to make a giant explosion instead of this relatively-small, "ladyfinger"-firecracker puff!

The terminal, manganese-steel, bus covers, line and neutral, were all blown off, burned, and deformed together with their conductor fittings. Even the bushing current transformers looked scorched, but the test man said his meter-lab fellows thought they were checking out alright so far. Leaning against the pipe rail, she decided that the one critical item in the whole horrible-looking mess was the B-phase line bushing; everything else could be "jury-rigged"—temporarily at least—to get the unit back on the line in a day or two. But, listening to all the dozen men, who were still ignoring her in their gloomy verbal appraisals of outages estimated to run up to a half year from a minimum of three months, she wondered where Joe was now.

Glancing at her wristwatch, she saw that it was now nearly five o'clock; and she tried to imagine what frantic maneuvers poor Frank was attempting in order to come up with a new plan of action—while the traffic policeman whistled at him at that busy intersection. Well, there was nothing she could do here—either for Frank or this stricken, old, veteran generator. Walking through the turbine-room ground level, she saw one of those new trail-blazing rarities like herself,—a female roving operator, standing beside a big, horizontal, motor-driven pump, which the nameplate proclaimed to be a service water pump. Smiling, she said, "I'm Marion Francis from Engineering. Can you tell me how to get to the Chief's office? I'm looking for Mr. Johnson, who is here somewhere. I—I don't want to bother everyone on the PA system when everything's so busy now."

"Howdy! I'm 'Sally' Lunn! I'm new here to-night—from River Shore—to help out! But I think you go down that aisle toward Unit 2—and then upstairs to the service gallery alongside Unit 1 turbine. I'd go with you to help you find the office, but I'm stationed here to watch the No. 3 control-room operator's first start-up of this pump after its bearing replacement and overhaul today. The machinists are waiting up in the control room to go to their next job after this trial."

Suddenly there was the startling whir of the motor, followed at once by an alarming metallic clangor, sounding for all the world like a Hallowe'en kid whacking a steel chain-link fence with a steel pipe as he rode past on a bike. As the girl operator looked around in obvious confusion and then began to run away from her visitor, she quickly called, "Sally! The stop button's right there on the column—at your left elbow!"

The girl halted and lunged for the button; and within seconds the nerve-shattering racket had ceased. "And, Sally, there's a PA phone—on that local panel—behind you—for you to call the control room now!"

In a couple of minutes, Sally had returned grinning sheepishly. "I don't know where anything is down here yet! At River Shore the buttons are conduit-mounted on the motor pads—with the PA on the nearest column. I'd probably have run all the way up to the control room—if you hadn't come along! Thanks! Gee! You won't tell anyone—about my messing up here, will you?"

"Not on my life, Sally! We girls have to stick together! Mr. Sellers once told me that when this unit first started up—about a quarter century ago—that a *male* operator was watching the initial start of a 1,000-horsepower, 4-kv, ID-fan motor—when smoke and noise caused him to ignore the pushbutton and PA phone beside him—and actually run all the way up to the control room—only to find that the operator there had already tripped the motor breaker upon seeing smoke coming from the switchgear! The smoke signal from the 'poled' motor had ascended the motor conduit faster than the running messenger! And that's a true story—with the joke on a man,—not a woman!"

As Sally laughed with her, she now looked at the service pump. "*That* fan motor had 'poled' due to incorrect bearing alignment between fan and motor. *This* motor is O.K., I'd say. But—the machinists have more work to do on the pump now! Well, so long, Sally! Keep everything under control!"

"Thanks again, Marion!"

It wasn't easy, but at last she stood outside a conference room, filled with more men,—including the cigar-puffing Joe Johnson, seated at the head end of the table. Unfolding a metal chair from the stack in the corner, she sat down quietly in the rear of the room.

But, within seconds of her arrival, silence fell upon the assembly; and Joe called out, "What kept you so long, Marion? You're an hour late!"

"Sorry, Joe, but I stopped by to view the remains. I've had a pretty good look-see at the corpus delicti."

She coughed; cigar smoke was one stink that made her ill. That's what came of being someone like Mr. Sellers, who didn't smoke, drink, chew, or swear!

Joe smiled. "Good girl! Well, what's your verdict? All these clowns say No. 3 will be down for many months,—and that ain't good."

As everyone craned their necks around to get a good gander at her, she took a deep breath.

"First, Joe,—have you a spare bushing? Or have you tried the vendor's service engineer?"

"I should have told you, Marion. No, we don't have a spare. Mr. Sellers always recommended that we carry spare bushings, but 'the roof never leaked before' anywhere! But the vendor has located *one* sold long ago to another utility, and it's on the way here by air freight right now. But what good is *one* when we need *three* line bushings?"

"Joe, a testman told me only one is cracked so that it leaks. The other two have glaze chips and minor porcelain spalls, but not in critical areas. They *could* be interchanged with the grounded-neutral bushings, but that's a lot of work! I'd say just a dielectric-paint job and a hi-pot check will do O.K. for a year or more. I understand that the scorched C.T.'s test O.K.; so—they'll need only taping and painting. The—"

Now Joe interrupted, "Yes, but—what about that iso-bus? The vendor said on the phone just now—that it'll take three to four months to get us new, special, manganese-alloy, nonmagnetic covers and fittings."

A young man, probably from the Test office staff, spoke up, "And you can't energize the bus conductors unless the covers are all in place—for flux shielding—or a through system fault will shatter the bus insulators and cause a *real* disaster!"

She waited a few moments to assemble her thoughts from remembering the generator-bus portion of Mr. Sellers' invaluable guide manual; then she said firmly, "That's correct for all these modern 'shorted' or 'continuous' aluminum-cover designs in the past twenty years or so, but this old one is an 'open-circuited' or 'insulated' cover type. Therefore, the porcelain insulators and copper conductors were designed to stand any through faults without the covers being in place. I can get out the old file data and calculations, but I'm sure that's the story. O.K.?"

Frowning, the young man scratched his head. "She's right, Joe. I should have thought of that myself. Well, Joe would you be satisfied with the high voltage danger signs and guard ropes around the platform area? Then later you could get Construction to put up vented asbestos screens? The Storeroom has copper flexes."

Now Joe grinned. "Then all we need is to get to work out there—pronto! We can get Test, Construction, and Operating maintenance crews busy around the clock—so that we'll be ready for that bushing tomorrow. Why shouldn't the unit be back Wednesday night if we all get the lead out of our, I mean, get off our—'duffs' and get with it! Well, what are we waiting for here?"

As everyone filed out, Joe clamped his cigar-free hand firmly on her shoulder. "Thanks for coming down here—after hours, Marion, and bailing us all out of this debacle. Frankly, I didn't think even you could think of any way to get us out of this one! And, then, now that you're a big-shot engineering supervisor, I was afraid you would be like all the others left up there—who hide away in their 'comfy' ivory towers! But, congratulations, Marion!"

"Thanks, Joe."

He grinned. "You're really doing O.K., aren't you? Making principal engineer—and then right on to supervising engineer,—all in only a couple of months! But, then, you *do* have fair hair, don't you?"

As she smiled in embarrassment, he relented, "Marion, I'm just kidding! Obviously you deserve it all, Marion. And that's more than I can say about *male* engineering bosses up there! I do hear that Ed King—has his eye on you; so—don't be surprised if you're tapped to move on up—fast now! And, when you do, just remember poor 'ole' Joe down here, Marion!"

She laughed, "I guess I haven't done anything to make Mr. King real mad at me—yet! And you really wouldn't like it up in that stuffy, old, ivory tower—away from all this,—now, would you, Joe? Now be honest!"

He laughed heartily. "No! But I could try to get used to it! You're alright, Marion! I won't hold you here any longer now. Thanks again!"

"Any time, Joe. Good night now!"

Her aching shoulder now released from his Ancient Mariner's grip, she waved cheerily to him and walked off with that happy girl-scout-good-deed feeling surging up within her. Striding past the guard-house with a casual exchange of "good nights", she was soon trudging along the dark, deserted, industrial highway alongside the railroad yards. Watching the shadowy forms of the parked autos and freight cars, she thought that it would soon be Hallowe'en. Suddenly she began to glance furtively—and fearfully—behind her as she searched for her Company car in the Stygian blackness of the night.

Instantly then terror gripped her pounding heart as a dark figure silently disengaged itself from the threatening shadows and slowly approached her. As the black silhouette loomed up in her path, she uttered her favorite prayer, "Lord, if it be Thy will, deliver me from evil." Her best chance seemed to be a speedy, screaming retreat along the dark, thousand-foot route toward the guard house; but, no doubt, the tall shadow could overtake her all too soon.

Drawing a deep breath, she was just about to put her emergency plan into action when the ghostly form spoke in familiar tones, "It *is* you, Marion! Thank God! I've been waiting for you in this crummy hell-hole for hours now,—locked up in my car most of the time!"

"Yes," she prayed quietly, "Thank You, Lord." Then, overcome by sudden relief, she laughed almost hysterically. "Oh, Frank Boone! You nearly scared the wits out of me! But—am I ever glad to see you!"

Now he ran towards her and took her hands in his.

"Why, Marion, you're trembling! You shouldn't be out by yourself in a dark, dangerous place like this! This dump has all kinds of bums, winos, thugs, drug addicts, hobos, tramps, smoke-hounds;—you name it. Marion, you've just got to—take care of yourself! Do you hear me? Are you listening to me, Marion?"

She had calmed down enough now to answer quietly, "Yes, Frank. But—how ever did you find me—down here?"

Solicitously he replied, "It wasn't easy! After five I put my car in a parking garage. I got your message from the lobby guard; Ann had already gone home, I guess. Marion, do you feel up to driving your Company car—or—?"

"Oh, yes, Frank."

"Then I'll follow you back to your Company garage. Where *is* your car? Come! Let's hurry out of here—while we're ahead!"

It was nearly eight o'clock before she was able at last to relax, safely beside him in his comfortable sedan, rolling along in the smooth velvet darkness towards home.

"Frank, for tonight—will it be alright with you,—in view of the late hour, if I just whip up some scrambled eggs, bacon, toast, and coffee—for a quick chuck-wagon snack for us? With apple pie a la mode for dessert?"

"That sounds good! It'll taste like heavenly ambrosia from the Elysian Fields,—coming from your hands, Marion!"

It was good she had remembered to phone Aunt Dinah to eat a snack and not wait for a late supper—unless she wanted to do so.

"Marion?"

"Yes, Frank."

"Keep steering me in the right direction—because I'm not very familiar with this part of town. And, about our repast tonight, I insist that you let me assist you—and also wash the dishes! Don't forget that I'm an expert bachelor's-hall veteran! And my reward must be a good-night kiss! Are you still listening, Marion?"

"Yes, Frank."

She smiled happily in the darkness. Aunt Dinah certainly will approve of Frank for her darling niece.

CHAPTER TWELVE

Uncle Bob

ON THE MALL BELOW her office window, she could see the trees leafing out on this wonderful April day. It had been a strenuous—but engrossing winter for her. As a supervisor she had attended Mr. King's quarterly management meetings and Manager Richards' daily morning staff sessions.

In January she had been selected to go to the Winter IEEE Power Engineering Society Convention in New York City to present discussions on several power-plant papers. There had been a number of visits to various consultants' offices together with many Company and vendor meetings. Through it all she and her group had kept "on top" of the calculations, drawings, studies, conferences, purchase recommendations, correspondence, reports, office routines, estimates, and field follow-up work. She had also made three factory visits; and she had been surprised at all the customer input required on manufactured equipment as to feedbacks on design and production deficiencies, desirable improvements, and necessary parameter specifications. The utilities had to inspect all equipment to remove all kinds of foreign materials, installed both in the factory and on the job, including bottles, bags, rags, pencils, and flashlights. Despite jigs, breakers wouldn't fit in their cells. Cables had absurdly eccentric conductors—and insulation replete with voids and inclusions. Motor and generator coils were loose; transformer coil bracing was inadequate. Every type of specified test had revealed deficiencies. Every control-wiring package contained hidden "bugs". Relays lacked restraint due to the use of second-harmonic data from obsolete iron. Cabinets and boxes were too small. Porcelain had firing flaws. She kept a list of all these items that filled a loose-leaf notebook; a similar collection of consultant and contractor shortcomings was even more voluminous and revealing, including 50% regulation in lighting runs—and welding outlets installed upside-down! In the future she wanted to guard against falling again into any of these hundreds of pitfalls; let her next troubles be new ones!

Her transformer-plant visit for River Shore had been especially memorable. As the first customer visitor of her sex, she had received kid-glove, red carpet treatment; and at last she had won promises of lower reactance—to improve stability—and also final agreement to relocate the low voltage bushings from the cover to the tank wall to save thousands of dollars in bus elbows and footage. While she had been on an escorted tour of the huge factory after a sumptuous luncheon, one of her Company's test inspectors had alerted her about suspiciously increased radio-interference readings during the double-frequency overvoltage tests,—the last before shipment of this Cliffside Unit No. 2 step-up transformer. Since the tests still had met all specifications by a close margin, the factory engineers had refused to extend the investigation. Then she had recalled Mr. Sellers' tale of his insistence upon the repetition of an unwitnessed motor-generator "hipot" test resulting in a failure due to a broken chisel point embedded in the winding; ever since, he—and now she—had crusaded against sloppy housekeeping in shops. After urgent appeals and threats to her suddenly reluctant hosts, she finally had persuaded the plant management to repeat the dubious test, which then had caused the transformer's failure, disassembly, inspection, and repairs. After transformer reassembly, testing was still in progress now—six months later.

Even without her commendably restrained "I-told-you-so's", the vendor had gotten the point that the customer had saved them both a bundle of money by detecting the fault at the factory instead of months later at the site. Curiously, the laboratory consensus was that the culprit had been a ten-cent cup of soft drink spilled on the million-dollar transformer's high voltage winding during assembly! And,—fortunately, for other reasons, the service date for Unit No. 2 already had been deferred *two* years later than Unit No. 1; for that stroke of good luck, she was very thankful.

During the March blizzard she had even driven and slogged on foot through the deep snow to check out overhead lines for emergency repair work for a week of Storm Patrol. In February Joe Knight had asked her to fly to New Orleans to give a five-minute talk before an industry-committee seminar on power-plant, motor-control practices, concerning policies for local, central, and redundant locations. She smiled as she recalled a woman on the plane asking her to hold her baby a minute while she went to the rest room. That minute turned out to be an hour; for a while it looked as if Marion Francis would become a bachelor mother.

Although it was now 3:30 p.m. on Friday, she had learned to accept the T.G.I.F. syndrome and now generally could take it in her stride. Glancing at Tom Fields, she recalled how he had pleaded with her to send him to an AEC—an NRC—meeting to argue why annual battery discharge tests were unnecessary and even detrimental to battery life and plant reliability; although she had tried to dissuade him from a hopeless mission, he had accompanied her—only to have the government men impolitely begin an internal discussion on another extraneous subject while Tom was still earnestly arguing his valid technical case. That one visit had sufficed for Tom.

Art was now ready to take over the group,—the *unit*,—at any time; his reports and studies were now coming out complete and authoritative almost every time. In fact, all his work was very competent. And Jane and she had enjoyed a thoroughly delightful Christmas-week shopping lunch together one bright chilly day with carols floating on the crisp air.

Ed was in seventh heaven with a younger technician to work at his direction; also, his bright assistant was in his same night classes, thereby easing her own tutorial burden. To the best of her knowledge, Ed never drank liquor any more, at least not on Company time. She had been rather firm with him at times,—as when he had phoned in one morning at seven-thirty to ask if he could go from home to his downtown dentist for a routine ten o'clock appointment. He had not been exactly happy when she had asked him to hurry on in to the office on time and work one and a half hours before leaving for his appointment. Last month at Easter, Ed had married a nice girl he had met in one of his nonengineering, elective, night classes,—apparently a levelheaded girl who should be good for him. At least the young lady had seemed so that wintry day Ed had proudly showed off his fiancée at the office, and Marion had since heard nothing to the contrary.

Among her many surprises during these past nine months had been the discovery that her major work—and, therefore, her principal problems—involved people rather than things, persuasive salesmanship of her ideas and recommendations rather than just economic and technical calculations, studies, and analyses. Portia-like, she had to argue her case, to sell her suggestions to vendors, consultants, contractors, and Company men,—even to her own fellows.

When operating men asked for more costly installations with more expensive features than she thought could be justified by evaluated maintenance, operating or reliability savings, they often questioned why she was so zealously concerned about cost reduction, anyway, when it all ended up in the rate base, on which the stockholders of their utility monopoly were allowed to earn a percentage return as specified by the Public Service Commission.

In rebuttal, she always replied that the PSC was, in fact, *not* allowing enough rate increases these days to earn the permissible rate of return on the plant investment even with the Company's best efforts at engineering economics. Therefore, most of the money for necessary, new, power-plant construction had to be borrowed rather than taken from the meager earnings; and capital venture funds were hard for utilities to obtain under present conditions. Also, the PSC could always compare the rate-base cost per kw of installed generation of one utility with that of a similar sister company elsewhere together with their generating costs in mills per kwh.

As to the alleged security of a utility's franchised monopoly, customers could—and some had—installed their own private generators—from small gasoline sets to diesels and fuel cells and even large steam turbines. Customers could even use nonelectrical power, including gas, oil, and other energy sources,—or they could even relocate to other areas.

Often she had to argue with Purchasing and Management for a *higher* first-cost purchase or installation but with an overall evaluated *lower* cost due to consideration of efficiency, maintenance, operating, and even somewhat intangible reliability and other factors. Sometimes her decisions were appealed over her head to higher echelons, and she had to plead her cause before rival managers and even vice presidents.

While nerve-wracking at times, each day's work was always different and very engrossing, never the same and not at all monotonous or boring. And at last Cliffside Unit No. 1 was now in service.

Now—in another hour—Frank would pick her up at the door to ride home in the luxurious style to which she had so easily become accustomed during the past half year. Frank had played tennis with her quite often, and now his superior masculine strength and stature bid fair soon to overtake her initial advantage of prior experience and expertise. Although he had not yet won a match—and would always detect and protest any attempt on her part to give away any points, she continually looked forward to that inevitable day when her apt and eager pupil would at last be the winner. He was always so obviously pleased with his consistent progress that she could scarcely wait to share his joy of hard-earned attainment when at last he would be the victor.

They also bowled; ice-skated; hiked on nature trails, which he illuminated so well with his interesting commentary; explored museums; attended plays and concerts; and often went to church together. Of course, it was on weekends when Frank and she had the most time to spend together; and most of the time they enjoyed best of all just being at home—with Aunt Dinah—and her company.

Perversely, she sometimes aroused his tender concern for her safety by recounting tales of job hazards, such as her witnessing a 13-kv potential-transformer fault with the exploding gas blowing open the steel cabinet door while she was standing nearby. She had told him of generators flying apart in other plants, killing several bystanders. Even about her own company, she related stories of engineers being electrocuted by inadvertently contacting lightning arresters and switchgear—and being fatally burned by an exploding oil circuit breaker. But, whenever he became alarmed over her hazardous occupation, she would turn the conversation to safer channels. Once they had even discussed the "new" peace symbol of a circle circumscribing an inverted Y on a vertical lower support line, and she had pointed out that modern youth had appropriated an ancient industry symbol for a wye-connected generator as shown on wiring diagrams since the 19th century.

And, at long last, tonight was the *big* night—when, after dinner—and a showing of some of Frank's latest animal and bird slides and sound movies, they would proudly announce their engagement. She could barely endure this last slow hour before quitting time today—of all days!

As the phone jangled her nerves now, she resolved not to answer it this one time. She would vanish into "the little girls' room." Slowly she lifted the receiver.

"Hello, Marion Francis."

"Oh, Marion! This is Midge. Can you come up to Mr. Blood's office right away? Mr. King has asked Mr. Blood to bring you to his office to meet with Mr. Sternly,—you know, the P.R. V.P. O.K., Marion?"

"Be right up, Midge."

Even after three-quarters of a year here, her heart still raced whenever she ascended into that rarified atmosphere of the executive suites on the upper floors. She wondered why it was that the chiefs, who always came to work later than the Indians, never got around to tuning up their war dances and pow-wows until quitting time.

Actually, Mr. Blood met her at the elevator door; and they rode down one floor together as he said, "Hello, Marion. I don't know what the Chief has in mind for us,—especially since Jim Sternly will be there, too."

As she entered Mr. King's office for the first time, she saw that Mr. Sternly was an undistinguished-looking, white-haired man in his sixties, standing in quiet conversation with the big boss.

"Hello, Ken. And, Marion,—this gentleman is Mr. Sternly,—Miss Francis. This shouldn't take long, but let's be seated."

She breathed a silent sigh of thankful relief at the promise of brevity.

Mr. King turned to Mr. Blood.

"Ken, after more than nine months, I know you value Marion's electrical engineering work—on cutting capital expenditures—while still expediting our necessary, multi-million-dollar, annual, power-plant, construction program. As your supervising engineer for that unit, she is turning in an excellent performance record in that important area. Isn't that right, Ken?"

"Yes, sir, Chief. Marion is doing a topnotch job for us there."

Looking next at Mr. Sternly, the Chief Executive Officer said quietly, "Now, Jim, you recall how I've been filling you in on Marion's attendance at various local club and civic organization meetings on environmental, rate, energy-crisis, and such topics—to present our corporate positions—in an effective, sincere, informed, 'grass-roots' approach?"

"Yes, Ed. Seeing the charming young lady here in person,—I can appreciate how she must come across very—uh—effectively—as you say."

"Right, Jim. Now—what do you think of getting the benefit of more of Marion's talents in this field? Not to downgrade your P.R. programs in the least, Jim; but—we certainly can always use more good image-building in these critical times,—especially some fresh, appealing, imaginative approach—like Marion here! Don't you agree, Jim?"

"True enough, Ed. What power company *can't* use a new approach these days—when environmentalists—through the EPA—make us burn costly foreign low-sulfur oil—despite the FEA—and delay our new nuclear plants with all kinds of quibbling—and then, putting on their consumerism hats, mob the PSC in rate-protest hearings? When can Marion go into the front-line trenches, protected by her construction-engineer's hard hat?"

Mr. King smiled with everyone else. "How about Monday—on a part-time daily basis? Effective then—she will be your new Manager of a yet-to-be-christened department for,—shall we say,—Corporate Public Policy Communications? She'll use that vacant office right next to yours, Jim. At first, she'll need reassignments for only a secretary—and a technician—and an office boy—until the program develops under Marion's direction. How does all that sound to you, Jim?"

"Great, Ed. I can't wait to welcome Marion to her new challenge on Blue Monday morning!"

"Fine! Now, Ken, I know you're concerned about losing Marion; but, as you must realize, the orderly, complete transition will be gradual, extending over the next year or so. I know Marion will work it all out with you in her usual competent style. I'd bet she already has her successor all picked out and groomed to take her place—in any emergency. Am I right, Marion?"

She smiled. "Yes, sir, I do."

Not only was Art ready for the job, but it didn't hurt any that he was Mr. Blood's second cousin,—one step beyond the corporate antinepotism limit. She had only recently gleaned this important bit of relevant news—not from the discreet Midge—but from Pat, who socialized up and down the building in all the right places to pick up reliable grapevine items.

Mr. Blood glanced at her sharply but said only, "Why, Chief, I'm sorry to hear that we'll be gradually losing Marion's expertise in that tough understaffed spot; but—we'll all do the best we can, of course, for the overall good of the Company."

Mr. King arose, smiling broadly. "Excellent! Oh, Marion, here is Personnel's little memo on your new position: initial salary, office location, title, first draft of your departmental and job description, and—starting complement,—and so forth. We'll all be imposing on you for the next year or two—as you change hats each half day! I hope you don't mind frequent elevator riding, Marion?"

"Oh, no, sir! I'm used to the ups and downs of life!"

They all chuckled; and, after Mr. Blood had left the room, the C.E.O. murmured in a confidential tone, "Jim, you and I are not getting any younger in these tough times, are we? We'll really appreciate having Marion up here with us—to get the benefit of her fresh new thoughts on everything—and to pass on to her the corporate backgrounds—in finance—as well as the other critical areas. You're not aiming to take a special early retirement on us, are you, Jim? You'll stick it out the full *three* years yet,—isn't it, Jim?"

Mr. Sternly scratched his head wearily. "Right now I think I'll stick around, Ed. Well, Marion, I'll see you in the morning,—this Monday? With Ken getting you back in the afternoon?"

She thought a second. "Why, Mr. Sternly, would it be alright if we turned that around—this first day on my new job? You see,—I'll need a few hours to set everything up in my engineering unit, you know!"

He smiled indulgently. "Oh, of course! This *is* right sudden, isn't it?"

She grinned. "Yes, sir, it surely is!"

Saying her "good evenings" to both men, she floated down to her office as she read and reread the incredible memo—with its combined two-job salary of $45,000,—a truly astronomical figure,—especially for a girl who had been drawing down only one third that amount last year up north—before she had been fired. She could hardly wait to read the notice on the bulletin boards Monday morning—about her being a *manager*!

By the time she had visited the rest room en route to her office, the eager crowds were already pushing past her down the hall; and, after hurriedly clearing her desk for a hectic minute, she hastily pursued the fleeing mob down to the thronging lobby.

Racing to the appointed curb inset, she arrived, breathless, just as Frank's car eased to a stop. Expertly slipping in beside Frank, she had—as usual—only a scant second for an instant kiss before the harassed traffic cop began to blow the whistle on them for delaying the rush-hour rat race. Bubbling over with her exciting news, a half hour later she was entering the front door with her smiling Frank before she had really finished her first enthusiastic recital of her day's epochal event. Then they had to make several trips before all of Frank's equipment was safely inside the entry hall.

"Frank, dear, shall we wait—to make our happy announcement at the dinner table?"

He kissed her tenderly in a snug embrace as he smilingly replied, "I'll try to endure the delay; but it won't be easy,—darling!"

As with their parents,—according to the courtship accounts told to their children,—in their own case, also, the course of true love had run very smoothly without any of those interludes of conflict which novelists and playwrights traditionally contrive to arouse the interest of their readers.

Now she smiled with Frank as they heard the melodious sounds of the soprano-baritone piano duet emanating from the living room. Last night it was "From Aunt Dinah's quilting party I was seeing Nelly home"; tonight she heard "Someone's in the kitchen with Dinah—" Tomorrow she probably would hear a male solo rendition of "Dinah! Is there anyone 'finah' in the state of Carolinah?"!

Her aunt's health,—appearance,—dress,—and spirits—had all certainly improved—unbelievably—this winter—since that autumn whirlwind romance and Christmas wedding. Why, Aunt Dinah now looked years younger than forty-eight,—positively radiantly beautiful! Of course, the two-year ordeal of Uncle Dan's long illness and death with its attendant loss of emotional and financial security had wreaked havoc with her aunt, but since then Cupid had done wonders. Smiling, she hoped Frank would soon have that beneficial effect upon her, also!

"Frank, darling, let's go in and let them know we're home—before I start dinner."

"Before *we* start dinner! Remember, Marion? I'm still your scullery boy! And bottle washer, dearest!"

"Thank you, honey! Yoo-hoo! We're home!"

The singing ceased as they entered the family room; and she exclaimed, "Oh, don't stop! It sounded real nice! Evenin', Aunt Dinah! Evenin', Uncle Bob!"

As she kissed them both as usual, Frank said, "Hello, Mrs. Sellers. Good evening, Mr. Sellers. Can you both stand my latest nature show tonight? After we join you in your sing-along—after supper?"

As they all laughed, she surreptitiously glanced at all three of her loved ones. Without Uncle Bob's advice each night—either to "second-guess" her decisions that day or to help her come up with tomorrow's promised answers, she never could have made it through these difficult autumn and winter months since his retirement; nor could she even think of the coming years without knowing that he would be here with his ever-ready counsel. And, despite his good-natured grumbling about the Company, he really wanted to keep up with all the developments.

She had been right in calling him "Mr. Sellers" instead of just "Bob" as the others had done in the office—because then it would have been more awkward for her now to add the prefix, "Uncle". And she must get Frank to call them "Aunt" and "Uncle", also, after the wedding!

"Oh, Uncle Bob! What are those jewels you're wearing on your watch chain? Let me see!"

He grinned. "In college we used to call that stuff 'belly brass'! Those two are my Newtonian math club key and Theta Xi social fraternity pin. This one is—"

"No! Let me guess! That's your Phi Beta Kappa key,—the same as my pin on my blouse. And that's your Eta Kappa Nu key! Why, we belong to the same, two, honorary fraternities,—sororities,—or societies, I should say today! Frank, Eta Kappa Nu is our electrical engineering honor organization. Frank has some of his own Ph.D. 'ology' scientific types, too! Like Sigma Xi. But, Uncle Bob, why didn't you ever wear yours at the office?"

"Oh, in my day, too much college education was to be hidden as a detriment to the rugged, practical, construction engineer's image. But, not today! It's all a brand-new ball game!"

He grinned as he stood with his arm around his smiling Dinah.

Hugging Frank's waist just as tightly, she happily steered him into the kitchen beside her. Once safely there, she whispered, "Dearest, does your nature show tonight, by any chance, include—a ground hog?"

He laughed, surprised. "Yes, it does, honey! You must be psychic! I'm studying the woodchuck's various hibernating peculiarities as related to its proverbial powers of meteorological divination! How did you guess? And—why do you ask?"

Since her curiosity had impelled her to peek at some of the slides she had just carried into the hallway, she ignored his first question and concentrated on the second query, "Well, darling, Uncle Bob will repeat his farmer uncle's traditional true story of the old hand who, when asked if he believed the ground hog could foretell the winter's severity and duration, replied, 'I don't think the Lord would entrust His business to a "mizzuble" "lil" varmint like that!'; so—I'm just alerting you—to laugh—as usual—when he tells his favorite anecdote! That's all! O.K.?"

"Marion, love, that's just one of the many, many reasons I love you so! You're always so thoughtful and considerate—of everyone's feelings! And—you're so—kissable, too!"

With that he took her tenderly in his arms and sampled another kiss. Their ensuing embrace was so timeless in its heavenly quality that the next thing she was even vaguely aware of in this everyday world was the lilting voice of Aunt Dinah, exclaiming laughingly from the kitchen doorway, "Bob, dearest, if we're ever to have even a bite to eat tonight, you and I had better take over out here from our newest love birds!"